Murray S

A Crooked Sixpence

Revel Barker
Publishing

First published by Doubleday & Company, New York, 1961
This edition published by Revel Barker Publishing, 2008

ISBN: 978-0-9558238-4-8

Revel Barker Publishing
revelbarker@gmail.com
66 Florence Road
Brighton, England, BN1 6DJ

There was a crooked man
And he walked a crooked mile.
He found a crooked sixpence,
It wasn't enough.

I

JAMES O'TOOLE looked around the public bar of the Earl of St Albans, which is in Russell Square. He found he didn't know anyone. He wasn't surprised. He had never been in that pub before, and he had not yet been a week in London.

One of the drinkers looked like his mother's favourite milk-man in Sydney; as far as his face went, anyway. The body and clothes were out of an English movie.

The bottles behind the bar had strange labels: the handles of the beer pumps, three in a row like a wicket, were new to O'Toole. So was sitting down to drink. The beer tasted weak and flat. Altogether, the place was a let-down.

Jennifer came in wearing a tweed suit he'd never seen before, with a velvet collar. She still walked like a duck. O'Toole tried to concentrate on this feature but it didn't work.

'Hello, James.' Nervously, neatly, like a doll that blinks and says 'Mama', she lit a cigarette. The case was pigskin, the lighter was covered in pigskin, and the pigs matched. Both were new. So, come to think of it, was smoking. Doll growing up.

'Hello, Jenny,' said O'Toole. 'I've never been in this place before but I didn't know where else to meet you. I just live round the corner.'

'Oh, I don't mind,' said the girl. 'How are you getting along? Have you started on the big book yet?'

'Not yet,' said O'Toole. 'I have some emotional problems to sort out first. May I get you a drink?'

'Only if you promise not to make a scene, James. Honestly, I can't take any more.'

'What would you like, apart from a quiet life? As I remember you're not a beer girl.'

'Oh, you pick something. Anything will do.'

O'Toole went over to the bar and studied the bottles. The bartender came up.

'Sir?'

'Could I have another of these beers, please.'

'A light ale.'

'Is it? And could I have one of those little bottles of champagne, isn't it?'

'Champagne Perry.'

'That'll be fine.'

The waiter took some silver paper off the dwarf bottle and poured the contents, bubbling, into a long-stemmed glass. O'Toole took it and his beer back to the table.

'Champagne,' said O'Toole. 'For a special occasion. It comes in a funny little bottle and the bartender has an extraordinary way of pronouncing Perrier. Or maybe I have. Anyway, here's luck.'

The girl smiled doubtfully and took a sip. O'Toole looked at her wrist. She was wearing some kind of gold thing.

'It's not a present,' said the girl, defensively. 'Honest, it isn't.'

'Of course not,' said O'Toole. 'You're in the money now.'

The girl was near tears. 'I shouldn't have come.'

'Please,' said O'Toole. 'Please don't cry. I'm trying to work up a bluff, fatherly manner. Help me a bit.'

'I've cried in every public place in Sydney,' said the girl. 'I can't cry any more. I don't know how anyone with such kind eyes could be so cruel.'

'Never mind the eyes,' said O'Toole harshly. 'I'm sorry if I'm being cruel. It's just the struggles of a wounded elephant.'

'I shouldn't have come. It's all over, you know that. I can't see what good this is doing, torturing each other.'

'I know it's over. I've got nothing more to say. I'm just trying to be a loyal, true friend. Of course, I can see your point of view. What the hell do you want a loyal true friend for? Anyway, I don't suppose I would pick you for a friend, either, if we'd been in the Navy together or something.'

The girl smiled through tears.

'There's a good girl,' said O'Toole. 'Drink up.'

She took another sip.

'What's this supposed to be?'

'Champagne.'

O'Toole took the glass and tried a sip himself. It tasted like bad apples. 'Just a minute,' said O'Toole. He carried the glass back to the bar.

'Something the matter, sir?' asked the barman.

'There's something wrong with this.'

The barman took a sip. 'Perfectly all right, sir.'

'What's it supposed to be?'

'Perry. Made out of pears. A lot of people like it with gin.'

'Oh.'

O'Toole went back to the girl.

'I'm terribly sorry, it's not champagne, it's some local rotgut made out of pears, I think he said.'

'Oh, it doesn't matter, James. I don't feel like drinking anything, anyway.'

'I'm sorry.'

'Don't harp on it, please.'

'I can't seem to open my mouth without annoying you.'

'Oh, it's not you, James, it's the way I feel. Restless. You're just the same as ever, I suppose. Don't worry about finding another girl. Heaven knows, I thought you were attractive enough.'

'Did you? I know it doesn't do any good to point out that I'm not looking for another girl. I've just got to write a new set of ambitions, that's all. I've been thumbing through my present set and they all seem to have a part for you in them.'

'Please don't torment me, James,' pleaded the girl. 'I know I'm probably letting a good man go. I just have to, that's all. It isn't there any more.' She lit another cigarette. 'Do you need any money?'

'Oh no,' said O'Toole. 'Don't try and squeeze the boot on the other foot. I'd rather hop.' O'Toole smirked bitterly.

'That's the trouble with you, James, you're too damn clever,' said the girl. 'No feelings, just these cheap wisecracks all the time. I'm worn out. I can't listen any more.'

'You may be right,' said O'Toole humbly. 'I seem to have feelings, just like anyone else: you know, hate, jealousy, remorse, all that stuff. But I've got to admit they're a lot more real to me if I can tie them up in a neat phrase. Perhaps all that ever happens to me is just something I read somewhere.'

'I can't sit here and listen to you parade your egomania any longer,' said the girl. Her lip was trembling.

'I'm sorry,' said O'Toole. 'Again. I'm really working very hard on the dignity angle. I'm not going to be the last to leave. The host doesn't have to put his pyjamas on.'

'I'll really have to go now,' said the girl. 'I think it would be much better if we didn't have any more of these ghastly farewells. I don't want to see you for a while.'

'It's hard to believe,' said O'Toole. 'We'll be strangers the next time. If there is…'

'Oh, I'll be seeing you around.'

'Well, this is it. Good-bye.'

'Good-bye.'

She almost ran out. Her drink was intact, like a bird-bath. O'Toole drank it, shuddering at the overripe taste. Then after a decent interval he walked slowly out of the bar, not following her.

The thing to do, thought O'Toole, is to concentrate on practical matters. Like what the hell do I do now.

There was a little low-lying mist, through which sly cats scattered as O'Toole went down the street. A man could live on them at a pinch, thought O'Toole. A new Ghenghis Khan, preying off the small cattle that roam the streets.

But by God she's beautiful, according to my own neurotic standards. A very personal thing. The way a Yale key feels about a Yale lock, worn smooth by a thousand late home-comings.

O'Toole ran a piece of dialogue through his head:

'Darling, put your arm around me.'

'Like that?'

'That's wonderful.'

'We seem joined, don't we?'

'I can't detect where you end and I start. A new local anaesthetic. Cheaper than novocaine. Leads to addiction, though.'

'Don't you ever stop thinking, lamb?'

'I've got a million of them. A million million million. Darling, I'm afraid…'

'I know, your arm is going to sleep.'

'Mind if I take it away?'

'Nnnnnnnn.'

'There, darling. Good night.'

'Goodnight.'

O'Toole screwed up his eyes. The mist had a stinging, acid quality.

I can't sell that, he thought. And I can't write anything else. I'd better get a job.

II

O'TOOLE sat at a round, rickety table in his one-room basement flat. His typewriter was in front of him and, on either side, in two piles, every national newspaper, daily and Sunday, published in Britain, and the London telephone book.

O'Toole was looking at the newspapers, trying to read the minds of the men who produced them. There appeared to be a lot of inter-breeding: the small, square ones had an incestuous family resemblance, weekdays and Sundays, too. The big broad ones looked like a couple of closely related parents with a brood of sub-normal children, a pair of identical twins on Sundays and a blunt, shy country cousin with no culture, no jokes, no fat black headlines and a strange obsession with the sins of the clergy:

THE CURATE AND THE CONTRALTO
VICAR'S BAFFLING DISAPPEARANCE
CHOIRBOY SAID: 'PERHAPS'

O'Toole decided that the same brisk, clear-cut, concise letter would do for them all.

The Editor,
The *Sunday Sun,*
Fleet Street, EC4

Dear Sir,
I wonder if there is an opening on your staff for a young Australian journalist looking for a break in Fleet Street, after a few days in the old country?

I know you're a busy man so I'll keep the details brief.

NAME: James O'Toole.

AGE: 27.

EXPERIENCE: Right through the mill with the Sydney *Star,* from the Prime Minister's conference to the hen that laid the four-inch egg.

In particular, reporter, sub-editor, feature-writer, art critic, gardening expert, etc, etc.

ACCOMPLISHMENTS: Fair shorthand note, halting French and German, ability to recognise news.

EDUCATION : Two years Melbourne University (Eng. Lit.).

AMBITION: The top, but ready to start as modestly as need be.

I am available for interview, with cuttings, any time to suit you, and my salary requirements are modest.

Yours sincerely,

J O'Toole.

O'Toole signed a legible signature, blocking the capitals in the manner of newspapermen, and typed up some envelopes. He thought that he, personally, would certainly interview anyone who sent him such a letter. It might not exhibit a typically English reserve: on the other hand, neither did the papers he had just read. He looked up their addresses in the telephone books.

O'Toole's flat had at one time been painted yellow, now fast going brown. The ceiling was criss-crossed by heavy pipes, doing something which involved periodic gurgling for the flat above. In fact, for the eight storeys of flats above.

He slipped his letters into his pocket and picked his way through milk bottles to the foot of the stairwell. The night porter scowled at him from his glass box as he left the building.

He turned into Russell Square. A cold wind rustled sad scraps of paper in a dusty corner. A grey-haired woman, face eroded by the spring rains of many years, reeled out of a pub as he passed. Staggering, thought O'Toole. Not a bad first line for a pop song:

When she walks, she's staggering.

He posted his letters, contrasting the twenty scarlet coats of paint on the English post-box with the single rusty coat at home, and hurried back to his flat. There is no rhyme for 'staggering', so there was another fortune gone west.

O'Toole looked down the grimy area way into his own windows. I'm sneaking up on the West End by the underground route, he thought. Hopping from cellar to cellar. Look well on the back of a Penguin.

The porter scowled up from his newspaper to see if O'Toole had brought a woman home, saw he hadn't and looked away.

Descending the unlit stairs, O'Toole kicked the milk bottles. Through

10

the door that faced his came a shriek: 'For God's sake let me go to sleep. Please. Please.'

O'Toole let himself in, undressed and climbed into the bed, which gripped him in a greasy calico clutch. After a few minutes he climbed out and opened the windows. Almost at once a heavy lorry rumbled by on its way to Covent Garden, rattling a set of dingy horse-brasses on the mantelpiece. He found an empty cupboard and pushed them into it. Then he put a pair of brass candlesticks beside them, two bleary water-colours off the wall and a floral-patterned dish mended with Seccotine.

Having stripped the room back to a bare cement box, O'Toole got into bed again. For a while he fought the lorries rumbling past over his head, the ceiling, unseen in the dark, pressing on his forehead, and the thought that she was staggering whatever she was doing.

Then he was suddenly back on Port Phillip Bay that glittering Christmas Day, and she was there, and everything was all right.

III

REPLIES trickled back to O'Toole over three days. All had expensively embossed mastheads of newspapers on top of the notepaper. Some began 'Dear Mr O'Toole', some 'Dear Sir', some 'Dear O'Toole' and one 'Dear James, I liked the frank approach of your...' All advised O'Toole not to give up hope, but to keep in touch, because he never knew when an opening might occur. Except this one:

THE 'SUNDAY SUN'
The Paper You Can Rely On.

Dear Mr O'Toole:
The Editor has received your letter and would like to see you.
Could you telephone me and fix an appointment?
Yours sincerely
(indecipherable)
Secretary to the Editor.

O'Toole found it among the morning's mail under his door. He looked at his watch in the orange gloom. Noon, near enough. He fumbled into clammy shirt and trousers, twisted sockless feet into shoes

11

and blinked up the stairs to the phone-booth by the porter's box.

A man answered at the newspaper's switchboard.

'The editor's secretary, please.'

A woman came on, against a background acoustically papered with typewriters and assorted office noises.

'Mr Barr's office.'

'This is O'Toole speaking. I have a letter from you suggesting I telephone for an appointment.'

'Oh yes, Mr O'Toole,' said the woman. 'Mr Barr is free about four this afternoon, if that is convenient to you.'

'Fine,' said O'Toole. 'Mr Barr is…'

'The editor. Oh, and could I give you a word of advice, Mr O'Toole?'

'Of course.'

'Don't expect too much. At four, then. Thank you.'

O'Toole put the receiver down as if it was made of china, and lit a cigarette. Fleet Street. He tried a manly handshake as he left the telephone booth. Mr Barr, I want you to know that…

When he regained his room he pulled back the curtains and noticed the light-coloured rings on the mantelpiece where the ornaments had been.

O'Toole walked briskly down Fleet Street at three forty-five, studying the bad architecture. The trouble, he decided, started when the shopkeepers in the printers' quarter got above themselves. Every building was an architectural gem, the Taj Mahal next to the Magnetogorsk ball-bearing works with the Munich Bauhaus fighting for breath in between. Megalomaniacs clamouring for attention, every building the latest architectural word when it was put up, and dated and pretentious twelve months later. Glass walls, Gothic fronts, Roman arches, art nouveau, Mussolini modern and business baroque. What happens when you try to translate news value into something that isn't thrown away tomorrow.

The display of Union Jacks, dense and assertive, reminded O'Toole of Greek Independence Day in Sydney.

The *Sunday Sun* occupied a strange building, each floor of which was stepped back from the one below, the same general pattern as the Aztec sacrificial pyramid. But there was no obsidian altar on top: this being a rainy climate, thought O'Toole, they tear the victims' hearts out inside.

O'Toole walked through a glass doorway. Above the lift was a mural incorporating blacksmiths, winged messengers and philosophers holding opened books. All wore Grecian drapes.

Underneath was an inscription:

'While the Press is in Chains, No Man is Free'

A doorman with a fat stomach in a brass-buttoned coat barred O'Toole's way.

'Excuse me, sir. You want to see someone?'

'I thought I could find my own way,' said O'Toole. 'I'm a reader.'

'I'm sorry, sir, we can't have people just wandering in like that. I'll have to ask you to fill this in. Would you give the name of the person you wish to see, and the exact nature of your business?'

O'Toole filled in Barr's name and his own. Under Business? he wrote 'seeking employment'.

'I have an appointment,' he explained.

'Just a moment, sir, I'll have Mr Barr see this,' said the doorman. He was obviously looking forward to telling O'Toole to leave or be thrown out.

A boy took the form and got into the lift. O'Toole studied the mural for symbolic meaning: Caxton was doing something to Pericles while the Pilgrim Fathers read all about it.

The boy came back and beckoned O'Toole into the lift. It stopped at the third floor. O'Toole followed the boy through a door marked 'Private' into a vast room. Desks arranged in rows, telephone cords dangling from the ceiling. Three or four men at typewriters looked up hostilely and a bald man turned and smiled at another. They didn't know O'Toole, and he didn't know them, but O'Toole thought they had a slight edge because they knew the geography. Love-fifteen. On the other hand, O'Toole could have been anybody, whereas it was quite obvious they were hired hands. Fifteen-all. Australia to serve.

The boy led O'Toole, concentrating on a glossy job-hunter's smile, to a smaller office on the other side. A tiny sweet-faced woman received him.

'Mr O'Toole? I'm Mrs Wilkins. Mr Barr is expecting you.'

She opened a communicating door into a carpeted office. A large desk had a glass top and a bust of Shakespeare. Behind it a middle-aged man, thin, in a brown suit, held out his hand.

'So you're O'Toole,' he said. 'Glad to see you. Sit down.'

O'Toole adjusted his smile and sat.

'I'll come straight to the point, Mr O'Toole. I liked your letter. Did you write it yourself?'

O'Toole's smile faltered but came back strongly.

'Of course. Writing's my business, Mr Barr.'

Barr liked that. He had the letter in front of him.

'We're a paper that likes to take chances. Frankly, I thought you were the Fleet Street type the moment I read your letter. Maybe you aren't. We've had a few Australians in the Street and they seemed to know their stuff. Tell me, are you just another hack?'

'I don't think so,' said O'Toole. It sounded weak, and he studied an impulse to start scribbling ideas on Barr's blotter, showing he had plenty. Barr kept on.

'Mind you, there's no room here for amateurs. We have a small staff and we want top-notchers, adaptable men who can turn their hands to all the small jobs. No need here for specialists and prima donnas. You with me?'

'Well, I don't know your local conditions here, of course, but I've been just about right through the mill,' said O'Toole. 'I've even had my by-line drawn in twigs on the gardening page.'

'Fine,' said Barr. 'We'll see if you've got what it takes, and we'll get to know you afterwards. Okay, boy?'

'Okay,' said O'Toole.

Barr pressed a button on a large intercommunication box and spoke into the receiver. 'Tom...? I've got this Aussie here. O'Toole. Send him out on something, will you?'

He motioned O'Toole to the door. 'Mr Jacobs is the news editor. He'll give you an assignment. If you can handle it, I'll see you again. If not, no hard feelings. Don't let me down, laddie.'

'Thanks, Mr Barr,' said O'Toole.

One of the men from the newsroom was waiting for him. He was balding, thirtyish, with eyes several sizes smaller than usual for a boyish face. He had a file of assorted papers in his hairy hands.

'I've got something here that should just suit you, Aussie,' said Jacobs. 'I suppose you've been everywhere, have you?'

'Lots of places.'

'Cairo, for instance?'

'For a day.'

'Great. You'll know the background. Just take a butchers at this.'

O'Toole studied the telegram Jacobs gave him.

SUNDAYSUN LONDON MEET ME 1700 PLANE FROM CAIRO LONDON AIRPORT GOT SOMETHING HOT POLLAK

14

'Interesting, Mr Jacobs,' said O'Toole.

'Tom,' said Jacobs. 'You've got the picture?'

'One or two questions occur to me,' said O'Toole. 'Who's Pollak?'

'Search me,' said Jacobs. 'This came in out of the blue. We have a lot of tipsters trying to sell us stories but I don't recall ever hearing of Pollak before. However, this cable cost him a couple of nick so Pollak must think he's got something good, whoever he is.'

'What's the procedure, exactly, with this sort of thing?'

'Use your nose for news. Meet Pollak and buy him a beer. If he's got anything, switch to Scotch. If he asks for money, be vague. Don't promise a definite sum, but indicate there's plenty here for him, and we'll get terribly annoyed if he tries to flog his story up and down the Street. Get him into a taxi and back to the office if he shows any signs of offering it all round. If his story is no good tell him to offpiss. Got it?'

'There's another small point, Tom...'

'Lolly. Never fear, Thomas is near. Write me an IOU for five and I'll let you have it out of the float.'

O'Toole scrawled IOU £5 J O'TOOLE on a sheet of copy paper and Jacobs exchanged it for five singles from a tin box, which held a small pile of notes and a bigger pile of paper.

'Only one beer, mind, unless there's a definite story. Times are hard.'

'I'll be careful,' said O'Toole.

In the taxi to the airport, he read the telegram again. Pollak is an unusual name for an Egyptian. On the other hand, anything can happen in Cairo.

Automatically, O'Toole began roughing out in his head a polished-up account of the day's events for Jenny. Then, painfully, he remembered.

IV

ONLY one of the people getting out of the plane could possibly have been named Pollak. He wore a crew-cut, bifocals and thick rubbersoled shoes, like a German trying to pass as an American. He was shepherding a family group through the Customs: the man, pale, unshaven, collarless and worried; the woman a plump young African, soot-black and motherly; a child in arms, obviously theirs.

'Mr Pollak? I'm O'Toole of the *Sunday Sun.*' O'Toole looked round warily for competitors, but saw none.

'Man, thees is a great article,' said Pollak, with an accent from the Barcelona Berlitz. 'These people have been through hell. This is Mr Sweeney and his family.'

O'Toole nodded.

'What they've done to these people will make your blood boil, feller.'

'I want to hear something about it,' said O'Toole.

'Look, man,' said Pollak, 'I'd write this one myself but I've got a million things to do. You take over, huh? I'll leave the money side to you. I often run across an article like this, and if the price is right... okay, feller? You can get me at this address.' He handed O'Toole a dog-eared card

HANK POLLACK, IMPORT-EXPORT

COLOGNE

LONDON

farewelled the family and left, his rubber soles squeaking on the polished floor.

O'Toole turned to the dazed father. The woman was staring oyster-eyed round the airline terminal.

'Well, Mr Sweeney, let me take you into town where we can discuss this in comfort.'

'We have nowhere to go,' said Sweeney hopelessly. O'Toole took a cheap fibre suitcase from the woman's hand, and led them to a taxi. Politely, he squeezed into the folding seat, and twisting, told the driver: '*Sunday Sun,* Fleet Street.'

O'Toole examined a number of conversational openings as the taxi went down the tunnel and turned into Western Avenue.

'Where've you come from, Mr Sweeney?' It was safe.

'Tanganyika.'

'You're in trouble?'

'I'm afraid I am. I was given two hours to leave the colony. We were married just an hour or so before we left.'

'They must have taken a dislike to you.' O'Toole tried to sound genial and sympathetic.

'The bishop put the authorities up to it.'

'Oh,' said O'Toole, puzzled. 'Religious trouble?'

'I suppose you could say that. I am a Catholic priest.'

O'Toole glanced at the child asleep in its mother's arms and then rapidly swivelled his gaze out of the cab window. The pub signs of Hammersmith flashed by, reminding him that no newspaper he had

16

ever worked for would print a line which might offend the breweries or the Catholic Church, or both.

'I won't distress you by asking a lot of questions, Mr Sweeney. Let's wait until we get back to the office before we go into this, shall we?'

'Look, Mr Towel,' said Sweeney, 'I'm in desperate trouble. My wife and I have no money and nowhere to go. Don't play with us, I beg you.'

'Take it easy,' said O'Toole. 'Perhaps we can do something for you. No one can harm you here.'

'I fervently trust not,' said Sweeney.

They swayed through the rest of the trip in silence. The doorman scowled as O'Toole led the family into the *Sun* office. Perhaps he thought O'Toole had brought his relatives to get jobs, too.

O'Toole showed the family into the waiting-room partitioned off a corner of the main newsroom, and reported to Jacobs.

'Which one is Pollak?' asked Jacobs.

'None of them, Tom. Pollak was on the plane and he handed them over to me. I'm afraid this is a pretty sticky story.'

'Fine,' said Jacobs. 'What's the lead?'

'The man is a Catholic priest, and it seems he had an affair with this girl in Tanganyika and was kicked out of the place as a result.'

'How much does he want?'

'Who?'

'Pollak.'

'He didn't say. He gave me his address and hinted he had plenty more stories where this one came from.'

'The crafty sod. We can fix him up later. How much does the priest want?'

'You mean, there's something in this for the paper?'

Jacobs grinned. 'The rain pounded down on my corrugated iron church as the priest and the man wrestled within me. Meanwhile, the gorillas howled through the jungle. Personally, I love it, but we'll see what Barr thinks.'

Jacobs went and returned a minute later with a beaming Barr. 'This is a great story, O'Toole,' said Barr. 'No good for the Irish edition but first-class for the Midlands. Is he broke?'

'I imagine so, Mr Barr. His luggage is pretty poor and I don't suppose he's got a job to go to.'

'Fine. Handle him carefully. Offer him two-fifty, signed and sealed and no punches pulled. Go to three hundred if he pushes, and not a penny more. He probably thinks he can come over here and ask the earth…'

Jacobs nodded in knowledgeable agreement at the priest's presumed rapacity.

'I haven't mentioned money to him at all yet,' said O'Toole.

'Just as well,' said Barr. 'Talk to him, give me a couple of slips of the story and we'll decide finally in the morning.'

O'Toole found a notebook and pencil and went back to the priest. The wife had started to unpack and turn the waiting-room into a home.

'Mr Sweeney, I may be able to make you a financial offer,' said O'Toole. 'But first, I'd like you to tell me the whole story. I'm just working in the dark until I know exactly what happened.'

Sweeney looked despairingly at his wife. There was no response.

'I went out to Tanganyika as a missionary, Mr Towel. As you may know, we're ordained before we undertake that sort of work.'

'You mean you re a proper, regular priest?

'There's only one kind of priest, Mr Towel. I have never had a parish, but I am ordained, certainly. Well, it was during my teaching work that I met Ada…'

O'Toole left the family in the waiting-room and found a typewriter. He had never handled a story of this kind before and, automatically, decided that it should be presented as straight news, in view of the number of people it would annoy.

A Catholic priest and his African wife have been expelled from the Tanganyika protectorate because, the priest alleges, of pressure on the Government by the local Catholic bishop.

The priest, Fr Francis Sweeney, claims that Government interference in a religious dispute violates the fundamental principles of British administration. He...

O'Toole looked up and found Barr reading over his shoulder.

'I'm afraid this pissology's no good to me, boy,' said Barr. 'What I want is the warm human drama, the heart-searing problem' – he stepped back and gestured dramatically – 'that is tearing this man's guts out. I want every detail of his tremendous struggle to master his hunger, the hunger he could not deny because he was a man under his clerical robes. That's the angle I want. Can you give it to me?'

'I'll do my best,' said O'Toole.

'Fine,' said Barr. 'Don't be too long, there's a train I can catch in an hour.'

O'Toole lit a cigarette and strolled unobtrusively to a file of the *Sunday Sun* displayed in a corner. He studied the paper closely for the first time. The basis of the prose style seemed to be words like LOVE and HATE and IN and OUT in capital letters.

Some were underlined as well, and here and there was a paragraph entirely in capitals with a black wiggly rule underneath. These were the paragraphs with the most banal ideas, generally concerning emotions the reader was urged to have about the story being told.

The whole effect was embarrassing to read, bathos swimming in goo topped with whipped clichés. But not all that hard to do. Just hold your nose and jump in.

Jacobs joined him by the file. 'Did they have it off behind the altar?' he leered.

'I'm not sure,' said O'Toole. 'I didn't even ask. I thought we left that part of it to the readers' imaginations.'

'Give this everything you've got,' advised Jacobs. 'Just let it run. This could be the page one lead on your first job, if you handle it right. The priest and the glamorous chief's daughter. I love it.'

'Is she the chief's daughter?' asked O'Toole.

'They all are,' said Jacobs. 'Use your head.'

'Sorry,' said O'Toole. 'It just slipped my mind for the moment.'

'Better get started, or Barr will smack,' advised Jacobs. 'Don't forget the gorillas.'

O'Toole wound a sheet of paper into his typewriter, took a deep breath and began:

It was the searing, destroying flame of LOVE that scorched the lives of this tragic couple—LOVE and HATE that brought them 6,000 miles from tropical AFRICA to find refuge in BIG-HEARTED BRITAIN.

He is a Roman Catholic PRIEST, a man bound by the most solemn promises known on EARTH, but still a MAN under his clerical robes.

SHE is the beautiful daughter of an AFRICAN CHIEF, a girl with thousands of adoring subjects to obey her SLIGHTEST WHIM.

They fell in love under the purple skies of Africa, while the rain pounded down on his corrugated iron church and gorillas sent through the steaming jungle the CRY OF NATURE!

WAGGING TONGUES drove them from their tropical love-nest to face the PITIFUL GLARE of publicity – the SCORNFUL LOOKS which stab these sensitive people to the heart!

CAN YOU REFUSE THEM THE CHRISTIAN CHARITY FOR WHICH THEY PLEAD?

This seemed a fair imitation of the style he had just read, perhaps a trifle on the sober side. Still, thought O'Toole, it's a serious subject.

He showed his effort to Jacobs, who read it quickly, roaring like a gorilla at the appropriate passage.

'Did you get her measurements?' he asked.

'I'm afraid not,' said O'Toole. 'Should I have measured her? I thought the story was more in the priest. He's about average height, I'd say.'

'Always get the measurements,' said Jacobs. 'Gives the readers something to slobber over. If they get shy, 37-25-37 is safe for just about anyone except Sabrina or Queen Salote.'

'I'll get them tomorrow,' said O'Toole.

'Otherwise it's fine, I'd say. I like your nose.'

'Nose?'

'The first paragraph.'

'Oh, the lead. I followed the general style of the paper.'

'So I see. I'll show it to Barr.'

Jacobs scratched his armpit, gorilla-style, as he went to the editor's office. Barr was out in a moment, enthusiastic.

'This is the real stuff, boy,' he said. 'Anyone else know about them? Was the *Pic* there, or the *People?*'

'Not a soul, Mr Barr, except myself. I collected them straight off the plane.'

'Fine. Take them home and keep them under wraps till the morning, at least, when we can sign them up. Don't let anybody else get a crack at them. Let me have a thousand words, tomorrow, or fifteen hundred if it's there. I think you've got a natural Fleet Street touch, laddie. Keep up the good work.'

'Thanks, Mr Barr.'

Barr returned to his office to get his hat and coat as O'Toole went to his guests. Barr passed him on his way out and glanced distantly at the family, as if they were no business of his.

The Sweeneys seemed to be settling down to camp in the waiting-room.

'Mr Sweeney, I think we can help you,' said O'Toole. 'In the meantime, you've got nowhere to stay. Would you like to put up at my place for the night?'

'Now, that's really very kind of you, Mr Towel.'

'O'Toole. My place is small, but I hope you'll be comfortable.'

O'Toole turned restlessly on the floor of his kitchenette. His head was in a dark corner under the sink; his feet projected into the living-room, where the priest was snoring loudly in O'Toole's bed. His wife was a shadow on the pillow beside him. The child slept happily in an opened suitcase.

Six hours ago I was unemployed, thought O'Toole. Now I have this warm human drama doing me out of my bed. This poor bastard is certainly in a tight spot, but where else can he get two-fifty for a load of nonsense, and somewhere to sleep thrown in?

V

O'TOOLE was finishing the story of the star-crossed lovers:

What does the future hold for this TORMENTED COUPLE and their innocent love-child?

Here, in HOSPITABLE BRITAIN, they hope to find the forgiveness they sought in vain in CRUEL AFRICA.

Father Sweeney wants a job. He knows no trade, has no qualifications except a little Latin, and the deep human sympathy of a man who has SUFFERED – a man who has the courage to start again.

Is there, IN THE WHOLE OF BRITAIN, an employer who will take a chance on this man, knowing that he has broken THE MOST SACRED LAWS of the Church and of Society?

The *Sunday Sun* has told his tragic story with one thought in mind – the hope that somewhere, among its thirteen million regular readers, there is someone who will show Father Sweeney that his FAITH IN BRITAIN has not been misplaced.

O'Toole's right thumb was tired from holding the shift-key, but on re-reading the story seemed not too bad. Some of this, he thought, comes close to home. I have no trade myself except a little Latin and the warm human sympathy of a man who needs a job badly. *Odi et amo. Da mi basia mille, deinde centum, deinde mille mille mille centum. At tu, Catulle, destinatus obdura.*

He had sneaked early out of his cellar, leaving bus fare for his sleeping guests. He reasoned that they would be along soon, as there was nothing to eat in the place. Everyone in London who charged money for food would help O'Toole kick the priest in the teeth.

'Mr Towel? Can you spare a minute?'

Sure enough, the worried Irish face around the door of the office, the apologetic Irish voice, and still no collar: he probably didn't have any non-clerical ones.

O'Toole gathered the typed slips of his story, waved the visitors into the waiting-room and followed them in.

The wife smiled brightly.

'Thank you for the hospitality,' said Sweeney. 'We were very comfortable. Can you do anything for us?'

'This is the score, Mr Sweeney,' said O'Toole. 'I'll come straight to the point. I've written an article, and if we publish it we'll pay you two hundred and fifty pounds. All I want is your signature on each page.'

O'Toole handed over the story, motioning the priest not to read it for a moment.

'Before you begin, let me say it's probably not what you'd like to read about yourself. I just work here, Mr Sweeney. I know what they want' – O'Toole noted as he spoke that *I* had become *they* – 'and I know what they'll pay the money for. You'll notice I've put an appeal on the end for someone to give you a job.'

'That's very thoughtful of you. May I read it now?'

'Go ahead.'

The priest turned the sheets with a marked, instinctive reverence for the written word. O'Toole watched uneasily.

'This is dreadful!' said the priest. 'No offence to you, Mr Towel, but this is a sensational vulgarisation of the whole situation. I know I have done wrong, but this...'

'I can probably get you three hundred,' said O'Toole. 'If you need the money, better get as much as you can. I can make a few alterations here and there if there's something you particularly don't like, but I might as well tell you frankly they want something along the general lines of this story, or it's no dice.' There's that *they* again, thought O'Toole. *We* give him the good news, but *they* put him under the chopper.

'You surely can't realise what you're asking me to do,' said the priest.

'I've got a fair idea,' said O'Toole. 'You've got something to sell, and I'm offering you the best price. You can hawk it up and down the Street if you like, but you can safely take my word you won't better our offer. If you don't want to sell, no hard feelings.'

'I understand. It's a lot of money, especially in my situation. When... when would I get it?'

'Tuesday. Cash if you like.'

'It would make all the difference to us. But, naturally, you're a businessman and you want your pound of flesh, if you'll pardon the expression.'

'I suppose I am,' said O'Toole. 'Personally, I don't know what I'd do in your position, and I know that's not much help. Look, here's a pound. Go and have breakfast, the three of you. No strings. Ring me when you've thought it over.'

'That's very generous. When do you want a decision?'

'I'm afraid I'll have to say, within a couple of hours.'

'Very well,' said the priest. 'I'll telephone you. And thank you again for your courtesy.'

Jacobs came up as the family left.

'How's the religious desk, Aussie?'

'I'm not sure. His Reverence is thinking it over.'

'You should have conned him into signing up on the spot.'

'I thought I'd better leave it to him.'

'You're crazy. So's he, if he doesn't take the lolly. What does he care what people think of him in Brighton or Bradford?'

'He's sorely tempted, I can tell you. The priest and the man are wrestling within him, to coin a phrase.'

'Nice line,' said Jacobs. 'Would you go and see Barr? He's asking for you.'

VI

THE bust of Napoleon hadn't changed, but Barr's manner was distinctly more fatherly.

'I thought you did a bang-up job on the Sweeney story, as soon as you got what we were after,' said Barr, warmly. 'Is he all signed up?'

'Not yet, but I think he will,' said O'Toole, with a modest smile.

'Your end of it was just what we wanted, anyway,' said Barr. 'Of course you can never be sure of these crooks until you've got them tied up, and sometimes not even then. As far as you're concerned, I think there might be a job here for you, if you can keep on delivering the goods.'

'Just try me out,' said O'Toole.

'That's just what I'm going to do, laddie,' said Barr. 'I'm putting you on a week's trial as from today. There are a lot of things you don't know yet, of course. I'm going to assign you to one of our top men to see how you shape on the team. You've met Norman Knight outside, have you?'

'Not yet.'

'I suppose you know he's the best crime man in Fleet Street. I've built him up over the years as the reporter who names the names. He can be a difficult man at times, but you might be the type to appeal to him.'

'What's the job?' asked O'Toole.

'Norman is doing a series on vice in London for me at the moment. He ties up the investigation side of it before the exposure actually starts running in the paper. Report to him and tell him you're working under his orders for the next few days. Right?'

'Right,' said O'Toole.

'Good luck, boy,' said Barr at the door of his office. 'There are big opportunities here in the Old Country if you're ready to work, ready to give us all you've got. There's Knight over there.'

O'Toole saw two men talking, or rather one talking and the other listening politely. One was about thirty-five, sandy-haired, with horn-rimmed glasses and a blazer with handkerchief tucked up the sleeve in the manner of naval officers and policemen, either of which, in a suitable uniform, he could have been.

The other man was very old, very tall and very long-grey-haired, a monument standing at the centre of a gentle snowfall of ash from a cigarette bobbing between busy lips. He couldn't possibly have been a crime reporter at any time after the case of Dr Crippen, so the other man must be Knight.

'You know what Lloyd George said to me, Norman?' the monumental personage was asking. 'He said he was too busy to see me. Didn't believe him for a moment, of course.'

'Of course not, Prof,' said Knight. He leaned forward and shouted. 'Excuse me a moment, there's someone here wants to see me.'

'The Kaiser tried the same thing on another occasion,' said the

24

personage. 'Remind me to tell you about it, Norman.'

'Another time, Prof,' shouted Knight. Then, turning to O'Toole, he almost whispered: 'You want me?'

'Mr Knight?'

'Uh-huh.'

'I'm James O'Toole. I'm new around here. Mr Barr told me to tell you I was to work with you.'

'You an Aussie?'

'Right.'

'I thought I recognised that twang.'

'I was going to say the same to you. You must be English.'

'Irish, actually, way back,' said Knight, laughing. 'Glad to have you aboard, Digger. As a matter of fact, I've got a job on in a few minutes that might just appeal to you. Come down to the car and I'll fill you in as we go.'

Knight drove carefully down the Strand, giving plenty of hand signals, like a policeman. O'Toole studied the ruddy, broken-nosed profile over his slug-grey raincoat.

'Done much in the Street?' asked Knight.

This is my first job,' said O'Toole. 'I'm very green.'

'I suppose you've been right through it in Aussieland,' said Knight.

'Pretty well,' said O'Toole. 'Courts, cookery, horoscopes, even a bit of culture.'

'Crime work?'

'Yes, a bit of that.'

'Read any of my stuff?'

'Afraid not.'

'Well, you'll soon get the hang of it. There's a lot of old bollocks talked about Fleet Street, you know: basically a newspaper's a newspaper wherever you are. Just at the moment I'm putting together some stuff for another series on vice in London. I more or less specialise in it, or I seem to have been lately.'

'Sounds interesting.'

'Well, there are a couple of basic points you want to get into your head. The secret of this game is, never open your fly. Not on the job, that is.'

'That's a concession.'

'It's just common sense, really: you'll have a lot of stuff poked at you, of course, but you're no use to me if it gets around that you're having it off with these whores on the side. Get me?'

'I think I do,' said O'Toole.

'Now here's the score on the place we're going to. It's owned by a dirty Maltese ponce with a record as long as your arm, including plenty of immoral earnings and a couple of malicious woundings. What we want is positive evidence that the place is a brothel. I can't go in myself because he knows me, but you're a fresh face, and with that accent he'll never rumble you. No offence meant, of course, Digger.'

'None taken,' said O'Toole. 'I suppose I don't announce myself as a new man from the *Sunday Sun.*'

'Good God, no,' said Knight. The idea gave him a lot of amusement. 'You'll be done up savagely if you do.'

'Who am I, then?'

'You're a sailor looking for a bit,' said Knight. 'Use any name you like. Got any special fancies?'

O'Toole thought. 'There's a newspaper columnist in Sydney named David McDougall,' he suggested. 'How's that?'

'Fine,' said Knight. 'Is he a pal of yours?'

'Yes, he used to be a sort of friendly rival,' said O'Toole. 'Writes on art and politics and that sort of thing.'

'Couldn't be better,' said Knight. 'Now here's the drill. I've been told that one of the girls in this place is called Eva. You go in and ask for her – say you've been recommended to her by a shipmate. Go and see her and establish definitely she's a prostitute.'

'How?'

'Well, you'd better get her to strip and name her price. That just about clinches it. Then you leave quietly, remembering you might have to go back if anything goes wrong.'

'What sort of information do we want?'

'Oh, just the usual. Ask her how much a short time and how much an all-nighter. We'll see what this Maltese is getting out of the place.'

'How do I get out?'

'That's up to you, Digger. You'll see some sort of opportunity. The big thing is, don't expose your person or commit a breach of the peace. Keep that in mind and you can't go wrong. If there's any rough stuff, you look out for yourself, of course, but no trouble unless you can help it.'

'Where will you be?'

They were passing through Earls Court and turning into a side street off Earls Court Road.

'I'll have a cup of tea in the ABC at the Tube,' said Knight. 'There's the place there. In you go, and good shooting.'

O'Toole felt improbably respectable as he approached the scruffy terrace house. A wild yearning for a disguise flashed through him, and he tried to slouch as the only thing available. Then, boldly, he knocked. A man with a dirty shirt under a navy-blue chin opened the door.

'I want to see Eva,' said O'Toole, with the sort of voice his parents had told him was common.

The man studied him without interest and jerked a black-rimmed thumb. 'Upstairs.'

O'Toole must have looked uneasy. 'Top floor,' added the man, looking up and down the street over O'Toole's shoulder.

O'Toole went down a dark corridor smelling strongly of cat's urine, up three flights of rutted stairs, and knocked on the only door on the top floor.

A voice, a girl's, in a mixture of Cockney and Cleopatra trilled: 'Come in, it's not locked.'

O'Toole walked into a narrow attic. A young girl showing signs of wear lay on a bed, dressed in some sort of housegown and evidently nothing underneath. She was reading a copy of *Tit-Bits*. A portable radio was giving out the BBC programme for schools.

'Eva?'

'That's me,' said the girl, smiling brightly. As she put down the magazine, O'Toole noticed that she didn't clutch the gaping front of her gown.

'I'm Dave,' said O'Toole. 'Dave McDougall. I got your address off a mate of mine. I'm just down in London for a couple of days. Off a ship. Liverpool.'

O'Toole felt a sudden fear that Liverpool mightn't be on the coast. Evidently it was.

'You're not a regular, are you, Dave?' the girl asked.

'No,' said O'Toole.

'Normally, I only do regulars in the afternoons,' said the girl.

'My mate didn't mention that,' said O'Toole. 'By the way, he didn't say how much it was.'

'What for?' asked the girl.

'Well, for a short time,' said O'Toole. The phrase sounded unlikely, like something you've been told to say to a Chinese waiter.

'Oh, three quid for regulars,' said the girl.

'How do I become a regular?' asked O'Toole, answering to himself by coming here regularly, of course, chump.

'You'll be all right, Dave,' said the girl. She began to remove the housegown. 'Slip your things off, love.'

'Er... How much for an all-nighter?' asked O'Toole.

The girl paused, the housegown half off. 'I only do all-nighters Mondays and Tuesdays. I've got plenty of time now, though.'

'That's great,' said O'Toole, desperately. 'Look, there's something I forgot to mention. I'll just have to nip down to the teashop to see a friend. He's... he's got the money.'

'Oh, I'll trust you,' said the girl. 'On second thoughts, I'll pop something on and come down and have a cup of tea with you.'

She's lonely, thought O'Toole.

'I'd like to take you,' he said. 'But... he's a friend of the wife's.'

'Okay, love,' said the girl. 'Don't be long.'

'Back in a flash,' said O'Toole.

The proprietor scowled at him suspiciously as he left. Knight, a solid British gentleman, was taking tea in the agreed place.

'How'd you go, Digger?'

'No doubt the place is a brothel, Norman. Your friend, Eva, wanted to come down and have tea with us.'

'Some other time,' said Knight. 'Now tell me exactly what happened.'

O'Toole recounted his story as they drove to the office. Knight seemed to enjoy it. 'Write it for me and we'll add it to the file,' he said.

'You mean, write it as a news story?' asked O'Toole. 'Girl offers body to phoney sailor – amazing revelations? Not exactly news, is it?'

'No, no,' laughed Knight. 'Just make a note of the facts, and you can give me a hand when I eventually put the whole series together.'

'Interesting people you meet in the newspaper business,' said O'Toole.

'Hang on a bit and they'll get a lot more interesting,' said Knight. The doorman at the *Sunday Sun* seemed to have got used to O'Toole: he hardly looked up when the pair went in.

As O'Toole was writing his account of the incident at Earls Court a light flashed on the telephone beside him.

'Hello, Mr Towel? This is Fa... Mr Sweeney speaking.' The priest sounded like a man afraid of the phone.

'Yes, Mr Sweeney.'

'I've come to a decision. You've left me no choice, really. I'll sign your... article.'

'Fine, Mr Sweeney,' said O'Toole. 'Could you come round to the office? I'll try to get some money for your immediate needs.'

'That's very thoughtful, thank you,' said the priest.

O'Toole went to give Jacobs the news.

'Father Sweeney has decided to do business with us, Tom.'

'Nice work, Aussie. Take him down to Trafalgar Square for a picture. The usual one with the pigeons. Better find him a hotel where the opposition aren't likely to get on to him: I think they'll take coloured around King's Cross.'

'He's very broke, Tom,' said O'Toole. 'I think if he had some money he'd be less likely to try for a better offer.'

'Okay, I'll give you a score in cash for him. Keep him going till he gets his cheque. Make sure he gives you a receipt. Looks like you've made the front page with your first story.'

'Just luck,' said O'Toole.

As Jacobs counted out the money from his tin box, O'Toole thought of the phrase, Thank You, Father.

That night O'Toole saw a movie: he was interested in the unfamiliar products advertised between pictures, and the fact that the audience were smoking. Afterwards he walked round Leicester Square, finding, unexpectedly, another bust of Shakespeare, with upraised arm pointing to an inscription, 'THERE IS NO DARKNESS BUT IGNORANCE', and beyond it to the dirty book stores.

Over a cup of coffee and a hamburger at the New Elizabethan Snackery, O'Toole contrasted the lost and regretted Jenny with the working girl he had met that afternoon: the innocent world of desire and make-believe he had left, the guilty world of make-believe he was entering. The bright, stunted, gap-toothed and over-painted people passing by sharpened the picture.

The hamburger was made of a smooth chemically treated artificial meat, with imitation onions on the side.

VII

THE NEXT day was Saturday, and when O'Toole came in at ten-twenty he was surprised to find the normally empty newsroom jammed with people.

On each one of the long rows of desks two, and in some places three, men were working. Others, all strangers, were walking about with papers in their hands. Along one wall sat a row of men wearing telephone headsets, with microphones round their necks, busy typing. The red light overhead which flashed for an incoming call was almost continuously alight. In the middle, like a hairy spider, sat Jacobs, bare-chested in shirt-sleeves, very busy.

'Ah, there you are, you Antipodean layabout,' he said. 'You'll have to show up earlier on Saturdays or Thomas will smack.'

'Of course,' said O'Toole. 'Your busy day. What have we got?'

'First of all you can go through the handouts,' said Jacobs, indicating a pile of perhaps three hundred letters. 'Won't take as long as it looks. You don't have to read them all. Anything with a roneoed address or a foreign stamp you can throw out straight away. Anything not sealed up likewise. Keep an eye out for handwritten ones containing warm human stories. Give me any invitations to parties you come across and God help you if you miss anything good.'

'Right,' said O'Toole. 'What then?'

'I've got some wills and the weather,' said Jacobs. 'Come see me when you've got through that lot.'

O'Toole took an armful of letters and selected a waist-high yard-wide wicker waste-paper basket. It was already half full.

The first letter he opened was from someone who made diesel engines. Out. Then some dog-lovers. Out. 'News Release from the World Ex-Servicemen's'... should have seen the foreign stamp. Out. 'The High Commissioner for Nigeria ...' Out. Just a tick, any free drinks? '...issued the following statement...' no, out. 'Atomic scientists meeting in Rome, this week called...' Out. Press Statement by J Carlton Zugsmith, President of the British Legion of Sun-bathers...' Show it to Jacobs. 'Sir: The people of Southern Zanzibar appeal to you in the name of...' Out. 'She'll be named Miss New Zealand Apples, pretty nineteen-year-old...' Out, and out, and out.

O'Toole threw out the last of the handouts and went back to Jacobs.

'There's a sunbather's convention you might be interested in.

Otherwise very ordinary stuff,' he said.

'Guess who's in the waiting-room,' said Jacobs. 'Your pal, Father Trickemup just arrived. Wants more lovely lolly, I expect. Go and see him, will you?'

The priest looked sleepless and haggard. He still had no collar.

'I'm sorry to trouble you again on this matter, Mr Towel.'

'Quite all right,' said O'Toole. 'What's the bother?'

'I hope you won't think me guilty of bad faith, but I'll have to ask you not to publish your article.'

'That's very serious,' said O'Toole. 'Might I ask what's happened?'

'They have been in touch with me.'

'The Church?' The priest nodded.

'You see, they have a procedure for cases... like mine. They have indicated a way out. Naturally, it won't be easy...'

'I don't suppose so,' said O'Toole.

'Of course, you can see that if anything is printed... if there's any public scandal... I've spent fifteen shillings of your money, I'm afraid, but I want you to take the rest back, and I'll repay you just as soon as I'm able.'

'I'm afraid it's not that easy,' said O'Toole. 'I'll tell the editor what you've told me, but I can't promise anything. It's not a question of the money, but the machinery has been set in motion. It's hard to stop,'

'I'll know you'll do your best, Mr Towel,' said the priest.

O'Toole went to Jacobs.

'The priest wants to renege, Tom,' he said.

'Some chance,' said Jacobs. 'He's signed up, hasn't he?'

'Yes, and had his picture taken, and collected an advance on his money.'

'Good enough. A deal is a deal is a deal. Better go and tell Barr, just the same.'

O'Toole found Barr in his office and told him.

'...and he says we'll wreck his welcome back into the fold if we go ahead, Mr Barr.'

'Oh he does, does he?' said Barr. 'The chiselling crook. If he'd come in yesterday, laddie, we might have done something, but now the whole thing's been wired to Manchester. He could build a couple of churches for what it would cost us to remake the page at this stage. Tell him we're sorry, no dice.'

'I'll tell him,' said O'Toole.

The priest seemed to take the verdict as the will of God, no appeal possible. 'This will put me outside forever, Mr Towel,' he said. 'Where can I turn?'

'I'm sorry, Mr Sweeney,' said O'Toole. 'The production of the paper has gone too far to be stopped, and there's nothing we can do about it.'

'Thank you, anyway, for your courtesy,' said the priest. 'I don't suppose I'll be seeing you again.'

'No,' said O'Toole. 'Good luck, just the same.'

The priest left the office reluctantly, like an old sheep on the way to the abattoir. O'Toole returned to Jacobs.

'I've fixed His Reverence up, Tom, and I'm ready for work,' he said. 'No more religion, please, for Christ's sake.'

'Right,' said Jacobs. 'Here's a quickie for you. We've had a tip-off from the local man that there's a public schoolboy working in a fish-and-chip shop in Huddersfield. The place is on the phone, and his name is Hetherington. Ring them up and check the facts.'

'What facts?'

'That he's really a public schoolboy, of course. I suppose you know what a public schoolboy is?'

'Eton, Harrow, boating in wing collars, that sort of thing?'

'That's it.'

'You mean he's run away from school?'

'No, he's probably fifty, if he's a day. The point is, he used to go to a public school.'

'Is that news?'

'No, but the fact that he's working in a fish-and-chip shop is. Bit of a come-down, isn't it?' O'Toole detected a touch of Bakerloo Line Cockney he hadn't noticed in Jacobs' voice before.

'Is it? I'm delighted to hear he's got a job. We don't want him sponging on the ratepayers, do we?'

'I'm too busy to explain it now, Aussie,' said Jacobs. 'Just check the facts, then use your imagination. After that, ring the Air Ministry and get the forecast for tomorrow. We don't want a lot of jaw-breaking crapology, just a simple, straight answer will do – will it rain or not. You'll see we use a little dinkus in red on the masthead of the paper. Find out which one to use. Got it?'

'Right,' said O'Toole.

He rang the fish-and-chip shop and Hetherington came to the phone, and said yes, he had gone to Winchester, and it's not a bad school, you know. Actually he was a bit of a socialist himself, and why the hell shouldn't he work in the fish-and-chip shop, the pay was seven-ten a week, they were decent people, and probably better than the blood-sucking bastards O'Toole was working for, but don't take any offence, old boy, because he thought the *Sunday Sun* was supposed to be the working man's friend, and if O'Toole proposed to put any class-conscious rubbish in the paper he might at least mention they changed the fat twice a day and made the tastiest chips in Huddersfield, and don't mention it, call again any time. The reference to fat gave O'Toole an idea for his lead paragraph, and, adopting the principle of maximum embarrassment which seemed to have worked with the priest, he wrote:

When he prepares six penn'orth of cod and chips, Henry Hetherington of the HUDDERSFIELD 'Sea Breeze' fish shop has to be careful – HIS OLD SCHOOL TIE MIGHT DANGLE IN THE FAT!

Yes, Henry wears the PROUD TIE of Winchester School among the FUMES and GREASE of a Midland fish-and-chip shop, but he claims the dignity of the old school ISN'T FRYING TONIGHT!

It's his POLITICAL OPINIONS which have brought Henry to this seven-ten a week job...

and O'Toole summarised the views he had heard on the telephone to complete his story. Then he rang the Meteorological Office of the Air Ministry.

'O'Toole of the *Sunday Sun* here,' he said. 'Could we have the forecast for tomorrow, please?'

'You're new, aren't you?' asked the voice at the other end.

'First week,' said O'Toole.

'Just the same, I don't expect you want the official forecast,' said the meteorologist, 'I've taken a lot of trouble with it.'

'No, I don't, as a matter of fact,' said O'Toole. 'I'm supposed to keep it bright and crisp. This is a family paper, you know. Just let me have an outline of the position in simple, non-technical language, please.'

'You're all the same,' said the official. He seemed to be annoyed about something. 'Well, here it is. There's a high pressure system building up over the Azores, with a corresponding cold front moving in the direction of Norway, accompanied by winds about Force Four or Five. That should mean early drizzle, with a possibility of later rain in the Home Counties, and a chance of...'

'Just a second,' said O'Toole. 'I'm afraid it's not much use me turning that in. Could you tell me if it's going to rain or not?'

'Just like all the others,' said the official. 'Look, you must be a man of some minimal education. You have to be, to work as a reporter, don't you?'

'I'm literate, if that's what you mean,' said O'Toole.

'I'm glad to hear it,' said the official. 'Well, surely you can understand the notion of a probability. When we say "there may be early rain", that's a scientific description of the situation as it is now. Sometimes it will, sometimes it won't, sometimes it might. That's not all that difficult, is it?'

'You have to see it from our point of view,' said O'Toole. 'We're supposed to be definite about these things. We have a set of little drawings which are printed in red next to the name of the paper, on the front page, of a girl in a bathing suit. If it's going to rain, she has an umbrella up. If it's going to be cold, she wears a sweater. All I want to know is, which drawing do we use?'

'Look, it's your irresponsible papers which have turned us into a standing joke,' said the official heatedly. 'Every time we say "it might" you chaps change it into "it will". Within the limits of our information, we give a good reliable service, but by the time you've finished altering what we say out of recognition, we're always wrong. Television has been the greatest thing that ever happened to weather forecasting and I hope it puts you out of business.'

'Now, now, no temper,' said O'Toole. 'Let's approach this another way. If you were a betting man, what would you put your money on here? Wet or fine?'

'Actually, this will help me get the position into your thick skull,' said the official. 'It's a two-horse race, wet or fine, and on my information I'd have to back them both. Does that make sense?'

'I can see your point,' said O'Toole. He was enjoying the debate, but Jacobs wouldn't expect him to take more than five minutes with the weather. He tried a long shot.

'By the way, what are you doing yourself tomorrow?'

'I'm working,' said the official.

'Bringing a raincoat in?'

'I keep one here,' said the official. 'I must say, you're a trier, though.'

'Thanks,' said O'Toole. 'I got the general drift of your forecast and I'll do the best I can with it. Don't worry.'

'I'll be on the television for a few minutes tonight giving the true facts,' said the official. 'I don't have to worry. Been nice talking to you, just the same.'

O'Toole hung up, walked unobtrusively to the office window and looked out. The sky was cloudless, even brassy, with a little heat-shimmer toward St Paul's. Looked as if it should hold for twenty-four hours.

He put a sheet of paper in a typewriter and wrote:

It's a fine sunny day for you. That's what the weather-man promises for tomorrow, although there's just a chance of a late shower.

Underneath, he added:

SUGGESTED DINKUS: GIRL IN BATHING SUIT

He gave both stories to Jacobs, who read the fish-shop account without comment, then studied the weather report.

'We don't need this bit about a late shower, only confuse people,' he said. 'Otherwise, fine.'

'I suppose you're right,' said O'Toole. 'The man at the weather office doesn't seem to like us.'

'None of them do,' said Jacobs. 'Bureaucrats. Too big for their boots. You can go out and eat, if you like.'

After supper O'Toole spent the rest of the evening talking with his new colleagues. He found most of them worked for other papers during the week, and worked Saturdays tax-free under assumed names for the *Sunday Sun.*

One man was spending a month's holiday from another paper working for the *Sunday Sun,* relieving a man who was spending his month working somewhere else.

They all blamed the high price of drink and cigarettes. None of them looked too well.

Then, when the first edition came up, Jacobs gave him a copy and told him he could go.

Put it under your coat as you leave,' he advised. 'Not supposed to get out of the office before three a.m. You might go up the street and flog all our lovely news to the opposition.'

'I've got integrity,' said O'Toole. 'See you Tuesday, Tom.'

In the lift, he found his story:

RUNAWAY PRIEST BEGS YOUR FORGIVENESS by JAMES O'TOOLE.

All there, not a word changed by the subs, with a twenty-four point by-line all on the front page.

As he tucked the paper under his coat, he caught the familiar, delicious scent of fresh ink and paraffin, the way newspaper offices smell all over the world, the way the *Manchester Guardian* and *Pravda* smell if you sniff them right up close under the big important ideas.

As he walked home, the streets were already shiny with rain.

VIII

O'TOOLE heard someone at the door as he woke up: he half-expected it to be the police inquiring about the priest's suicide, or the editors of rival papers queuing up to offer him jobs.

It turned out to be the porter pushing a crisp blue air-letter under his door, with the two-shilling stamp decorated with aboriginal art, snakes and boomerangs in brown and white.

The stamp, designed by a man who arrived in Sydney from Vienna in 1947, gave him a stab of home-sickness. So did the letter:

Dear Shoulders:

I got the news that you cracked it in Fleet Street a few days after it happened. The rumour in Sydney is you're getting forty rugs a week to begin with and lots more very, very soon. I shouldn't be surprised if bums started pouring off the boat into your flat any minute demanding food, drink, clothes, women, etc. (What else is there, anyway?)

Short Cummings, who seems incapable of keeping his sticky hands off anyone's relationships, is spreading it all over town that you've broken up with Jenny. The way the story goes here, she's supposed to have been rushed by the papers the moment she got off the ship and, on the strength of a few mammary pictures, landed some sort of big part. According to the stories which are being generally distorted around, this is about the last you saw of her. Another version says you got married secretly but naturally the first one is getting a better hearing.

It's hard to imagine you two apart after all this time, but I'm not in a position to send a correction around the grapevine until I get something definite from you.

How does it feel to make the Big Time on Fleet Street? Bowler Hat? Striped Pants? Powder-blue suit? I want to know what sort of clothes I'll need.

If the Jenny story is true, let me remind you as an old friend there are plenty more fish in the sea if you've still got the right bait. I know it's an alarming thing to be wiped off like a dirty arse but, basically, you just have to sweat it out like everyone else. The only real cure is another girl but don't start looking too soon. Just relax and spend some of your big salary.

I'm assuming the Cummings story is true: if not, delete it from the copy.

I'll cable you when I'm fifty quid short of the fare. You won't miss a day or two's pay.

Love
Jowls,

PS –Don't insult T S Eliot. Leave him for me.

O'Toole cooked two sausages and an egg, the smoke hanging in the air of his basement in geological layers. Then he consulted a list he'd prepared in Sydney of people he knew in London, and finally picked

Ruth Flagg
Houseboat Mistral
Chelsea Reach
Chelsea

He found a bus going the right way. Chelsea, please. What part? Just Chelsea. Town Hall? That'll do. Eight, please. Eight what? Eightpence. Oh, sorry. Thanks. The conductress had a little machine that poked out a long tongue of ticket.

O'Toole walked down the Embankment, and by Chelsea Bridge found a flotilla of houseboats lying line abreast on a mudbank. They were festooned with electric cables and joined by a rickety gangplank. A couple of tobacco-stained swans were mooching through the empty bottles and rusty tins on the mud between the boats. Shanghai, S W, thought O'Toole.

One of the boats, cream with a red funnel, was called *Mistral*. O'Toole picked his way along the gangplank to an open hatchway, looked down and wondered what to do. Knock? Shout? Blow a siren? A girl in velvet slacks, roll-neck sweater and long red hair solved the problem by appearing at the bottom of the wooden well.

'Look who it is, James O'Toole! Come on down!'

O'Toole descended, thinking that he ought to be going backwards as, strictly speaking, this was at sea.

The boat turned out to be one long room, divided by curtains. At one end was a cooking-stove, at the other a doll's house door which must be the john. The place had a faint smell of chemical toilet, masked by old face-powder.

'Well, well,' said the girl. 'Get sick of the easy living back home?'

'I just arrived in town a few days ago,' said O'Toole. 'You've got pretty exotic quarters here, Ruth.'

'Not too bad except in the winter,' said the girl. 'Where are you living?'

'I've got a suite of cellar over by Russell Square. It's a bit cramped, although I managed to squeeze a priest and his family in the other night.'

'A priest?'

'I've been doing some work for the *Sunday Sun*. I think I've got a job there, as a matter of fact. They're very interested in religion.'

'How did the priest come into it?'

'They bought him. I was minding him.'

'Really, James. The *Sunday Sun*. Not much of a paper, is it? I mean, what's wrong with *The Times?*'

'Look, it's very hard to break into Fleet Street at all,' said O'Toole. 'I needed the job badly. In fact, I haven't even got it yet. Don't point the bone at me before I start. Besides, there have to be some crummy papers to show the Press is free, what with the insistent demand from crummy people. Someone has to keep them happy while you top people read *The Times'*

'All right, all right. Where's Jenny?'

'No comment.'

'Like that?'

'Just like that.'

'Did she come over with you? She seems to be doing very well.'

'I forget. How are you getting along?'

'Oh, I've a job with an advertising agency in South Audley Street and I get a thousand a year which is a lot for a girl in London and I know hundreds of people.'

'When do I meet them?'

'Tonight, if you're around you can meet quite a lot of them. I'm having a party. If you feel like getting a bottle or two you can come, if you like.'

'I'd like to. What's a cheap drunk? Emu Sherry?'

'Good God, no. I suggest you go up to the Anglesey and get some cider. I've already got quite a bit laid in.'

'Pretty tame stuff, isn't it?'

'Not on your life. Try some first and see.'

'Before I start investing in this, could you give me some idea who I'm going to meet?' asked O'Toole.

'Well, you'll meet Ralph. He's my lover. He's a big producer at the BBC. He's ever so sweet really. I'm the first mistress he's had since he got married.'

'Oh,' said O'Toole. 'First time?'

'What?'

'Married.'

'No, I think he's been married a couple of times. He's a bit older than you. He writes books and does talks and he's really terribly bright.'

'I can see you're still a romantic old-fashioned girl,' said O'Toole. 'Where do I go to get this stuff, exactly?'

O'Toole spent the first hour of the party sorting out who belonged to who. There seemed to be a couple of females to spare. One was a good four axe-handles round the seat, with red meat right down to the heel: the other no more than two axe-handles around, an overwhelming advantage in the narrow, crowded cabin of the boat. Two-handles had long black hair, eyes of an unobtrusive functional colour and not a bad face, by any means. O'Toole brought her a drink.

'Here, try one of these,' he said.

'Do you happen to know what it is?' she asked. She was English.

'It's some sort of local health drink,' said O'Toole. 'I've never tried it myself, but it looks harmless.' It looked brown, oily and vicious.

'It tastes vaguely like apples,' said the girl, taking a sip.

'Do you the world of good,' said O'Toole. They both drank. 'What do people talk about at parties in this country?' he asked.

'You've only just arrived in London?' asked the girl politely.

'More or less,' said O'Toole. 'I suppose it's obvious.'

'It is, rather,' said the girl. 'Oh, sex, politics, religion, what's going to become of the world. All the usual things.'

'I don't know that I can help you much on your political problems here,' said O'Toole, expansively. 'I'm a classless society man myself.' The air in the boat was thickening with cigarettes, talk and a noisy record-player.

'Surely you've got classes wherever it is you come from... New Zealand, is it?'

'Australia. Well, I must say I never noticed them. My mother used to tell me I must try to speak better than the common little boys down the street, and my old man used to say if I didn't study hard I'd wind up cracking stones. Is that class?'

'It sounds like the beginnings, anyway,' said the girl laughing.

'However, I'm getting that strong French Revolution feeling over here,' said O'Toole. 'I think that it happens to the mousiest Australians in a set-up like this, they start to see Lenin's point of view.'

'Oh, that's silly,' said the girl, but tolerantly. 'I think it's rather nice if people are different, don't you? I mean, it's a bit boring if everyone's the same as everyone else.'

'I know what you mean,' said O'Toole. 'I think I'd better explain the colonial reaction more clearly. The only class struggle I've ever had any real contact with is the international one, seen at a great distance: you know, we're a hell of a lot better than anyone else, especially the elite-conscious English.'

'But don't you have people that everyone looks up to?'

'Well, you know the sort of stuff you see in the social column of the *Evening Standard*. Derek Nochin, who is engaged to the younger sister of the Honourable Tony Sloping-shoulders, the heir of Lord Lacknuts. There is a sort of equivalent of that in the Australian newspapers, but they're pictures of sheep-farmers sour around the socks dining with raddled wives in restaurants run by immigrant Greeks. And a couple of minutes of their conversation on intellectual topics would pack them in at the Palladium, I can tell you.'

'Well, somebody has to be on top, don't they?'

'We go in for more democratic forms of snobbery. We even make a fuss over Americans, poor Americans, because the girls like their haircuts. We also like people who have good jobs, especially if they're ignorant, and we love crooks of every description. Rich ones, of course.'

'Sounds dreadful,' said the girl. 'At least we don't have that sort of thing.'

'Well, I've only been here a few weeks,' said O'Toole. 'But I must say I've noticed people aren't exactly hail-fellow-well-met with one another.'

'Oh, we're friendly enough when you get to know us,' said the girl.

'You don't quite get what I mean,' said O'Toole. 'The picture that this country projects overseas is completely top-heavy. Take me as a typical example: before I'd arrived here I'd never heard of a football pool, although I knew that South Audley Street was okay as an address. There's no point in me trying to learn about football pools, because the proles are just as damned exclusive as the others. Anyway, a stranger anywhere won't recognise the local social ladder unless there's a spot for him right at the top. Otherwise, he just wants to turn the whole thing over. So I'm an equality man.'

'Where would you put me on our social ladder, for instance?' asked the girl.

'Search me,' said O'Toole. 'Where were you born?'

'Just outside Chelmsford.'

'Don't know where it is,' said O'Toole. 'Even if I did, I don't know which side of the tracks it's on. In fact, I can't even locate the tracks. We could make a fortune with a really useful map of London, showing the tracks with arrows pointing to the right side and the wrong side. For foreigners only, of course. Start a revolution if the English saw it.'

'Would it help you if you knew I went to Oxford?' asked the girl.

'I've really caught your interest, haven't I?' said O'Toole. 'Where do you work? Or do you, or is that the wrong sort of question?'

'No, that's quite in order,' the girl laughed. 'At the War Office.'

'What do you do – make war?'

'Only in a very minor way. I read newspapers and magazines and things like that and make reports.'

'Now, there's a funny thing,' said O'Toole. 'I'm more or less of a travelling newsman myself. You know, with a bicycle, a green tennis eyeshade and a bag of plumber's tools on my back.'

'Really?' asked the girl. 'From the great outback?'

The boat was by now jammed with people, the floor slowly getting stickier with spilt beer, wine, cider and crushed dog-ends. O'Toole was looking behind him to see he didn't tread on anyone, when a man of thirty or so joined him and the girl. The newcomer had pink cheeks and heavy horn-rimmed glasses.

'This is Nigel Porter,' said the girl. She evidently knew him, and didn't particularly want to know him any better. 'This is an Australian friend of Ruth's.'

'James O'Toole,' said O'Toole.

'I accidentally heard what you two were talking about,' said Porter. 'I don't know why you wogs come over here if you don't like the way we do things.'

'My great-grandfather was transported,' said O'Toole. 'Possibly by yours, if a Porter ever got as high as the county bench. I'm the first member of the family who ever got the fare back again. I'm here to get even.'

'How are you going to do that?'

'By taking all the women, of course,' said O'Toole. This seemed to touch Porter on a psychological boil.

'Some chance,' he said.

'I hear it's not a crowded line,' said O'Toole.

'What do you mean?' asked Porter, truculently.

'Never mind,' said O'Toole. 'We're having a serious discussion here. Why not get us all some drinks and join in?'

As Porter fetched the drinks, O'Toole asked: 'Friend of yours?'

'Not lately,' said the girl.

'Got it,' said O'Toole. Then, to Porter returning with the drinks. 'Nicely carried, old man.'

'Now, what were you saying about our social system?' asked Porter.

O'Toole took a long swallow. 'Here's how I see it,' he said. 'All caste systems are based on foreign conquest. The untouchables are the aboriginal inhabitants, Welsh and Britons and cattle of that sort. The Saxons turn up, conquer them and set them to work, where they are to this day. Then the Normans, a sort of good German type, come over and kick the living be-Jesus out of the Saxons. Everyone kept racially pure, so you have the framework of the present three big social divisions. Collaborators of course got honorary membership in the next group up. Now, how do you like that?'

'Rubbish,' said Porter. 'The last invasion was a thousand years ago, thanks to the Royal Navy.'

'Of course things have got a bit blurred,' said O'Toole. 'On this scheme the present middle-class got their mystique from the Saxons, who were bad Germans anyway, and being conquered conquerors would make anybody twisted. Everyone admits the middle-class are the biggest bastards of the lot. No personal offence, of course.'

'You make it sound like a continuous civil war,' said Porter. 'It just shows how ignorant you are of the real spirit of Great Britain, chum. We're a very united people. You should have been here during the war.'

'So should half the actors in Hollywood,' said O'Toole. 'Just the same, something very queer is going on here. Look at the conspicuous absence of the British Dagwood.'

'Dagwood?' asked Porter.

'You couldn't draw a Dagwood strip for a British paper,' said

O'Toole. 'An average, everyday family with a part for everyone to identify with.'

'There are millions of average Englishmen,' said Porter.

'Maybe,' said O'Toole. 'But try to imagine what the English Dagwood does for a living. Does he go to the dogs, the races or the bookie in the tobacco kiosk? Blackpool, Frinton or the Riviera?'

'He suits himself,' said Porter. 'He's independent.'

'No matter how you handled him, half the population would say "Thank Christ I'm not one of those",' said O'Toole, taking another long swallow. 'That's where the Royal Family come in.'

Porter didn't like this twist. O'Toole did. 'They're the Dagwood Bumsteads of England,' he said. 'A happy tale of family life, with a part for everyone, and they even get a big bang out of dogs.'

'You've got a nerve coming to this country and insulting the Queen,' said Porter.

'Easy, Jack,' said O'Toole. 'This isn't the Forbidden City we're talking about, you know. They abolished prostration some years back.'

'You ignorant clot,' said Porter, swinging a wild whistling blow. It missed by a yard, and so did O'Toole's counter. Drinks spilt in a radius of two paces, and a rush of guests separated them. There was no sign of a race riot developing.

'Don't take any notice of him,' said the girl. 'He's had too much to drink.' Porter had moved some distance away and was explaining his side of the dispute to an appreciative circle, who turned from time to time to scowl at O'Toole.

'Does this place have an annexe?' asked O'Toole. 'We need quiet for a serious discussion.'

'Well... there's an empty boat, three boats up,' said the girl. 'We could take a walk up there, if you like.'

'Fine,' said O'Toole, grabbing a bottle as they left the party. The tide had covered the mudflat, and there was dark water under the swaying gangplank linking the houseboats. Red and green lights, of the hard chemical colour of milkshake flavouring, winked over the river. O'Toole lowered himself into the third boat, a twin of the one they had left, and caught the girl as she followed. She dropped lightly into his arms, so he kissed her. She clung, warm and luxurious like a cashmere sweater. 'You know,' she said, 'you're rather nice.'

The boat seemed much like the other one inside, but empty. They sat on the bed. O'Toole shivered.

'Are you cold?' whispered the girl.

'No violence,' said O'Toole. He had passed slightly beyond rational speech. 'No prisons, no wars, no wounds, no rough stuff. Have pity on me.'

'I haven't a violent thought in my mind, silly,' said the girl.

'They all have,' said O'Toole. 'Poison you with tears.'

'No one's crying.'

'Not yet,' said O'Toole. 'Or maybe never.'

Women, seemingly, wear much the same underneath, everywhere.

'You be kind to me,' whispered the girl.

'Everyone's kind to everyone, it's a great world,' said O'Toole. He was just past the point of talking. The bed was impossibly narrow. The floor had a long ridge down the middle, but it was better.

Suddenly, the boat rocked in a long, shuddering heave, reverberating in O'Toole's head.

'She's come off the mud,' said the girl, softly.

'Shipboard romance,' said O'Toole thickly. Floating, the floor seemed gentler.

'My sweet, my sweet,' said O'Toole.

The boat swayed softly on the incoming tide.

IX

O'TOOLE and the girl were having breakfast in a rundown restaurant in the King's Road, the first they had found open. In the window a peeling gold-letter sign said TEAS backwards. On the counter was a glass case containing cigarettes, staling buns and fruit pies in boxes, and near it a gas-fired coffee-machine. The chrome on the machine had been polished off in places, showing copper underneath. A notice said ORDINARY COFFEE, 8d. CUP. Around them, honest working men were consuming sausages and mash and egg and chips.

O'Toole and the girl were drinking ordinary coffee out of thick chipped mugs. He felt as if he had been extensively tenderised by the iron spine of the boat. The girl looked fresh. Tough people here, thought O'Toole.

'You know, this country has some marvellous old traditions,' he said. The girl's mouth was full. 'Look at that.' He read a sign over business premises across the road. 'Thomas Crapper and Sons, Sanitary Engineers, by Royal Appointment.'

The girl twisted round to look. 'Don't start on the Royal Family again,' she said.

'It couldn't be a coincidence,' said O'Toole. 'He must have started the whole thing himself.'

'Who started what?'

'Crapper. The original of the gentleman dapper probably stepped right out here into the King's Road.'

'Stepped out of what?'

'The original crapper. Dunny. Jakes. Cabinet.'

'Oh, you mean the loo.'

'Is that the word? Loo.'

'I thought Sir Walter Raleigh invented them.'

'Just a middleman,' said O'Toole. 'It's hardly possible that someone named Thomas Crapper should just drift into the game, or is it? Or maybe it's one of those occupational names, like Farmer or Porter. Speaking of names – now, steady yourself – I never did catch yours.'

'Oh, Elizabeth.'

'I know that much,' lied O'Toole. 'What's the rest?'

'Le Galliene.'

'Ah. Norman blood,' said O'Toole. 'It's the best.'

'No, I think Huguenot originally. But everyone in this country isn't obsessed with their background, you know.'

'I'm just getting to grips with mine,' said O'Toole. 'Chains and leg-irons, guilty, seven years, next case. God Save the Queen, No Fishing by Order, all that sort of thing.'

'Does it bother you?'

'It's a complex emotion. One side is the prodigal returning to find that veal is off the menu. Another is a suspicion that the same old gang are on the job, only now they only transport them as far as obscure provincial universities or council houses in Barking. Then there's the reaction: don't tempt me with any of your lousy fatted calves, Jack, I've learnt to eat beef and like it in the wilderness. And the final stage is, you did me a good turn: it's the judges and juries who ought to be pitied, they left themselves in gaol and they set us free by mistake.'

'I love the way you say "a" in "mistake",' said the girl. 'What was all the rest?' She drank some more coffee.

'I get the message,' said O'Toole. 'There are a lot of things I'd like to ask you now that we're so chummy, but I'm shy.'

'You're what?'

'Shy,' said O'Toole. 'Guilt piled on guilt. This Porter seems to fit in somewhere, for instance.'

'Porter is out,' said the girl, conclusively.

'I guessed as much,' said O'Toole. 'At one point I thought I might be using you as sprain liniment. Perhaps you are, too. That's pretty blunt for a shy man.'

'Very,' said the girl. 'It could be the basis of an interesting arrangement.'

'Where do I get in touch with you?' asked O'Toole.

'You don't have to,' said the girl. 'Not at all.'

'Don't come over all British on me,' said O'Toole. 'Don't you have a phone number?'

'You can phone me at the War Office,' said the girl.

'I will,' said O'Toole. 'But that isn't a promise. Just a dispassionate prediction.'

'We'll see,' said the girl. 'I'll have to fly or I'll be late. Thank you, James. It's been very interesting.'

'I thought so, too,' said O'Toole. 'Look after yourself.'

O'Toole finished his coffee alone. He wished he felt more cheerful.

'What sort of a week-end did you have, Aussie?' Jacobs, in shirt-sleeves, was stirring his tea. His eyes were still too small and close together, but friendly.

'Wearing,' said O'Toole. 'I tried some of this London vice you read about.'

'Not like home, eh?'

'Bit more primitive.'

'Well, you're loosened up for a day with your pal Knight. But first of all, I want your expenses.'

'To tell you the truth, I haven't had any to speak of. What's the score here?'

'You must have had some. What about the priest? They're big spenders.'

'I could remember some.'

'Barr expects you to make a fiver or so on what you actually spend every week. More than that is pushing it and you need a real story to back it up.'

'What do I do?'

'Fill in the form. I want rigid proof of every item, of course, restaurant bills and so on.'

'I lost them.'

'Never fear, Thomas is near,' said Jacobs, opening his desk drawer and bringing out a handful of blank restaurant bills. 'A bob each. It's a little sideline I run. Don't forget, I didn't get them for nothing myself. Vary the handwriting a bit.'

'I'll take three,' bringing out some change.

'Here's a strict kosher place I've had on my hands for weeks,' said Jacobs. 'Nice religious flavour.'

Writing with his left hand, O'Toole prepared bills for three large meals. Better stick to plain, wholesome food, he thought. Steak and Kidney Pudding with Veg, three times, seventeen and six. Apple flan and custard eight shillings. No cigars or minerals. Paid with thanks. He transferred the total to an expense sheet:

Meals for Sweeney Family	£2 12 6
Taxis: London Airport and return	£1 10 0
Reciprocal hospitality	10 6
Advanced to Mrs Sweeney	£1 0 0
Baby Food	17 6

O'Toole could think of nothing else. A rough cast showed the total a bit low for the recommended profit margin. There was a line left on the sheet so he added

Gratuities	10 0

and handed the documents to Jacobs.

'Not bad,' said Jacobs, screwing up a miser's face. 'What are these gratuities?'

'Good will,' said O'Toole. 'Every time I saw an open hand I thrust two bob into it, mentioning Cameron Barr. Gives the paper a good name.'

'Okay,' said Jacobs. 'You'll be working for Norman Knight from now on until further notice, so I advise you to clear out of the office before you get it.'

Knight was on the other side of the newsroom talking to the personage with the Dean of Canterbury haircut.

'I'm a theoretical Monarchist but a practising Republican,' said the personage. 'I used to tell the old King that...'

'Very interesting, Prof,' shouted Knight. 'Afraid I have to go. I've got a job on with O'Toole.'

Knight took O'Toole's arm and swept him toward the lift.

'Wonderful old chap,' he said. 'Won't be any more like him in the Street. You cleared for action, Digger?'

'What's on, Norman?'

'We'll stroll up to Soho, take a cup of tea and lay out the week's programme.'

Knight and O'Toole paused in front of a newsagent's window in Greek Street. The front part of the window was crammed with fly-spotted magazines, cracked kewpie dolls and similar unselling and unsaleable merchandise. The back was occupied by two big boards on which were thumb-tacked dozens of small white cards, some printed, some typed, some handwritten. O'Toole studied them uncomprehending: perambulators for sale, flats to exchange, Italian lady gives private massage, furniture confidentially removed.

'Which ones are we interested in?' asked O'Toole.

'The bent ones,' said Knight. 'Anything not above board. These ads here are offering you just about everything there is in the vice line from dirty books to flagellation and even straight sex if anyone's interested in that.'

'How do the customers tell which is which?' asked O'Toole. 'Come to that, how do we?'

'There's always something about the wording,' said Knight. 'See that one, "Confidential French lessons"? Private, perhaps, might be on the square, but not confidential. That's a whore calling you, boy. Make a note of the phone number; she might have something to tell us.'

'How about the perambulators for sale?'

'They're straight. Put a lot of people off sex, I should think. But see "Relaxing massage with corrective treatment"? That will be flaging. Anything mentioning corrective means the old whip and the chains.'

'I think I can guess what "chubby youth amenable to discipline" does for a living – or, rather, has done to him,' said O'Toole, reading from a card. 'But how about "Miss Maria welcomes old and new friends"?'

'She'll welcome you all right,' said Knight. 'And a rough half-hour you'll get.'

'I suppose these models with own studio, lights, camera and film are whores?'

'That's it, business girls. Let's go back to the office and phone for French lessons.'

'There's a phone box over the road.'

'I want someone listening to the call. You'll see.'

In the deserted newsroom of the *Sun,* Knight and O'Toole each had a telephone hand-set to his ear. The switchboard had connected the two phones together. As a distant bell rang Knight, hand over the mouthpiece, said to O'Toole:

'You talk to her, Digger, and I'll make a note. Find out what you can about her business, as long as she doesn't rumble you. Tell her we'll be straight down.'

O'Toole nodded. 'Hello,' said a distant voice, business-like.

'Hello,' said O'Toole, 'Miss Raymonde?'

'Miss Raymonde speaking,' said the voice, with a sausage-and-mash London accent.

'This is Major McNaughton,' said O'Toole. 'I saw your ad.'

'Oh yes, dear.'

'I'm ringing to ask your terms.'

'It's a guinea for friction and three guineas for the full course,' said the voice, in a rehearsed tone.

'Oh,' said O'Toole, glancing up. Knight, grinning, was making notes.

'How far do you go into the French language for three guineas?' asked O'Toole.

'Can't you pop round and see, dear?'

'That will be best,' said O'Toole. 'I'd like to bring my friend, Colonel Williams along. We're just back from India.'

'I suppose that will be all right,' said the voice. 'I'll get a pot of tea on.'

'Make it strong,' said O'Toole, replacing the hand-set. Then, to Knight, 'What's this about friction, Norman?'

'She's probably got a dozen ads up all over London offering French lessons, corrective massage, manicure and anything you fancy. She doesn't know which one you've seen. Let's go and have a look.'

The mews house was freshly painted. O'Toole pressed the button marked 'Miss Raymonde' and a plump woman about forty, in a tweed suit and rabbit-wool jumper, came to the door. There was a blast of cheap scent.

'Miss Raymonde?' asked O'Toole.

'Are you the gentlemen that called?' Her elocutionist had skimped the job.

'Major McNaughton and Colonel Williams,' said Knight.

'Oh, come in,' said Miss Raymonde.

The flat was commercially feminine, with china and chintz curtains.

The embroidered chairs had transparent plastic covers on them.

'About the French lessons,' said O'Toole.

'The terms are three guineas – each,' said the woman. She looked uneasily at Knight. 'I don't normally have two clients at once, and if one of you gents wouldn't mind waiting...'

'Oh, I won't bite,' said Knight, expansively. O'Toole thought he was doing the officer-from-India act superbly. 'Gentle as a lamb, y'know. Just tell us about the full course, m'dear.'

'Well, I teach that French kind of love you know,' said Miss Raymonde, putting an arch curve into her sagging body.

'You mean you're a prostitute?' asked Knight. He sounded as if he couldn't believe his ears.

'Now don't be old-fashioned, ducks,' said Miss Raymonde, put out. 'I'll do whatever you like.'

'This is absolutely disgusting,' said Knight. 'We're officers back from India brushing up our French for the Civil Service exams, and you're trying to get us to engage in immoral acts. Outrageous.'

'Now don't get on your high horse, dearie,' said Miss Raymonde, startled. 'If you really want to learn French you can get free lessons from the LCC. But wouldn't you like me to be nice to you, like?'

'There's been a misunderstanding here, Madam,' said Knight. 'We're not sailors. We shan't take up any more of your time. I can see that it's valuable.'

'Won't you stay for a nice cup of tea, dear?' asked Miss Raymonde.

'Certainly not,' said Knight. 'Come along, Major.'

Knight laughed silently as they walked out of the mews. 'We frightened the life out of that old sow, Digger. There's nothing much for us in a one-woman show like that. Let's go and try some corrective massage.'

The address in the advertisement was a boxlike tenement in a grimy row off the Tottenham Court Road. Against a bell-push was a roughly printed sign: MASSAGE. With his finger on the button, Knight gave last-minute instructions:

'We're normal clients looking for massage. We've got arthritis. This doesn't look much like Harley Street to me, but we've got to make sure.'

'Okay.'

The door clicked electrically open. The pair followed signs thumb-tacked at intervals up a dark stairway to the third floor. A woman wearing a stained white overall dress was sitting behind a desk in a parody of a doctor's waiting-room, complete with dog-eared magazines.

'We're here for corrective massage,' said Knight.

'Three pounds each,' said the woman. 'I'll take it now. Only one at a time. Who's first?'

Knight gave her three pounds. 'I'll see if the treatment does my friend any good first,' he explained. 'He needs it more than I do.'

The woman opened a door and motioned O'Toole into the adjoining room. Another woman was standing beside a low divan covered with a greasy sheet: in the purplish light squeezing in between heavy drawn curtains it was difficult to guess her age. The frayed carpet and Victorian sideboard were old enough.

'Strip off!' barked the woman, as the door closed behind O'Toole.

'I'm here for massage,' said O'Toole uncertainly.

'I know,' said the woman. 'Strip off.'

O'Toole, reasoning that no one is going to massage you through a gent's two-piece suit, obediently removed jacket and shirt.

'The lot.' The voice was inflexible. O'Toole took off his underwear.

'Lie down.' O'Toole thought it was still faintly possible that this was a seedy centre of the British medical profession: very faintly possible.

'Now where's the trouble?'

'Arthritis,' said O'Toole. The woman moved closer. 'Here.' He raised his hand to the small of his back.

'Awwwww!' O'Toole felt a searing pain, like a hot wire across his bare backside. He twisted half upright. The woman had armed herself with a heavy, short-handled whip. She pushed O'Toole back on to the divan and raised her arm for a second stroke. The whip had started to descend when Knight burst through the door, the other woman holding him by the arm.

'Stop!' said Knight. 'You've indecently assaulted this man.'

The woman with the whip turned to face Knight.

'He's here for corrective treatment, isn't he?'

'I wanted massage for my lumbago,' said O'Toole. 'I didn't come here to be assaulted.' He dressed rapidly.

'What are you lot, coppers?' asked one of the women.

'We're not police officers,' said Knight. 'We're respectable businessmen.'

'Oh, you've come for a free look,' said the woman with the whip. 'Well, there's nothing to see.'

'We want our money back,' said Knight.

'We'll see about that,' said the whip-woman.

The other woman had gone out, unnoticed, and was back with two men in braces and shirt-sleeves. They had necks like elephant's knees.

'You mugs stirring it up or something?' asked one.

'We're trying to get our money back,' said Knight.

'Just a minute, I know you,' said the first man. 'Aren't you Norman Knight?'

'I'm not going to discuss my identity with you,' said Knight.

'We don't want any reporters nosing about here, see? You two hop it if you know what's good for you.'

'Who are you to order us about, anyway?' asked Knight.

'Friends of these ladies. Now, are you going to get out or are we going to do you?'

The lady of the whip nodded endorsement of the threat.

'You'll hear more about this outrage,' said Knight.

'Why don't you get a man's job, you nosey bastards,' said the first gorilla, swinging a fist like a mouldy ham. Knight stepped back to the stairhead, saying to O'Toole, 'Coming, Digger?' He slipped his glasses into his top pocket.

O'Toole followed him down the stairs, keeping carefully out of range. The medical quartet did not follow.

Outside, the Tottenham Court Road was seedily uninterested.

'That's what happens when they rumble you,' said Knight. He was polishing his glasses.

'Who are your friends?' asked O'Toole.

'Ponces', said Knight. 'They're probably there to see that the owner of the business gets his cut. Nice types, eh?'

'Who does own these buildings?'

'I'm just going down to the council office to find out. You go back to the office and hold the fort. This should be a good one.'

Barr's secretary beckoned O'Toole as he walked into the newsroom. 'Mr Barr would like to see you, James, if you're free.'

Barr was behind his desk, looking through a pile of pin-up photographs.

'Sit down, O'Toole,' he said, smiling. 'I liked the way you handled the priest story. Real feeling.'

'Thank you, Mr Barr,' said O'Toole.

'We have our own free-lance clergyman and I nearly put him on it,' said Barr. 'But he's C of E and I didn't want any sectarian trouble. As it turned out, I don't think he could have improved on your story.'

'That's nice to know,' said O'Toole modestly.

'I also liked the little feature on the public school boy in the fish-shop,' said Barr. He smiled appreciatively. 'Witty, laddie. Very witty.' He pronounced the word 'wi'y', using the glottal stop as a Cockney says 'Ge' along nah.' O'Toole gathered this was funny and made an appropriate expression.

'The priest chiselled a lot of money out of us, but the circulation report indicates he was worth it,' said Barr. 'How would you like a job here?'

'I'm trying to get into Fleet Street,' said O'Toole.

'I think you've got what we're looking for,' said Barr. 'Heart and guts. And hard work, that's what we want.'

'I'm ready, Mr Barr,' said O'Toole.

'Fine, laddie,' said Barr. 'I can't offer you a lot in the way of salary to start. Things are pretty tight, you know. Newsprint very dear, advertisements slow. I might be able to get the directors to agree to twenty-five guineas.'

'I'm ready to start low, Mr Barr,' said O'Toole.

'That's the spirit, boy,' said Barr. 'Mind you, most newcomers start at eighteen. Still, I think you've got what it takes. When the purse-strings get a bit easier, I'll keep you in mind, of course.'

'I'll take the job,' said O'Toole.

'Good lad,' said Barr. 'Are you tied up at the moment?'

'I've been helping Mr Knight with his vice series,' said O'Toole. 'I think we've got a job on this afternoon.'

'Tomorrow morning will do for what I want, first thing,' said Barr. 'Here's a big chance for you, right at the kick-off. Have you heard of the Honourable Michael Macedon?'

'I think so,' said O'Toole. 'He's been running round with some Czech film-star, hasn't he?'

'That's him,' said Barr. 'Son of Lord Epping. I want the full story of the romance. Every stolen kiss, every little tickle, with plenty of big names and nothing left out. First person, of course.'

'We'll pay for it, I suppose.'

'Start him at five thousand. Not a penny more than ten, unless it's really good, and twelve is the absolute limit. Mind you, for twelve thousand I'd want the stains on his underwear.'

'What do I do if he accepts?' asked O'Toole.

'Rough me out five instalments and bring him in,' said Barr. 'If the outline is okay, he can sign up and get his lolly. Know where he lives?'

'I'm afraid not.'

'My secretary will give you his address. It's somewhere in Kensington. A number 9 bus will take you near enough. Short walk will do you good. Now, remember, not a penny over ten thousand unless it's really sensational. Use your judgment.'

'I'll do my best, Mr Barr,' said O'Toole.

'You'd better,' said Barr. 'I've got a lot of faith in you.'

Dazed, O'Toole found his desk. He was contemplating the sum of twelve thousand pounds, divided by twenty-five guineas, when Knight bustled in. He was beaming.

'I think we're on to something good, Digger,' he said. 'That building we were in belongs to an outfit called the North-South Trading Company. That tells you a hell of a lot, doesn't it? They buy it in the north and sell it in the south, whatever it is. Sounds like the knuckle-crushers.'

'The what?'

'Freemasons. Never mind. I've checked up on the company. Hundred-pound capital, dodgy set of directors. They seem to own some more property. You busy tonight?'

'No. I've got a job on for Barr in the morning, that's all.'

'I'll pick you up at your place about nine and we'll do an observation on one of their other places. If my guess is right, the whole lot are brothels.'

O'Toole and Knight were sitting in Knight's car, parked opposite a house in Queen's Square off the Bayswater Road. Dusk had just faded to the luminous London dark. Knight brought out a notebook and pencil.

'That's the place over there, Digger,' he said, indicating a four-storey house with nothing special to mark it out. 'If our theory holds up, the girls ought to be getting into their stride for the night's work. We'll just keep an eye on it for a bit.'

'What are we looking for?' asked O'Toole.

'Just who goes in and out.'

The pair smoked as they watched the doorway, up five steps from the footpath. After a few minutes a young woman came down the street with a man, and let herself in with a key. Shortly after, another girl with a man. Then the first man came out alone, and a minute or two later the second man. Then both women left the house, and chatting together, walked down the street in the direction of the Bayswater Road. It was too dark to see much of the women, except that they were not sensational.

'We've struck oil here all right,' said Knight. 'There'll be more along presently. I'll keep a note of when the customers go in and out. You keep an eye on your watch and let me know how long each one is inside.'

O'Toole checked the glowing hands of his watch. Nine-twenty. No sign of the women.

'Good job you haven't got a wife if you're working these hours,' said Knight. 'You leave one back in Aussie, Digger?'

'Not exactly a wife,' said O'Toole. 'Anyway, she left me.'

'Oh?' said Knight. 'There's the first one now. Let me know when he comes out and how long he's had for his money.'

Knight noted the time. 'What do you mean, not exactly a wife?' he asked.

'We sort of had the honeymoon first,' said O'Toole. 'That went on for a couple of years. We often thought about making it legal, but we never seemed to be willing on the same day of the week.'

'You broke up over there?' asked Knight, in a kindly voice.

'Yes, pretty messy,' said O'Toole. 'I decided I had to get out of town and come over here. As it turned out, she beat me to the boat.'

'She's in London?'

'Yes. Doing very well. Someone spotted her for television before I could do anything about it. Not that I would have, of course.'

'You see her?'

'Once or twice,' said O'Toole. 'We're not moving in the same income bracket these days.'

'Ah, carrying the torch,' said Knight.

'I brought that Olympic torch back with me,' said O'Toole. 'I keep it at home as a reading light.'

'Sorry to hear that,' said Knight.

'One of those inevitable things,' said O'Toole. 'Sort of teacher-pupil deal. You know, newspaperman shows struggling young actress the bright lights. The trouble with running a drama school at home is, graduation day arrives. You hate to see them go.'

'He's just out now,' said Knight. 'How long did he get?'

'I make it twelve and a half minutes,' said O'Toole.

Knight wrote the figure down. 'I saw another go in about the time he went out,' said Knight. 'Start him off, will you?'

'Right,' said O'Toole. 'You don't want to hear my troubles, anyway.'

'Well, I know you're getting a bit now and again, just the same,' said Knight.

'I'm keeping the rust off,' said O'Toole. 'How about you, Norman? Respectable married man, I suppose?'

'Used to be,'said Knight. 'Separated.'

'Oh. Getting a divorce?'

'Can't, old boy,' said Knight. 'I'm a Catholic. Aren't you?'

'I'm a baptised but unconfirmed Anglican,' said O'Toole. 'Renegade spiritual Titoist. Did you think I was a Catholic?'

'The name suggested it, I suppose,' said Knight. 'Sorry.'

'Oh, no offence,' said O'Toole. 'We might have been once, but I think the O'Toole who went overseas to make good left his religion in Liverpool Gaol. There's a family tradition he was a Tolpuddle Martyr or Dreadnought Boy or something of the sort. More likely he was a horse thief. Anyway, he got an hour a week off the chain gang for Church parade, so he became C of E in a flash.'

'I hope you didn't take my reference to the knuckle-crushers amiss,' said Knight.

O'Toole laughed in the darkness. 'Good God, no. My old man was a general or something like that in the Masons, but I never got interested in it.'

'He's out,' said Knight. 'How long did he get?'

'Eleven minutes,' said O'Toole.

'This is a real short-time house,' said Knight. He noted the new figure. 'You come from a knuckle-crushing family, then.'

'You might say so,' said O'Toole. 'It doesn't bother me. But you're in a tough spot, aren't you, Norman? Does that mean you can never get married again?'

'Not in a church anyway,' said Knight. 'If you've got a religion, old lad, you can't just forget what it says when it suits you.'

'I can see the point when it's a question of children to be protected, or the property of rich men's daughters,' said O'Toole. 'Up to a point the prohibition of divorce works for women's rights. But in your case it's just a prison, isn't it?'

'There's another one going in,' said Knight. 'Got the time? Yes, I suppose you're right, looking at it from a commonsense point of view. Still we believe that God won't have it, and that's that.'

'Surely the Church has changed its mind before,' said O'Toole. 'You know, money lending and all that.'

Knight laughed. 'God hasn't changed his mind, Digger. Maybe, as you say, the Church is making a mistake on this one.'

'How about the question of birth control?' asked O'Toole. 'Must make marriage pretty tense for a Catholic.'

'Our break-up was over something like that,' said Knight. 'It doesn't make life particularly easy, especially if your wife has ideas of a career. I've seen a hell of a lot of people leave the Church in their twenties and come back when they're fifty and the pressure's off. There he is coming out again.'

'Fifteen minutes,' said O'Toole.

'His zip must have stuck,' said Knight, noting the new figure. 'These two birds between them must be clearing close to a score an hour.'

'Tax free,' said O'Toole.

'Tax free,' said Knight. 'No, getting back to the problem you mentioned, I must say I sympathise with anyone who just can't stick it and follow the rules. I can't pretend I've sorted it all out myself. Still, a man must do what he's been brought up to think is right, and as far as the Church goes, you're either in or you're out. There's another one going in now.'

O'Toole glanced at his watch. 'Well, I admire your sincerity, Norman,' he said. 'Business seems to be picking up here.'

The two men smoked in silence.

One thing, the answers aren't in there, thought O'Toole. Not even if you get a whole half-hour for your money.

X

THE NEXT morning O'Toole, after the fading but still fierce stab when there weren't any letters, took a solitary breakfast and went to see Macedon.

The building was a solidly-constructed one near the South Kensington Tube. O'Toole pushed open a door eight feet high and heavy enough for a stockade in unpacified territory to find a lift installed about the time of the Boxer Rebellion. It no longer worked. It looked as if it hadn't worked since the early thirties. The stairs, however, were brassbound and likely to last the monarchy out.

O'Toole climbed and knocked at the door on the top floor. A man about thirty, boyishly good-looking in a well-cut dark suit showing signs of wear, answered.

'My name is O'Toole,' said O'Toole. 'I'd like to speak to Mr Michael Macedon. On business.'

'He's abroad,' said the man, a shade annoyed at something. 'In Spain. Probably gone for good.'

'Oh,' said O'Toole. 'Then I suppose I can't give him a message.'

'Quite out of the question,' said the man. 'Sorry.'

'That's a pity,' said O'Toole, ninety-nine parts out of a hundred certain about the identity of the man facing him over the doormat. 'As a matter of fact I wanted to make him a financial offer for some assistance. A very handsome one. But it's no use unless I can find him quickly.'

'Oh?' said the man. 'You're not here to collect from him?'

'Just the reverse,' said O'Toole. 'He stands to gain quite a bit.'

'Better come in, old boy,' said the man. 'I'm Macedon. I don't suppose you want to discuss this on the doorstep.'

'Thanks,' said O'Toole. 'I won't take up a lot of your time, if you're just leaving for Spain.'

'No need to twist the knife,' said Macedon, grinning. O'Toole followed Macedon into the room. It was about forty feet long, with the air of an antique shop nearly sold out of stock. Part of the sloping ceiling was glass, drawn curtains showing a blue north sky. In one corner loomed a grand piano, with a yellow brocaded settee next to it and a gilded wooden angel looking down from a striped wall. On a painted wooden chest stood a set of fisherman's glass floats, entangled in yards of net. A bust of Macedon in bronze stood in another corner. There was no carpet on the warped floorboards.

'Sit down,' said Macedon, waving to the yellow settee. 'Now, what sort of business do you want to discuss?'

'I'm from the *Sunday Sun...* ' began O'Toole.

'I'm frightfully sorry, old boy,' Macedon broke in, 'but there's absolutely nothing doing. You're about the tenth newshound that's been round, you know.'

'Well, you can guess what I'm here for,' said O'Toole. 'I won't beat about the bush. I'm here buying, not begging.'

'It's nice to hear it,' said Macedon patiently. 'The trouble is, there's nothing to sell.'

'Possibly not,' said O'Toole. 'But just let me suggest a price if there was something to sell. I like the sound of the words.'

'Go ahead, suggest.'

'Ten thousand pounds?'

'You're talking my language,' said Macedon. 'As a matter of fact, I didn't know that accent could be so charming. Could I offer you a cup of tea?'

'I just fancy one,' said O'Toole.

'Fiona!' Macedon called through the flat. The head of a pretty girl appeared round the door. She looked annoyed but smiled perfunctorily at O'Toole.

'Could we have a brew-up, do you think?'

'Coming up,' said the girl, disappearing.

'What you want, of course,' said Macedon, 'is the story of my affair with Miss Dvorak, every stolen kiss, every secret meeting, with nothing held back and plenty of big names. In the first person, of course.'

'That's about it,' said O'Toole. 'Nicely summed up.'

'That's exactly what the last man wanted,' said Macedon. 'At less than half your price, I might mention. Look, I don't want to hurt your feelings, but you'll have to hear the truth sooner or later. Frankly, old boy, there never was an affair. I've never even had a nibble with the girl. I've only seen her twice in my life, both times through an alcoholic haze. Mind you, I wouldn't mind, if she didn't, but it's just never happened.'

'Nothing there at all?' asked O'Toole, intent as a doctor asking where it hurts.

'Nothing,' said Macedon. 'Frankly, the girl's a bone-head. Not that I'd object to that, normally, but there has to be a limit.'

'Well, that kills that.'

'Afraid so,' said Macedon. 'You certainly haven't offended me with your offer, old boy, and I suppose at a pinch you and I could cook up something to satisfy your ravenous readers. The trouble is it would land me in all sorts of trouble, family and that sort of thing. Might cost me more than you're offering in the long run.'

'I quite understand,' said O'Toole. 'It wouldn't help to raise you a thousand or so, would it?'

'Not really,' said Macedon. 'Not that the cash wouldn't be handy just at the moment. But it's right out of the question. Don't go, though, tea's up in a moment.'

The girl reappeared with a tea-tray. She was wearing a housegown and grubby mules, but she looked even prettier. O'Toole decided she had put lipstick on in the meantime.

'This is Miss Spenser, Mr... ' said Macedon.

'O'Toole.'

'Yes, O'Toole. He's another reporter.'

O'Toole and the girl exchanged nods.

'You've just arrived in the land of opportunity?' asked Macedon.

'Few weeks,' said O'Toole. 'I've just started with the *Sun.*'

'Found somewhere to live?'

'More or less. Bloomsbury, underground.'

'Bit depressing, isn't it? The reason why I mention it is that one of my lodgers has just moved out and I'm looking for another one. You might be interested.'

'No objection to coloured?' asked O'Toole.

'Not at all, racial or political,' said Macedon. 'We're very free and easy here.'

'What sort of rent are you... asking?'

'Three-ten a week. Plus sixpence per bath per mistress per morning. Lodgers' baths in with the rent, within reason. I've had to put this rule on because some of the lodgers' women were washing me out of house and home, so to speak.'

'Seems reasonable.'

'Would you like to see the room?' asked Macedon. 'I was just going to advertise it down at the tobacconist's.'

The room was a bright little box, with a painted floor and a blue and white striped bedcover. The window looked out over the Imperial Science Museum.

'Very pleasant,' said O'Toole. 'Quite a different flavour from my present place. If I took it, when could I move in?'

'Right away,' said Macedon. 'Week in advance, if that won't put any strain on you: times are hard.'

'I'll phone you and confirm.'

'I think you'll be happy here, so far as a bed can make anyone happy,' said Macedon.

'It might be better if you paid the rent to me,' said the girl. The prospect of O'Toole as a neighbour hadn't seemed to affect her either way.

'Probably be better,' said Macedon. 'Considering the way things are.'

O'Toole put his head round the door of Barr's office. Barr, writing on a proof, looked up impatiently.

'Macedon wasn't having any at any price, Mr Barr,' said O'Toole.

'Come in, laddie,' said Barr. 'Just the man I want to see. Did he throw you out?'

'Not at all,' said O'Toole. 'Quite a friendly type. But he claims there isn't anything in the romance angle, not even for ten thousand.'

'You can't always count on co-operation from these people,' said Barr, unexpectedly tolerant. 'What are you doing at the moment?'

'I've been helping Mr Knight with his vice.'

'He can spare you for a day or two. I've got something you can really get your teeth into. Frankly, I'm not sure you can handle it, but I'm going to give you a chance. Have you met Nick Starsh?'

'No.'

'Nick's the production editor. My right-hand man.' Barr pressed a button on the internal telephone and spoke into the box: 'Spare a minute, Nick? I've got O'Toole here now.'

A thin, round-shouldered man came in, evidently from an adjoining office. He had an olive Levantine face, thinning hair and bright mouselike eyes behind horn-rimmed glasses. Unexpectedly, his voice had a touch of Lancashire.

'You must be O'Toole. I'm Nicholas Starsh. How do you do.'

'Hullo,' said O'Toole.

'I'm just giving O'Toole a run-down on the idea we discussed, Nick,' said Barr. 'Thought you might like to sit in.'

'Of course,' said Starsh. 'I'll be handling your copy when you've finished the job,' he explained to O'Toole. 'You'll soon find I know what I want.'

'Nick's a perfectionist,' said Barr. 'That's why he's so useful to us.'

'I'm here to learn,' said O'Toole.

'That's the spirit, boy,' said Barr. 'Now here's the picture. Your friend Macedon has let us down badly. Series are the life-blood of this paper. Almost all of our sales, you understand, are over the newsagent's counter, or from a street corner seller. Therefore, we must have some good compelling reason in the paper every week why people should buy it the following week. That means long stories in instalments, two or more running at the same time so that when one ends, another is going full blast. Got it?'

'It's like the old serials at the cinema,' explained Starsh. 'We have to leave the heroine hanging over the cliff. The technique comes straight from the old silent days, or perhaps they got it from us.'

'It doesn't matter,' said Barr. 'O'Toole's got the general idea. Now you might have to adjust your news sense a bit, O'Toole, but you'll soon get the way of it. We've got quite a different approach to the dailies, because their readers buy the paper automatically every day, whereas ours have a week every time to break themselves of the habit. Which is just what we don't want. They have to buy the paper before they can read a spot-news story, and they'll forget it in a week. That means that the biggest news story on earth, if it's a oncer, is almost valueless to us compared with a good gripping serial which will have them gasping for more – and people can't forget a story when they don't know how it finishes. Clear on that?'

'Where do you get them from?' asked O'Toole.

'That's the perpetual problem,' said Barr. 'We always seem to have a crisis about the beginning of summer, which is just when we want a really good series – people start to go out more on Sundays and there's a tendency for them to cut down on newspapers. We want something they can't miss even if they have to stay home. Now this time last year we picked up a little series from America for practically nothing – what did it cost us, Nick, the one about the Negress who kept a brothel at the age of twelve?'

'Five hundred,' said Starsh.

'Dirt cheap,' said Barr. 'It astonished us all by putting on two hundred thousand copies right at the beginning of the holiday season. We want to do the same again.'

'I see,' said O'Toole.

'Now that your pal Macedon has done the dirty on us, there's absolutely nothing in sight,' said Barr. 'Mind you, I was never very optimistic about him. Of course, there's always something on offer but what's around at the moment is worse than useless. I've had a try-on from a nun, but they're a drug on the market.'

'It runs in waves,' explained Starsh. 'One nun sells her story and they all want to. There've been three nuns confessing everything in different Sundays in the past six weeks.'

'Homosexuals are out, too,' said Barr. 'The public's sick of them. The same goes for prison reminiscences. There's a hangman doing the rounds, but he wants the earth for it, and anyway, it's mainly a rehash of old murders most of which we've had. We did a dope fiend last month so they're out. In short, boy, the cupboard is bare.'

'I can see it's tricky,' said O'Toole. 'It's the old problem of trying to arrange for unpredictable things to happen on a timetable.'

'That's just it,' said Starsh. 'A problem common to all newspapers, but we have it in a particularly severe form.'

'Quite,' said Barr. 'Now Nick here has one or two ideas. We'll kick them round and see if they appeal to you, O'Toole. Then you knock us out a sample instalment and an outline of another four. You should bring a fresh approach to this and we might get something a bit different. Let's have it, Nick.'

'I don't think we can ever go wrong with "don't put your daughter on the stage",' said Starsh. 'We've served it up a dozen different ways and it always goes down well. There's been a lot in the news lately about models and how they take to whoring. What I had in mind was to tie them up together.'

'Mothers, beware of model agencies,' said Barr. 'They may train your daughters for a life of shame. Sounds okay.'

'We could start this girl off in Bradford,' said Starsh.

'Our heaviest circulation is up that way,' explained Barr. 'We like to start a series off well away from London.'

'I see,' said O'Toole.

'Well, she's working away at her dreary job in t'mill,' said Starsh. 'But she dreams of the bright lights of London. Foolish girl, she thinks that being a model is the way to the West End.'

'Do we carry any advertising from model agencies?' asked Barr.

'Not that I've ever seen,' said Starsh. 'Nor do the other publications of the group, to the best of my knowledge.'

'Oh, let them look after themselves,' said Barr. 'After all, we have a duty to print the facts.'

'Now I think she might start off by trying to get on the stage up in the North,' said Starsh.

'How does that sound to you, O'Toole?' asked Barr.

'Is she pestered by stage-door Johnnies in tweed caps who ply her with Guinness and fish and chips?' asked O'Toole.

'That's it,' said Barr. 'You're getting the idea. Don't mention Guinness, of course.'

'Bad Spanish wine,' said O'Toole.

'Better,' said Barr. 'Now what happens next, Nick?'

'She could leave Bradford, disillusioned with men, and hitch-hike her way to London,' said Starsh. 'Then she sees an ad for a model agency. The job turns out to be a seedy dress warehouse in the East End.'

'Rats running everywhere.'

'If you like,' said Barr. 'On second thoughts, no rats – we want this to appeal to women, too.'

'Right, no rats,' noted O'Toole.

'Then I see her being chased round racks of twenty-nine-and-six sun frocks,' said Starsh.

'By a podgy piece-goods salesman,' said Barr.

'His fingers glittering with diamonds,' said O'Toole.

'Fine,' said Barr. 'Nice touch. Then the dirty old sod collapses with a heart attack just as he's closing in for the kill.'

'He dies?' asked O'Toole.

'That's a bit drastic,' said Barr. 'After all, this is for family reading. No, I think he just gets a good fright, and perhaps she could revive him to show she's got a heart of gold.'

'Then champagne suppers in Mayfair,' said Starsh.

'With a Marquis, I think,' said Barr. '..."I thought he was a gentleman just because he was a lord." The head for that instalment practically writes itself.'

'Then nude reviews in the West End, a life of shame and she sees the light in the last few paragraphs,' Starsh finished.

'How about her old boy-friend from Bradford rescues her?' suggested Barr. 'He's down here to see the Cup Final, and he spots her hawking it round Piccadilly but nobly forgives everything.'

'I like that,' said Starsh.

'As soon as she sees the light, get her off quick,' said Barr. 'We haven't got any space to waste tying up loose ends.'

'Just chop it right off,' said O'Toole. 'I get the idea.'

'Fine,' said Barr. 'Now who can we get to confess this little lot, Nick?'

'I thought one of Knight's women might do nicely,' said Starsh. 'He ought to be able to pick us up something cheap.'

'We only want a name and a couple of profile pictures,' said Barr. 'Most of them use phoney names anyway, I imagine. What do you think is a fair price, Nick?'

'Oh, fifty should do,' said Starsh.

'I'll just have a word with Victor about the layout,' said Barr, pressing another button on the intercom. 'Got a moment, Victor?' he said into the mouthpiece.

An apologetic man came in. He was short and thin, with protruding ears and the wide, sterile pink grin of National Health dentures.

'This is the art editor, Victor Sprogg,' said Barr. 'This is O'Toole, the new man. He'll be writing a series for us about a girl from Bradford who leads a life of shame.'

O'Toole and Sprogg exchanged nods.

'I think we should emphasise the mystery angle in the layouts,' said Starsh. 'You know, we're not telling you too much about her to save her from the intolerant scorn of narrow-minded neighbours.'

'Masked portrait?' asked Sprogg.

'Looks a bit phoney,' said Barr. 'No. I think a sort of profile in silhouette would be better. Norman Knight will get hold of a model for you.'

'Dramatic crosslight, perhaps,' said Sprogg.

'That's it,' said Barr. 'Now, we'll be building the heads round the word SHAME, and I want you to dream up a really striking treatment.'

'How about letters which look as if they've been whitewashed on a wall, dripping?' suggested Sprogg.

'People might wonder what they're dripping,' said Barr. 'But I think the idea of brush strokes is good, and we might have the letters sort of jagged, different heights, to suggest twisted emotions. The rest of the heads in a heavy gothic, with the girl's by-line in a good bold box, perhaps with an arrow pointing to her picture.'

'What's her name?' asked Sprogg.

'Don't know yet,' said Barr. 'We'll keep it short – probably Anne something, or perhaps Joan. Let me have a dummy as soon as you can, and some ideas for a poster.'

'Right,' said Sprogg.

'Now, do you think you can handle your end, O'Toole?' asked Barr rhetorically.

'I'll do my best,' said O'Toole.

'That's the spirit, boy,' said Barr. 'Don't be afraid to pile on the emotion. Nick will see it's okay from an obscenity point of view, so don't worry about that. Just put your whole soul into it.'

'Right,' said O'Toole.

XI

O'TOOLE was wrestling with the mill-girl's confession. He had spent the morning reading the clippings in the *Sun* library filed under the headings MODELS – VICE – BRADFORD TEXTILES and, irrelevantly, the personal file on JENNIFER TAYLOR. She had a part in a TV play the following week, had opened a bazaar at King's Lynn and been interviewed for a rival Sunday paper, overstating her education and understating her age. But no new personal information, so O'Toole returned to the shadowy mill-girl. There was nothing filed under the heading SHAME and only three yellowing clippings on the subject HITCHHIKERS. He had also read two series previously printed in the *Sun* on similar subjects. O'Toole decided that he knew all that he was ever going to about the perils of the modelling profession.

Then the light on his phone flashed, and the overhead buzzer sounded.

'*Sunday Sun,* O'Toole speaking,' he said.

'James?'

'Yes.' It was a female. English.

'It's Elizabeth.' O'Toole had paused a fraction too long. 'The girl on the boat.'

'I know,' said O'Toole. 'It's rather noisy in here. Presses whirring, shouts of "Boy!", people being fired. You know. I can hear you all right now.'

'I've been expecting you to ring,' said the girl.

'I've been meaning to,' said O'Toole. 'Terribly busy. I'm trying to grind out something on this girl who led a life of shame and it's hard going.'

'Which girl?'

'I'll tell you when I see you.'

'When and where will that be?'

'This evening, perhaps?'

'I'd love to. Where?'

'I've just changed my address,' said O'Toole. 'I've moved to a smarter part of town, just near the South Kensington Tube. There's a coffee-house there with a whole mess of bird cages, string, pot plants and stuff in the window. Know it?'

'I think I do,' said the girl.

'It's right opposite the Tube,' said O'Toole. 'I'll be there about seven, if you can make that.'

'I think I can,' said the girl. 'In fact, I'm sure I can.'

O'Toole returned to his typewriter, wound in a sheet of paper and began:

Only a few months ago (but it seems like a lifetime) I was an innocent mill-girl in Bradford.

My Mum had been a mill-girl before me, until she had married a handsome lad from the mines.

66

They didn't have much money, but they had each other, and soon there were eleven little ones. We were a happy, united family.

But somehow I was restless. I didn't realise I had ALL THE IMPORTANT THINGS IN LIFE.

I couldn't keep my mind on the warp and woof of my loom: all I could see was the GLAMOUR I had read about in magazines, the BRIGHT LIGHTS OF THE WEST END I had seen at the cinema.

I laughed at my dear old Mum when she told me that London was HEARTLESS AND CRUEL! But how I wish I'd listened to her! How much I'd give to be back at my loom, to change my DIAMONDS AND FURS for my old cotton overall and my clogs – and a CLEAR CONSCIENCE!

Girls, if you think there's an easy way to the top, read the story of how I slipped down the path which leads to SHAME.

It all began when I was offered a tiny part by a repertory theatre close to my home town.

The producer explained that the takings had been poor, and he took me to supper of stout, fish and chips.

I was intoxicated by it all, the bright lights, the greasepaint, the cultured atmosphere of the theatre.

Later, it was to be champagne and caviar, as I will reveal in subsequent instalments.

It was that same night I discovered that the producer – like all the other men – was not really interested in my career AT ALL!

O'Toole re-read his first page. The authentic note of heartbroken remorse was there, all right, but the next bit was tricky: how much biological detail did the *Sun's* readers want about the mill-girl's first disillusionment? Better consult Starsh, he thought, before I write too much of this guff the wrong way.

The production editor was sitting at his desk writing, and chewing gum. One hand held the end of a long grey filament from his teeth while his other flew over the paper, covering it rapidly in green ink.

'Sit down a minute, O'Toole, there's a good chap,' he said. 'I'm just on the end of this.'

O'Toole sat. Starsh spun several more threads of gum and filled another sheet with the swift green squiggles.

'There,' he said, throwing his gum into the wastepaper basket. 'Filthy habit. I just gave up smoking. Got to do something with my spare hand while I churn out this crap.'

O'Toole must have looked startled.

'Just polishing up the astrologer's stuff,' Starsh explained. 'Hottest stargazer in the business, but he's inclined to be careless. Predicts disaster for the same people two weeks running. Result: they switch from us to the *Pic*. I have to watch him like a hawk to make sure he rations out the bad news, no more than once every six months for each set of bulls and goats and virgins and so on. Now, what's your problem?'

'If you have a minute, I'd like you to glance at the mill-girl,' said O'Toole. 'Want to get off on the right note, you know.'

'Of course.' Starsh took O'Toole's copy and read it intently, unsmiling. 'What's this about warp and woof?'

'Isn't that some sort of technical jargon connected with weaving?' asked O'Toole. 'I just slipped it in for colour.'

'Risky,' said Starsh. 'In principle, colour's fine, but you've got to be very careful about details. Our customers don't know much about champagne suppers in the West End but they know a hell of a lot about mills. One jarring detail, and the illusion's gone.'

'I'll check it,' said O'Toole. 'How does the rest of it sound?'

'Not too bad. Sincere. Perhaps the teaser about what happens to her next week ought to go right at the end.'

'Finish up hanging from the moral cliff?'

'Exactly.' Starsh's dark face showed prominent teeth. 'Just like the silent serials. It probably strikes you as crude, and it certainly strikes me that way, but I can tell you it sells papers. A good strong sexy situation at the end of a confession one week can put half a million on the figures for the next.'

'Do you enjoy reading these things yourself, Nick?' asked O'Toole. 'I assume it's in order to call you Nick.'

'Of course, dear boy. We're one big happy family here. I can't say the subject matter thrills me a great deal, but the technical problems certainly interest me. I came here just as a job in the first place, but I soon became absorbed in the technique. Talking to the masses in their own language. This business is a kind of sociological laboratory, with the results of Sunday's experiment available in the circulation returns the following Tuesday. By a long process of trial and error, we've discovered just about what they want.'

'The condition of the working classes in England in 1960,' said O'Toole. 'Engels with an adding machine.'

'I was fairly left myself at one stage,' said Starsh. 'Probably gives me a lot of insight into the workers. We'll take this up some other time, dear boy. Just now, I've got work to do, and you ought to get back to your mill-girl.'

'Just one other thing, Nick, while I'm here,' said O'Toole. 'You've noticed I've left the producer groping under the table as they bring on the fish and chips. How far do we proceed with this line? I mean, how much of the steamy details can the readers stand?'

'I'm afraid you have to leave nearly everything to the imagination,' said Starsh. 'The *News of the World*, with their carefully cultivated archaic layout and expensive politicians writing on the leader-page to add tone – they can get away with enumerating the exact pieces of underwear the bus conductor tore off the waitress behind the gasworks. We go in for catchy headlines and sexy pictures, so we have to be terribly careful about what we actually say. It's the old story about the policeman who books every sports-car driver on sight for speeding.'

'Bit of a let-down for the panting reader, isn't it?'

'That's why we need real writers here. Getting back to your mill-girl, I want you to work plenty of personalities into it. You're not writing a degree thesis, you know, so never mind the generalities. Let me have a bit more about the house she lives in, her boss at the mill, and so on. And could you let me have the first instalment within a day or two, like a good chap?'

'You can't rush genius, Nick,' said O'Toole, 'but, boy, talent can move.'

The girl was waiting in the appointed coffee-house when O'Toole arrived. Seeing her, he realised she was the first person in London he'd recognised out of a crowd. In the first few days, he'd studied people in the street, expecting to see someone he knew round every corner, startled and disappointed by the continual echo of faces he knew, always of people who couldn't possibly be in London. After a week or so, he'd given up looking for acquaintances: there weren't any.

'Hello, Elizabeth,' said O'Toole, enjoying the minor miracle of her continued existence. 'How's the War Office?'

'Hello, James,' said the girl, smiling. 'Pretty dull, as usual. Actually I'm not supposed to talk about it outside, if you could possibly think of some other form of greeting.'

'Sorry. Strangely enough, I'm probably the only reporter in town your secrets are absolutely safe with. I can't think of a thing that could happen at the War Office that would possibly interest my employers.

Especially war. But we can keep your business quiet if you like. What'll you have?'

'Just a small black, please. Slimming.'

And not a second too soon, thought O'Toole, and beat the thought back. You have to allow a certain amount of room for manoeuvre in the matter of figures, and too much always has the edge on not enough.

'What about this girl who leads a life of shame?' asked the girl, after O'Toole had ordered the coffees. 'Was she nice?'

'She's just an innocent mill-girl from Bradford,' said O'Toole. 'I'm writing her confession in five instalments. As a matter of fact, I left her being chased down a back street by a seedy stage-door Johnny in a cloth cap.'

'What happened?'

'I'm not sure. I think she's going to win. The *Sunday Sun* is a paper for family reading, so I've been told.'

'You mean, you're making the whole thing up?'

'In a way, yes. It's life, but hotter, stronger and neater.'

'What a peculiar way to earn a living,' said the girl. 'Do you tell your readers it's all made up?'

The coffees arrived. O'Toole sugared his heavily, publicly, wondering if he was being spiteful and if so, what about.

'Not in so many words,' he said. 'In fact, not at all.'

'Isn't that just a teeny bit dishonest?'

'Good God, no. I mean, if you'd been connected with the other branch of the newspaper game you'd probably find it a relief.'

'Tell me about the other branch,' said the girl. 'I'm fascinated.'

'I don't believe that either,' said O'Toole. 'But you asked for it. You have to understand that newspapers are all, more or less, in two distinct kinds of business. There's the intelligence side. You know, meat will be dearer tomorrow, the president of Peru just shot himself, bond-holders beware. That sort of thing's supposed to be true. The other side's the one the money's in.'

'That's what you're in.'

'Right. It's called human interest, and it's really a branch of show business. Non-stop vaudeville, changed every day, and always leave them laughing. If you can write revue sketches and begging letters and you can clean up dirty jokes, you've got what it takes. The only difficult part about it is to get members of the public to take part in your productions.'

'This is the side that doesn't have to be true.'

'Not in the pedestrian, literal sense, no. But it has to be true within a set of conventions called "a nose for news". All women under fifty-five are attractive. All Frenchmen are hairdressers. Every time an aeroplane crashes someone had a dream warning them not to go, a broken doll was found in the wreckage, and priests gave absolution to the dying. That's what people want to read, so that's what I write. It's of no importance that the mill-girl doesn't exist, except that it saves me the trouble of convincing some deluded little girl that the things that have to happen to her really did happen. It also saves my employer some money.'

'You really despise it, under your big tough act, don't you, James?'

'You may be right about my act,' said O'Toole. 'But you're quite wrong about my attitude. Most of the time, I love it. It's got the warm friendliness of clean, uncompromising dishonesty. None of your barrow-boys polishing up the apples on the front of the stall. Mind you, I've got to admit that everyone I ever knew who was in a dirty racket said exactly the same thing: what I like about this game is it's good, clean dirt.'

'But it's such a waste of ability.'

'Oh, I don't know. We're entertaining people, too, and T S Eliot would use exactly the same line of defence for his racket. It can be a very congenial atmosphere to work in. The one thing you don't have to be is sincere.'

'Except with the public.'

'I forgot them. Around the office there are one or two people you have to keep a straight face with, of course, but everyone else knows the whole thing is balls. And they know you know it, too, and so on.'

'But it must be terribly unsatisfying, isn't it?'

'You have to remember we've all got something wrong with us,' said O'Toole. 'Booze, wrong class, hungry for power, can't do anything else. There's always a psychological club-foot or a nasty secret somewhere.'

'What's wrong with you, for instance?'

'Oh, I'm lazy. I need some bastard cracking the whip over me before I can write a line and then some other bastard telling me what great stuff it is as I go along. I like the sensation of power, phoney as the power is. Also, I'm an honest man.'

'Making up stories about mill-girls?'

'I'm too honest for business, let's put it that way. I don't have to convince myself people like their milk watered.'

'Couldn't you be just ordinary old-fashioned honest without all these excuses?'

'You're making me uneasy,' said O'Toole. 'Tell me some more about yourself, if the subject hasn't become irrelevant by now.'

'There's not much to tell, really,' said the girl. 'You already know what I do for a living. You mightn't know I'm engaged to a very nice chap named Henry, so there's an item for you.'

'Henry Something or Something Henry?'

'Henry Something.'

'Is he around?'

'He's been out in Ceylon planting tea for a year or so. He's coming back to marry me in eighteen months. Unless I get a better offer, of course.'

'Perhaps he might.'

The girl laughed. 'Perhaps. I'm very fond of Henry but he's a bit... well, stuffy, you know.'

'But a good man.'

'As you say, a good man. I'm afraid I'm going to have a lot of trouble staying physically faithful to him.'

'I can offer no comment,' said O'Toole.

'You don't have to. He's nothing to do with you, really.'

'This makes me slightly uncomfortable,' said O'Toole. 'But would you like to come up and inspect my new place? I'd like to see how you get along with my landlord.'

'I'd love to.'

'It's not the most thrilling of evenings, I know. Also, it will cost sixpence.'

'Sixpence?'

'I presume you like to take a bath now and again,' said O'Toole.

Outside, it was cold and already dark, and the air smelt of smoke. Unexpectedly, as the girl took his arm, O'Toole felt at home.

XII

IT'S AWKWARD to lie abed with a comparative stranger, and O'Toole was up and dressed and smoking before the embarrassment had worn off. So he was punctual to the office.

The newsroom was deserted. But in a minute Starsh, bird-like and busy, bustled in.

'Ah, James,' he said. 'You've just got half an hour to get your train. You're going to see something of our English countryside. Liverpool is particularly lovely at this time of the year.'

'What's the job?'

'Did you see the Liverpool golfing murder in the papers this morning?'

'I haven't had time to read one.'

'Oh?' said Starsh. 'Well, never mind, you can pick it up on the train. Briefly, this woman – a Mrs Green, I think – was found relaxing by the fire at home with her head bashed in. Just a routine murder, but both husband and wife were keen golfers, and the golf angle lifts it out of the rut.'

'A full-blooded iron shot.'

'Anything you like. Naturally, suspicion favours the husband.'

'Why?'

'Murderers seldom pick on people they don't know. It's the family who have to look out when Dad cuts loose. From the story in the mornings, the police have been grilling hubby all night without result. That's where you come in.'

'I grill him some more?' asked O'Toole.

'Not quite,' said Starsh. 'If we accuse him of doing his old lady in, he'll sue us for millions, and if the police can't prove it, we've got no chance: Besides, no one says he did it.'

'Well, what do I ask him?'

'We have to be subtle about this. As a matter of fact, Norman Knight invented this technique, but he's not about at the moment and he suggested you might be able to handle it.'

'Very nice of Norman. What technique?'

'We can't even say that gossip accuses Mr Green: that's highly libellous, too. However, if Mr Green himself says that gossip accuses him, that's altogether different. A man can't libel himself. Prior consent. We're completely in the clear.'

'Does he say this?'

'Handle him right, and he will. Norman's a wonder at this sort of thing. Frankly, I wouldn't know how to start: that's your department, dear boy. What I want is his denial, with alibi, and the longer and more unlikely, the better. Oh, and one more thing... '

'His measurements.'

'Not this time. I don't need to tell you, this is risky stuff, and it's only worth it if you get to him first and get him really tied up. Take your typewriter along and get the whole thing written down. Then I want his signature at the end and his initials on every sheet. With that, we're completely safe.'

'Just one more point, Nick,' said O'Toole. 'Does it matter if he did it or not?'

'Makes no difference,' said Starsh. 'I don't want to know, either. That train goes in twenty minutes.'

Everyone in Liverpool seemed to know where Mr Green lived, so O'Toole found the house without trouble. It was a neat brick box in a machine-made suburban street. A hundred yards from the door O'Toole passed a patrolling policeman, and avoided his eye, for no reason he could think of.

On the doorstep, he felt immensely improbable and alien with his typewriter in his hand and a phoney story about reading the gas meter half-formed on his lips.

Idiotically, he found himself remembering an undertaker who had called to measure his dead grandfather, years ago on the other side of the world. He twisted a grin off his face and in the same impulse knocked heavily on the door.

It was opened by a middle-aged man with heavy black eyebrows and black-rimmed glasses over a pale fleshy face. He wore braces and carpet slippers.

'Mr Green?'

'Yes.'

'I've heard about your trouble, and I've... er... come to help.' O'Toole stumbled and recovered smoothly. 'I only want a couple of minutes of your time and I can save you a lot of bother.' He moved toward the door, and Mr Green moved forward at the same time. They were closer than comfortable face-reading distance.

'It's a personal matter,' said O'Toole, standing his ground. 'I really can't discuss it here.' He glanced at the policeman, who now had his back to the scene. Mr Green backed an inch or two.

'Just a couple of minutes,' said O'Toole. 'In privacy.'

'Better come in,' said Mr Green. O'Toole wondered why he'd weakened. Probably lonely, like everyone.

The house was inhospitable, deathly-neat. Mr Green led O'Toole to a cramped living-room with a cold, sepulchral empty fireplace.

'Sit down,' said Mr Green. As he folded, O'Toole recognised that the easy-chair must have been the last resting-place of the late Mrs Green, but completed the sit without a noticeable stiffening. Involuntarily his eyes flicked from the polished fire-irons to heavy brass candlesticks to a set of golf clubs standing in a corner. None was bloodstained.

'Now, what's this all about?' said Mr Green.

O'Toole leaned forward to project a bluff, honest friendliness. 'I've been hearing some terrible rumours about you, Mr Green,' he said. 'Wicked, horrible rumours. I think you should know what they're saying.'

'Like what, for instance?' Mr Green vibrated with suspicion.

'I've heard them in the pubs round here,' said O'Toole. 'On the buses, too. They're pointing at you behind your back, Mr Green. They're saying you did it.'

'Did what?'

'They're saying you were responsible for your wife's death, Mr Green.'

O'Toole glanced at the fire-irons again, but Mr Green didn't notice. He didn't answer, either.

O'Toole leaned further forward.

'You've got an honest face, Mr Green,' he said. 'I just want the truth. As man to man, did you do it?'

'I'm innocent,' said Mr Green.

'That's good enough for me,' said O'Toole, straightening. 'We can crush these rumours, once and for all – scotch them right at the source. I'm from the *Sunday Sun*' – he was talking rapidly, and the dangerous moment passed without Mr Green bridling – 'and we want to publish your side of the story. Straight from the heart, putting paid to these wicked gossips.'

'You'll just make them worse,' said Mr Green, but he seemed interested.

'You're wrong, Mr Green, terribly wrong,' said O'Toole. 'People are asking why you are silent, why you haven't said a single word in your defence. The whole nation is waiting, Mr Green. They're whispering that you have something to hide. That isn't so, is it?'

'No.'

'Of course not,' said O'Toole. 'We'll show them you've got a clear conscience, no secrets to hide. You've heard the rumours, haven't you?'

'I suppose people must have been talking,' said Mr Green. 'Some people ain't got no feelings at all.'

'Wicked scandalmongers, they're everywhere,' said O'Toole. 'But don't you worry, Mr Green, we'll put a stop to them. Luckily I've brought my typewriter along so we can get your side of the story – the truth, the whole truth and nothing but the truth. We'll write it down word for word, with no possibility of mistakes.'

Mr Green showed no sign of gratitude, but he didn't decline the offer. O'Toole dragged his machine on to his knee, whipped off the cover and kept talking as he wound in a sheet of paper. Mr Green studied the typewriter with interest.

'You swear that you're innocent, don't you?' said O'Toole.

'That's correct.'

'I swear that I am innocent,' O'Toole typed.

'You know what they're saying?'

'You just told me.'

'I know what they are whispering,' typed O'Toole. 'But it's lies, all lies, wicked, heartless lies.' He read as he typed. Mr Green nodded. 'Can you prove your innocence, Mr Green?' he asked.

'I was nowhere near this house at the time,' said Mr Green solemnly.

'I am innocent of this dreadful charge and I can prove it – prove it up to the hilt,' typed O'Toole. 'Here is my alibi.'

'Now where were you, Mr Green?'

'I was at work. It's a good quarter of a mile from the house.'

'Where do you work?'

'In the dockyard.'

'You were working all that day?'

'Oh, yes. Except for lunch and my tea break, of course.'

'Now, don't get me wrong, Mr Green,' said O'Toole. 'I'm here to help you prove your innocence without a shadow of a doubt. Would it have been possible – remotely, conceivably possible – for you to have left the dock?'

'Of course not. The chap on the gate would have recognised me.'

'I see. How many people work in the dockyard?'

'About fifteen hundred, give or take a hundred,' said Mr Green.

'Hmm,' said O'Toole. 'Do you know the man on the gate?'

'Not personally, like,' said Mr Green. 'There are a dozen of them. But I would have been recognised, all right.'

'Just let me get that down,' said O'Toole. He typed: 'I could not possibly have left my place of employment at the time this dreadful crime was committed. One of the twelve doorkeepers would have been bound to have recognised me.'

'Now why would he have recognised you, Mr Green?'

'I'm not an ordinary-looking chap,' said Mr Green. 'My moustache, for instance. Very noticeable. And these glasses.'

'I have a very distinctive appearance, as I wear a moustache and horn-rimmed spectacles,' typed O'Toole. 'I do not know the gatekeepers personally because there are 1,500 men working with me, but I am absolutely certain one of the gatekeepers would have recognised me.'

'I think we should make this pretty clear and definite, Mr Green,' said O'Toole. 'If you had left your job – I'm not saying you did, of course – you'd have had to walk home, of course. How long would that take?'

'Oh, a good twenty minutes.'

'Each way?'

'No, there and back. I ought to know, I often nip home for lunch.'

'Not this time, of course.' O'Toole forced a good-natured laugh.

'Oh, no. I wasn't hungry that day.'

'Now, let's get that down,' said O'Toole. He typed: 'I could not possibly have come home and returned to work unobserved, as I would have had to do if there was a grain of truth in these filthy rumours. It would have taken me a good ten minutes each way, and someone would have missed me.'

'Now where do you work in the dock, exactly?' asked O'Toole.

'Oh, I'm in and out of ships. Sort of moving about, like.'

'Perhaps we'd better leave that out,' said O'Toole. 'Don't want to give the wrong impression, do we? Anyway, the neighbours would have been bound to see you, wouldn't they?'

'Oh, yes. There was a bit of mist about, but that wouldn't make any difference.'

'Of course not,' said O'Toole. 'I think we'll just put a bit on the end in which you appeal for justice, which you're so richly entitled to. Something like this: "So I appeal to you, fair-minded people of Britain, to study my watertight alibi and see how cruelly these thoughtless gossips have wronged an innocent man." How does that sound?'

'All right, I suppose.'

'Well, that should do the trick,' said O'Toole. 'There's only one other little formality, Mr Green.' He snatched the sheet of paper from his typewriter. 'I'd just like you to sign the end of this – just as a guarantee that not a word will be changed, of course.' O'Toole smiled sincerely.

'Well, how much?' asked Mr Green.

'I beg your pardon?' O'Toole dispensed with the superfluous smile.

'What do I get for signing this lot?'

'I don't quite understand, Mr Green,' said O'Toole. 'I'm here to get justice for you. Suppose it leaked out we'd actually given you money, then it'd weaken your case, mightn't it? I mean, what would people say?' O'Toole implied that giving people money was worse than murder.

'I think I ought to get something,' said Mr Green.

'I quite understand,' said O'Toole. 'More in the way of expenses. I'll tell my editor what a dreadful time you've been through and I'm sure he'll be generous.'

'Well, if that's the best you can do,' said Mr Green doubtfully.

'Leave it to me,' said O'Toole. 'It's the policy of our paper to see that no reader asks for justice in vain.'

'I'd like it in cash,' said Mr Green.

'I'll do my level best, don't you worry,' said O'Toole. 'Now, if you'd just sign here...' He thrust a pen into Mr Green's hand. Mr Green signed. O'Toole blinked, recovered, pressed on.

'Better put your initials on the bottom of each page, too. You don't want us to slip a page in, do you now?'

'You'd better not. I still don't know if I've done the right thing or not.'

But he initialled, and O'Toole softly clicked his typewriter shut, pocketed the statement and stood up. Mr Green maintained his hard grudging suspicion to the last. There seemed no point in wishing him luck (at what?) or hoping for better times.

'You'll be grateful to us for clearing your name,' said O'Toole on the doorstep.

'We'll see,' said Mr Green.

As O'Toole turned to go, the policeman over the road quickly turned his blue-coated back. Mr Green looked up and down the street, then shut the door. Fog was gathering round the street lights.

XIII

IT WAS three in the morning when O'Toole, sour in the mouth, arrived at Euston. He had smoked and dozed alone in his dusty plush first-class compartment, while slivers of a pork pie he'd bought in Liverpool fermented back to their original chemical components between his teeth. The dying gasp of the locomotive hung, yellow-white, between the matt black girders of the station roof. Three pimply young soldiers clicked ahead of him off the platform. The cabby didn't want to go to South Kensington, or anywhere else. Even the whores had gone home from Park Lane. London was empty and dead, except for the automatic traffic lights drilling along Oxford Street, the control boxes tapping in thought on the street corners as they directed invisible streams of cars and buses through the night, like sleepless policemen in a malted-milk ad.

'How much will that be, driver?' asked O'Toole, outside his house.

'Five bob, guvn'er, normally like.'

O'Toole found a ten-shilling note. 'Give me a couple of bob,' he said. The cabbie started to fumble. O'Toole leaned back against the cab door, indicating he had plenty of time. The cabbie found two shillings and handed it over.

'Good night,' said O'Toole, but the cabbie turned the square backside of the cab at him, broke a cloud of diesel smoke and derisively fut-futted off.

The typewriter was a dead weight to drag up the three flights of stairs. The keyhole was hard to find in the dark.

Inside, the flat was silent, but with a spacious, echoing feel. O'Toole, hearing no sleeper in the studio, risked the light.

The room was empty. Bare. Stripped. The piano, the painted chest, the glass globes and the fishnet had vanished.

Then Macedon, yawning, in his underwear, came in.

'Oh, there you are, old boy,' he said. 'How nice to see you. There's been... an incident while you were away. Thought I'd better give you the score. Not to worry, though, it will soon be sorted out.'

'Burglars?' asked O'Toole. 'Surely not. Not everything.'

'Not exactly,' said Macedon. 'Bailiffs. Estreated my chattels, I think that's the phrase. Just a minute, I'll find you the form.'

O'Toole put his typewriter down and sat on it. Macedon came back with a printed form. The type faces were the sort popular for playbills around 1890. O'Toole glanced through the text:

'Greetings. By these presents be it known... estreat the aforesaid chattels... distrain, seize, remove... whomsoever shall conceal, or attempt to conceal the aforesaid chattels SHALL SUFFER SIX MONTHS RESTRAINT IN THE HOUSE OF CORRECTION... God Save the Queen.'

'I gather this is an official document of some sort,' said O'Toole.

'Seems to have a very patriotic flavour.'

'My word,' said Macedon. 'It's a court order.'

'Exactly what does "estreat the chattels" mean?'

'Take away the furniture, old boy. Of course, I'll get a chance to buy it back myself. Damned decent of them, when you come to think of it.'

'Didn't they leave you anything?'

'They left a bed, table and chair. That's the law.'

'Only one bed.'

'Only one. Mine. Yours had to go. I'm sorry old boy, just couldn't be helped.'

'Couldn't you have told them I was sleeping on it, Michael? Appeal to their better nature, or something like that?'

'Sorry, out of the question. I couldn't let on you were living here. This is partly about some rent owing, you see, and I'm not supposed to sub-let the rooms, I couldn't tell them I had a lodger, so I told them it was the guest-room. They've cleaned it right out, I'm afraid.'

'How about my clothes?'

'They're all right. I told them they were mine. Gift parcel of hand-me-downs from a relative in Australia. From you, as a matter of fact. They seemed to be quite touched and left them all.'

'Are you much behind in the rent, then?'

'I am a bit, as a matter of fact. About four and a half years, to be exact. No need for panic, though, they'll never find anyone else to pay the rent I'm paying, or rather not paying, if you see what I mean.'

'Am I right in assuming I'll be sleeping on the floor?' asked O'Toole.

'Don't get bitter about this, James, really,' said Macedon. 'I thought you people were used to roughing it.'

'Beaten earth's what I'm really used to,' said O'Toole. 'I'm looking forward to a nice soft, wooden floor.'

'Not a bit of it,' said Macedon. 'After the vultures left, I pondered, naturally, about the plight of the lower ranks, telephoned a few people, and a friend in the LCC put me on to a perfect substitute. You'll be as snug as you please.'

'Let's have a look,' said O'Toole.

He opened the door of his room as an archaeologist opens a pharaoh's tomb. The bed, striped cover, wardrobe, carpet and curtains had gone. His clothes were neatly piled in a corner, and in the middle of the room was a thick green rectangle about five feet long.

'What is it?'

'It's your new bed,' said Macedon. 'Temporary, let me emphasise. It used to be a bus seat. I picked three of them up from a disposals place for five bob each. Marvellous, really, soft and springy.'

'It's a bit short, isn't it?'

'You can curl up. It's not a cold night, so you won't need blankets and sheets, and they've gone anyway. Just curl up in some old clothes, with your overcoat over you, and you'll sleep like a baby. It might be a good idea to sneak your typewriter out of here in the morning.'

'But it belongs to me. They can't take that.'

'I'm afraid they can,' said Macedon. 'That's where the part comes in about concealing the chattels and going to the House of Correction. Everything here is supposed to belong to me, or at any rate people are not supposed to bring their belongings to a place which is being combed over by the bailiffs. They've put another notice on the front door warning everyone off.'

'That means I'm liable to the House of Correction even if I do take it away in the morning.'

'Yes, technically you are,' said Macedon. 'However, there's only one bailiff coming round, and I'll install the fellow in the kitchen, which is where he belongs anyway. When he's settled down you can sneak out and Bob's your uncle.'

'If there's no other way,' said O'Toole. 'Just in passing, where is the House of Correction?'

'Haven't the foggiest, I'm afraid I'm a bit out of touch. By the way, there's another bit here you'll like. The threatening part of the form finishes up: "Six months in the House of Correction without bail or mainprize".'

'I'm familiar with bail,' said O'Toole. 'What's mainprize?'

'You'd better go quietly in the morning, or you might find out,' said Macedon. 'Whatever it is, it hurts like hell when you can't get it for six months.'

'I have an idea what it might be,' said O'Toole.

'We all have our pet fancies,' said Macedon. 'Whatever it is, we must get as much of it as we can while there's still time. Sleep well, old boy, and don't worry, I'll soon get this sorted out.'

'I have great confidence in you,' said O'Toole. 'Anyway, I've been doing without mainprize for months.'

He put on a sweater and two pairs of socks, arranged his overcoat on the bus seat and slid his train-stiff body under it. The seat sloped alarmingly. In the dim starlight from the uncurtained window he got up again, pushed the seat against the wall and crept into the valley so formed. His knees creaked as he bent them.

Mainprize, thought O'Toole. The thing most desired. The thing you can't have. Not so hard as wood, or so soft as soap or so wet as water or so warm as wool, but a thing you don't know you had until you don't have it any more. Losing your mainprize *is* the house of correction.

O'Toole woke in a stabbing violet light from the naked window. His mouth was wounded and bruised from too many cigarettes. By his watch it was ten, late for the office with the high-spot of his career. He forced stiff limbs into clothes and walked as briskly as he could manage to the kitchen.

Macedon was talking to a square-built man in braces and a collarless shirt fastened with an artificial ruby stud. To be more precise, with this man, it *had* to be an artificial ruby.

'I really think you've gone far enough, Hicks,' Macedon was saying. 'How long are you planning to stay in my kitchen?'

'I'm just as anxious to go as you are to see me go, Mr Macedon,' the man said briskly. 'I always make a point of explaining that to me customers. We know people aren't all that glad to see us. I've seen hundreds of these unpleasant cases, and I always try to be civil and helpful, if you know what I mean.'

'You mean you're going to sit here until I pay up?'

'You could put it more nicely than that, Mr Macedon. Let's say I'm going to remind you about certain matters you ought to attend to.'

'There's no need to adopt that hypocritical snivelling tone, Hicks,' said Macedon. 'We both know what you're here for.'

'Don't take it too hard,' said Hicks. 'I've got me job to do.'

'You're sure you're comfortable?' asked Macedon. 'I suppose you left that chair behind so you could sit on it yourself.'

'Oh, I'm right as rain, Mr Macedon. I'll just sit here quietly doing me pools, and you needn't give me a second thought. I've had a world of experience with this type of case, you know.'

'I'm sure you have,' said Macedon. Turning, he noticed O'Toole. 'Ah, good morning, James.'

'I just dropped in as I was passing the flat,' said O'Toole, glancing toward the bailiff.

'How thoughtful,' said Macedon. 'Let's go and – er – stand in the other room, shall we?'

They went to O'Toole's room.

'That's the bailiff, is it?' asked O'Toole.

'That's him,' said Macedon. 'Name of Hicks. He's the man in possession, I think the term is. He's costing me two guineas a day which all goes on what I owe.'

'He seems very respectful.'

'Of course he is. Knows his place, Hicks. Quite a decent chap, really, if only he'd go away. By the way, I forgot to tell you, I'm having a party tonight. Too late to cancel it. Drop into the studio on your way home from the office.'

'I'll come for a few minutes, anyway,' said O'Toole. 'Are you asking Hicks?'

'Be reasonable, old boy. There has to be a limit somewhere. He'll be quite happy in the kitchen. Now, I'll keep an eye on him while you sneak out with your typewriter.'

Starsh was waiting in the newsroom, frowning:

'This really won't do,' he said. 'An hour late. Where have you been?'

'Sorry,' said O'Toole. 'A minor domestic crisis.'

'Mustn't let your personal life interfere with the work of the office,' said Starsh. 'Did you get the story?'

'Yes.'

'Good lad! He signed up all right?'

'Here it is.'

Starsh skimmed through it. 'Not bad at all,' he said. 'We were banking on this, and I can tell you Cam would have had your blood, if you'd missed. Late, too.'

'Well, there it is,' said O'Toole. 'I can hardly believe it myself.'

'I'll go and touch it up a bit before I turn it over to the editor,' said Starsh. 'I think he's got the head done already, as a matter of fact. In the meantime, you've got a visitor.'

O'Toole peeped through the glass door of the waiting-room and saw the grey ghost of Father Sweeney.

'It's Sweeney,' he told Starsh. 'You remember the priest who heard the rain beating on the tin roof of his church while the jungle drums et cetera et cetera.'

'What does he want? More money?'

'No, I don't think so. The story didn't turn out the way he expected and he's been worrying me about it.'

'He's got a nerve.'

'You wouldn't like to explain that to him, would you, Nick?'

Starsh jumped back in real fright. 'Oh no, dear boy, please don't,' he said. 'You're here to protect me from the public. I don't want to talk to him under any circumstances. You get rid of him and then come and see Cam.'

O'Toole went into the waiting-room. Sweeney, anguished, rose and grabbed his arm.

'Mr Towel, you've got to help me, you must,' he implored.

'Now, sit down and take it easy, Mr Sweeney,' said O'Toole. 'What's the trouble?'

'I'm desperate,' said Sweeney, wringing white hands. 'I haven't had a moment's peace since that dreadful article was published. I'm a branded man, Mr Towel.'

'You're still in trouble with the Church?'

'Terrible trouble. They say I must undo some of the harm I have done them before they can offer me any help. I can't find any kind of work because everyone seems to have seen your article, and as soon as they see my name or my face they turn me away. Can't you print a little note, just a few words to say I wasn't responsible for what appeared in your paper?'

'I'm afraid not,' said O'Toole. 'The owners of this newspaper are prepared to do almost anything for a reader, but one of the things they won't do is deny a story they've paid money for.'

'But it would cost you nothing, Mr Towel, and it might mean a new life for me.'

'The trouble is, it would spoil the gay, generous tone of the paper,' said O'Toole. 'I know that's hard to follow from your point of view, but I assure you that's the case.'

'It's no use seeing your editor, is it, Mr Towel?' asked Sweeney. 'Even appealing to him in the name of Christian charity?'

'That was just a formal flourish in the story,' said O'Toole. 'I wouldn't attach too much importance to it. Look, could I lend you a few pounds? Might help to keep you going.'

'No, thank you' said Sweeney. 'I've still got the greater part of your paper's money left – I've been desperately trying not to spend it, hoping that I might be allowed to give it back.'

'There's no point in giving it back,' said O'Toole. 'None at all.'

'I was afraid so,' said Sweeney. 'I don't want money, Mr Towel. All I want is a chance to remove this dreadful brand – you've made me a whining, sponging, hypocritical good-for-nothing.'

'You'll have to find some other way, I'm afraid,' said O'Toole. 'I don't think this paper can do anything for you.'

The priest bowed his head, then rose hopelessly.

'Thank you, anyway, Mr Towel, for your courtesy,' he said, slowly.

'It's part of my job,' said O'Toole. 'I wish I could do more.'

O'Toole's hands were damp as he left the waiting-room. Starsh, ferret eager, was coming toward him.

'Nice work, dear boy,' he said. 'Cam loved the story. Did this golfing chappie ask for money?'

'I told him we'd consider his expenses.'

'For doing his old lady in? He must be crazy.'

'The way he explained it sounded reasonable. He's not very bright, but I think he has a dim suspicion he's helping us to sell papers.'

'Rubbish. We're fighting for justice on his behalf. The murderous sod. I hope you didn't sign anything promising payment.'

'No, he did all the signing. I had to talk fairly fast at that.'

'It always amazes me how you fellows do it. Norman Knight will be proud of you.'

'As a matter of fact, Nick, I'm feeling a bit uneasy.'

'What about? Mr Green?'

'No, the priest. Sweeney. I feel I ought to put his case to someone.'

'Bring your problems of conscience to me,' said Starsh. 'Let me tidy Mr Green up and we'll go out and have a bite to eat.'

O'Toole ordered a beer and a ham sandwich. Starsh had egg and tomato, and a whisky with water. 'Molotov's favourite tipple,' he explained to O'Toole. 'Now, what's the problem about the Reverend Father?'

'I need hardly to tell you that the piece we published over my signature was hardly to his liking,' said O'Toole.

'That's why we paid him,' said Starsh, almost mechanically, like a chess-player who is trying to see three moves ahead. 'Quite a whack, too, as I remember. What then?'

'I've been trying to explain to him that he's had his shame and embarrassment money, that a deal is a deal, that it's no use crying over spilt milk of Christian charity, and that the publicity will be great for his novel. In short, I've done my best to fend him off, as we learn to do in our trade.'

'Good boy,' said Starsh. 'Then what?'

'His Reverence is a trier,' said O'Toole. 'It seems that his superiors in the Church are prepared to have him back, but they want to see some action from him to correct the public scandal which he's caused. All he wants is a line to the effect that he was incorrectly reported, and when he shows it to his boss, he's back in like Flynn. As I was explaining to him for the umpteenth time that we couldn't help him, it suddenly occurred to me: why can't we? Would it really wreck the paper if we played along? We could camouflage it, of course: something like "Priest Sees Light, Come Back, All Forgiven Wires Archbishop". You'd have to polish it up, of course, but something like that?'

'I'm sure you know why it's out of the question,' said Starsh. 'It would undermine the whole foundations of our operation. You could never convince Cam you'd done the fellow any harm, to begin with. Nor our readers, for that matter. They've welcomed him back to big-hearted Britain, and that's that. By the way, why are you so concerned? Think of the Inquisition and what they did to Galileo.'

'I'm just putting this to you as a matter of form,' said O'Toole. 'I'm the last man to be catty, Nick, but I must say your disinclination to face the anointed Sweeney yourself was a bit marked.'

'Very true,' said Starsh. 'You've just stumbled on a fundamental social principle.'

'What's that?'

'It's a lot easier to give the orders if you don't have to do the dirty work yourself. Conversely, the unpleasant jobs are easier if someone else takes the responsibility. I'm thinking of you, dear boy: you'll be happier in your work if you leave the moral decisions to higher authority, until the day comes when you have to make them, and, of course, draw a commensurate salary.'

'Do you make and draw accordingly?'

'No, I'm but a humble labourer in the vineyard myself. There has to be a captain on the bridge to bring the ship safely home.'

'And we're all going where he's going. Do you get a turn at the wheel, for instance?'

'Cam reposes a great confidence in me. He consults me about many things.'

'That's nice to hear,' said O'Toole. 'I take it you'll worry about the priest as long as I see him. Or, if pushed, you'll pass the worry higher up.'

'I'll do the same for any of your little problems of conscience,' said Starsh. 'I used to have them myself, once. Now drink up, dear boy, we really must be getting back.'

'Don't let my conscience worry you, Nick,' said O'Toole cheerfully. 'It's just a hooked, half-drowned conscience flap-flopping on the deck.

Go on, hit it on the head. It wants to die, anyway.'

'I'll use that as a letter to the editor,' said Starsh.

They had given O'Toole's story a heart-warming run on the front page, with a six column streamer head and boxed by-line. It really looked convincing.

GOSSIPS DRIVING HIM TO THE GALLOWS
They whisper: 'He killed His Wife'
GOLFING HUSBAND'S GRIPPING PLEA
by James O'Toole
Yesterday, his eyes filled with tears and the Bible held to his heart, Henry Green said to me: 'I swear I am innocent.'

'I know what they are whispering – that I brutally murdered my wife. But I swear by everything I hold dear that what they are whispering is lies.

'I DID NOT sneak away from my job. I DID NOT hurry home through the darkened streets of Liverpool.

'I DID NOT BATTER MY LOVELY WIFE TO DEATH WITH A GOLF CLUB!'

'Here is my alibi – the alibi which proves my innocence to the hilt, which must bring the BLUSH OF SHAME to the heartless gossips who are ruining my life, already blighted with tragedy...'

O'Toole glanced up from his fascinated reading to find Jacobs reading over his shoulder.

'Nice work, Aussie,' he said. 'You've certainly got this boy set to rights. If anyone hasn't thought of hubby already they'll certainly think of him now.'

'There's just a slim chance he didn't do it, Tom,' said O'Toole, warmed by the praise just the same.

'Bollocks,' said Jacobs. 'They'll top him for sure after he comes out with this ridiculous alibi.'

'I helped him compose it.'

'Good for you. Well, it looks quiet. What time are you on till, eleven?'

'Unless I'm doing the late trick.'

'No, I think you've had enough for today. Get on with your mill-girl confession piece, and you can quietly offpiss about ten-thirty or so.'

O'Toole read the rest of the first edition, savouring as always the smudgy ink and paraffin aroma of newspapers five minutes off the press. The astrologer said things would soon begin to look up for him, which might be right at that.

He carried a typewriter to the monastic calm of the waiting-room, wound a sheet of paper into it and searched for the mental state of the star-crossed mill-girl. It came quicker than usual:

'It was the word "model" which drew me to the advertisement in a London newspaper (not the *Sunday Sun).*

'I copied down the address, that of a wholesale dress warehouse in the East End.

'Little did I guess that the proprietor of this establishment was a MONSTER IN HUMAN FORM who used the word "model" to lure young girls into the MOST SHAMEFUL EXPERIENCE a woman can endure!'

I really must go easy on these capital letters, thought O'Toole. I'll start to talk like that if I don't watch it. Now, what, for publication, is the most shameful experience that a woman can endure?

Wrenching himself back from the recollection of shameful experiences he had helped women endure, he typed on:

Hopefully I put on my best dress and my little lacy gloves. I found the address in the ad, and my spirits sank. It was sleazy and decrepit, and the windows had not been cleaned FOR AGES!

The proprietor was a fat, oily individual. I glanced at his fingers, and they were podgy, and glittering with REAL DIAMONDS ! But while I looked at them, HE was coarsely ogling my curves (I'm 39-21-32). I sensed that this OGRE wanted me for more than just showing off his scruffy sun-frocks to bored buyers from provincial department stores.

O'Toole re-read the page critically. The HE seemed to have a theological touch quite out of place in the text, so he marked it for lower-case letters. In the margin he made a note to ask Starsh for an expert opinion on whether there was a hint of anti-Semitism about the anonymous villain, considering he was in the rag trade. It might be safer to say straight out he was a Greek, now Cyprus had quietened down.

Then it was ten-thirty and a decent time to go home. Barr had come out of his office and was holding his customary Saturday night court in the big office, the hour or so every week when he was a newsman reminiscing among newsmen and whatever happened to Fred

Paperback who used to be on the old Bristol *Morning Star* before it sank in the West? Barr beamed in answer to O'Toole's nod, and he felt he was being praised behind his back.

Arrived home, O'Toole found the party in full swing, but strangely quiet to his notion of a party. The flat was still naked of furniture, except for the bus seats: a half-dozen people sat on them and the rest, about a score, stood about.

The women were all skinny, with tubular calves and no perceptible ankles. Many wore cocktail dresses vaguely out of date: all their lipsticks seemed creased and too orange, or perhaps O'Toole was just tired.

The men wore either dress-suits tight over the chest and shiny at the seat, or roll-neck sweaters, horse-riding twill trousers and plimsolls.

Although there was no drink in sight, they were all talking fast, using a razor-sharp short 'a'. There was a strong smell of burning grass, or incense; stale old incense that might have gone bad on the incense-dealer's shelf.

Macedon was glad, but not too glad, to see him.

'Glad you could come along, James,' he said. 'I can't afford gin at thirty-five bob a bottle, for reasons well known to you, so we're smoking reefers. Do have one. They're a great success, really. Cleaner, tidier, and less like work. You smoke them like this.'

He showed O'Toole, holding the cigarette between his little and ring fingers and dragging the air, whistling, through his clenched fist.

'I think I've seen the Lascars smoking that way on the P and O boats,' said O'Toole.

'We have to break away from our hidebound European point of view, you know. Come and meet some people.'

O'Toole lit his cigarette as he followed Macedon. It tasted like a mildewed Weight. He coughed, and didn't catch the name of the pair in front of him.

The girl had lank hair and a horsey face and wore a white dress with a cesspool-green sash. The man with her was pimpled, with a prominent Adam's apple which dived and surfaced from his roll-neck sweater as he spoke.

'You're the friend Michael has told us about,' said the girl. 'From Owstralia.'

'That's right,' said O'Toole.

'That's a long way, isn't it?' asked the girl brightly.

'Yes,' said O'Toole. 'It's out Japan way. We use standard Tokyo time.'

'Well, that's interesting, isn't it, Rafe?' the girl asked the man.

'Very interesting,' he said.

'What are you doing over here?' asked the girl, smiling as one does to a child if one doesn't like children. 'Studying?'

O'Toole couldn't feel that the girl's looks rated the patronising tone. What else entitles women to be superior these days? In England, a lot of things. But a fast answer was called for, or he'd be stupid as well as whatever else was wrong with him.

'I know enough already to make a living,' said O'Toole. 'I work for a newspaper.'

He *was* stupid, on that showing. The girl pounced for the kill.

'I have a friend on the *Guardian,*' she said. 'He does field sports now and again. Perhaps you know him.'

'I don't,' said O'Toole. 'I work a different line of territory.'

'Which paper do you write for?' asked the man.

'The *Sunday Sun,*' said O'Toole.

The man tried to catch someone's eye on the other side of the room.

'I'm afraid I don't read it,' said the girl.

'Our readers live under stones in Liverpool,' said O'Toole. 'You only see them very early in the morning, on their way to work.'

The girl pretended not to understand. Perhaps she didn't.

'I'm afraid I don't follow you,' she said, with a brass-tasting little laugh.

'Someone has to entertain those scruffy old workers,' said O'Toole. 'I like it. We're not as dangerous as people think. Less harm is caused by Jack believing the *Sunday Sun* than by his master believing *The Times.* Assuming *The Times* was ever wrong, of course.'

'You've got some sort of peculiar chip on your shoulder,' said the man. 'I don't imagine your newspaper makes much difference, one way or another. If you like working for it, that's your business.'

Macedon came up.

'We're discussing my employer,' said O'Toole.

'Great fun, writing the old tittle-tattle,' said Macedon.

'Look, I think I'll go off to bed,' said O'Toole.

'Someone's sitting on it,' said Macedon.

A protesting couple rose from the bus seat against the wall. O'Toole, as he shouldered it, felt unkempt and noticed his fingernails were dirty. He muttered 'Good night' to no one in particular and no one answered.

His room was still empty. He took off his shoes, found a sweater among the heaped clothes and put his feet in the sleeves. Mouldy smoke and a thin dribble of chatter came under the door.

He was quickly asleep, lone, old, unattractive, hating everybody.

XIV

O'TOOLE woke stiff and cramped, a dull pain in his knee where it jammed against the wall, a cold contour where he extended over the edges of the bus seat. A soft autumn morning shone without malice through the naked window. A striped blue air-letter, with the familiar brown and white aboriginal art stamp had come under the door. O'Toole reasoned it must have arrived the day before, and been kept for him by Macedon. His knee creaked as he fumbled it open.

Dear Shoulders:

So you made it into the aristocratic set. I'm not surprised. It's hard to keep a good man down the social scale, and as I remember you hardly ever belched at table. Your mate Macedon doesn't look too bad in *Debrett,* apart from a bit of second son of second son stuff a few centuries ago. We can overlook that as long as the family dough is intact, which your new address certainly indicates.

You wondering how I get this news so quickly? I can only report that London is alive with gossip-peddlers and professional no-hopers with nothing better to do than send wildly inaccurate stories home. At least, I assume they're inaccurate, in particular some unspeakable versions now going the rounds of how you came into flat-sharing range of Macedon. Anyway, you'd never pass for a Guardsman, with or without the fairy at the bottom of. Stories which are also getting round that he has hired you as a domestic servant I am denying whenever I hear them.

I now have independent confirmation of the rumour that you and Jenny have split up. With the additional information that you're taking it hard. If you'll forgive me leaving a few finger-prints on your personal affairs, the trick in a case like this is to distinguish illusion from reality. Of course this is not easy, particularly if you yourself figure as a big hero in the illusion. The reality makes you a prize chump, and this is hard to swallow. I don't recommend indiscriminate tail-chasing, but a nibble now and again will convince you that the difference between the various brands is largely a matter of advertising. This is my experience, anyhow, and as you know I've tried 'em all. Of course, a mass clean-out of all your illusions is going to leave you pretty shaken, so be sure to stop in time. You're still going to write for posterity, for instance. A bit of healthy hatred helps, too.

Nothing much is happening here. At a party at Short Cummings' the other night John Neville's girl-friend disappeared into a bedroom with some bloke not identified in the gossip. Neville found the door locked. Just then Willy Armstrong minced by and made a full-of-hidden-meaning remark. Neville grabbed a walking-stick from a convenient hat-stand and beat him until his arm was tired. It was like a man killing a snake. Armstrong of course felt that honour was fully satisfied. There's illusions for you!

I'm still waiting for that letter describing how the big-time newsmen operate. If Jean-Paul Sartre happens to visit London, detain him on some pretext until I get there.

Won't be long now.

Your old cobber,

Jowls.

O'Toole tottered to the kitchen and made a cup of tea. There was no sign of the bailiff: evidently they didn't estreat the chattels on the Sabbath. Macedon's phone, in the hall, was a public four-pennies model. O'Toole found the coins and dialled.

'Elizabeth?'

'It's James, isn't it?'

'These trick accents have some uses.'

'How are you?'

'Shaken. Hangover from work. I was just wondering what you do on Sundays.'

'Oh, the usual things, wash the smalls and so on. No church.'

'I wasn't going to suggest it. In fact, I don't have anything very thrilling to suggest. But I thought you might like to show me a bit of the town.'

'Let's go for a walk in the park. That's the thing to do on Sunday afternoons.'

'Which park?'

'Kensington Gardens. From your place, it's straight up Queen's Gate.

I'll meet you by the Round Pond.'

'It will take me an hour or so to have breakfast, so we'll make it about an hour and a half.'

'That will be just right. When you get to the pond, start walking round it. I'll be somewhere round the edge.'

'You walk clockwise and I'll walk anti-clockwise.'

The girl laughed. 'Sounds like a military operation. But this is the age of science, isn't it? Don't be late. 'Bye.'

O'Toole shaved. The face of Mr Green's betrayer looked sickly in the mirror. Or Mrs Green's avenger, or the conscience of the public, or some nosey bastard with no business in the Greens' lives at all, but no great physical specimen this particular morning, at any price.

Walking up Queen's Gate, O'Toole peeped into the barred windows of the basements, but saw nothing more rewarding than a rumpled bed or an odd piece of underwear hanging on a chair.

There has to be some sense behind these basements, he thought. Why dig a hole in the ground and start building from there? You still have to have foundations, so you don't save anything, and you condemn a good section of the population to living down in Jenolan Caves. But of course, you save the gentlefolks who live up higher a flight of stairs. And you have a visible proof that some people are way up and others are way down, just in case anyone hasn't noticed it already. People will pay more to live on the ground floor if they think someone else is living in the cellar, and that covers more fields of study than architecture.

The rising ground of Kensington Gardens showed bare trees on the skyline, indistinct in the soft, moist light, which flattened the colours of women's coats. The men and children out walking with them were nicely camouflaged in various shades of grey. People and trees close to hand seemed unnaturally real, because the world dissolved into grey soup a few yards behind them. The Round Pond looked as big as the North Sea, the other side on the horizon.

O'Toole joined the procession walking round the pond, going anti-clockwise as promised. The people passing had the strange sameness of an English crowd, the emotionless faces, the products of chain tailors, chain chemists, chain bootmakers, chain restaurants and mass newspapers.

Elizabeth came up, waving, then smiling. She was carrying a copy of the *Sunday Sun.* Apart from that, she wore the black skirt, an open topcoat and a transparent blouse showing receding planes of misty lace.

Her shoes, thought O'Toole, are a touch too sensible for the rig, like all these women's.

'You don't look all that sick to me,' she said, and sounded relieved.

'I'm not sick,' said O'Toole. 'My landlord was entertaining about thirty head of the upper orders. They were being devils and smoking reefers, and the stuff stank the house out, I lay writhing in bed full of hate, hate, hate. No one gets a good night's rest on that.'

'I see there's an article of yours in the paper,' said the girl. 'That ought to cheer you up.'

'I know. Mr Green. I really do work for the *Sun,* but I suppose you're entitled to your doubts.'

'It seems very suspicious to me,' said the girl. 'Not about your job, but about this person, Green. He makes such a fuss about his alibi, doesn't he? What was he like? Do you think he was telling you the truth?'

'You suspect he might have been tricking me – not coming clean?'

O'Toole enjoyed these questions and was ready to smile at the next one, if the standard kept up.

'Yes, rather like that,' said the girl. 'There seems to be something very insincere about what he says. If he said it that way, of course.'

'Ah, the worm has crept in,' said O'Toole smiling. 'Yes, he said it, all right. What's more, he signed every page.'

'Talkative chap.'

'Let's be fair to him,' said O'Toole. 'I wrung every word out of him by posing as a bosom friend. He thought he was using me for some dirty little game he's up to, and I thought I was using him. The big difference is, this was his first murder case, and about my thousandth newspaper story.'

'Did you try to get him to confess?'

'Not a bit of it. I wanted him to deny it, and the harder, the better.'

'Why? Didn't he do it?'

'I've got no idea. I saw some signs indicating he might have, but I dismissed them as irrelevant.'

'Well, what's the idea of the article? I know I must sound dreadfully naive.'

'I was there after a story,' explained O'Toole. 'We're not in an area of truth or falsity here. He had a role to play and I stage-managed him, that's all. Not too badly, either, if I say so myself.'

'Ah, it's show business again.'

'That's it. This was supposed to be entertainment. Once you've read it, that's all there is. I'll never see him again and nothing will happen. In fact, I hope everyone forgets the whole thing by tomorrow. Except my name, of course.'

'But Mr Green mightn't be able to forget it. He might have the police after him, for instance.'

'He might. The trouble with the newspaper game is, you don't get the choice of who you're making trouble for. It's a game of chance. Blind-man's-buff played with straight razors.'

They had reached the far side of the Round Pond. O'Toole, liking his phrase, noticed they were walking anti-clockwise. His direction. Then he saw a middle-aged clerkly man in wading boots fending off a model sailing-boat with a stick. Beyond was a scattered squadron of model boats.

'No son about,' he said to Elizabeth.

'He's sailing it for himself,' said the girl. 'He's probably been here every Sunday since he was a boy.'

'Ah, more tradition,' said O'Toole. 'Now, there's a thing that really makes me feel like a foreigner. What possible bang can a grown man get out of toy boats?'

'He likes them,' said the girl.

'Now, just a minute,' said O'Toole. 'This is the twentieth century. You can't just say a man likes something. How does sailing these boats make him feel more loved or sexually potent or one up on his mother?'

'Why don't you ask him?'

'I would for the paper,' said O'Toole. 'Not for me. I got human feelings, too, on Sundays.'

'Well, talking about getting a bang out of things, as you put it, what sort of a bang do you get out of seeing your name in the paper?'

'It's not a fresh, virgin bang,' said O'Toole. 'It's happened before. I suppose I think it helps me get what I want.'

'Which is?'

'Mainprize,' said O'Toole.

'Main what?'

'It's the secret of the universe. Everyone's after it. Without being certain what it is. I'm not ready to swear it's the same for everybody, of course.'

'How are you going to get it by going round making trouble for people you don't know, so as to entertain a lot of other people you don't know either?'

'Like a drunken knife-thrower,' said O'Toole. 'Once a week we hit

95

the fat lady in the belly-button by mistake, but the show must go on. Don't forget I'm not a solo act. I can always say to the victim, or to myself, "the gang sent me." I need regular money, I have no application, no purpose, nothing to say and I hate to get up in the mornings. In view of all that I think I'm in a very suitable line of work.'

'You know, I don't believe a lot of this,' said the girl. 'Every time I ask you about your job, we get this rush of words and your big tough pose mixed up with something that sounds a lot like whining self-pity. You could easily get a job in a bank or something if it's the money you're worried about.'

'A man's job,' said O'Toole. 'Funny thing, a man said that to me just the other day. But you've got me wrong. Perhaps we're not quite sure of our values, but I could say the same about your employers down at the War Office.'

'It's not that I mean,' said the girl. 'There seems to be something gnawing at you. As if you're trying to get even with the world.'

O'Toole contemplated this, and looking around saw another man in gumboots with a boat in his hand. This was a model speedboat, and the owner was tugging at a string coming out of its navel. After a couple of tugs a tiny motor started with a bee-like whine. The owner, a younger man than the sailboat enthusiast but still old enough to have convincing thinning hair, put the boat in the pond and it curved away, throwing a light grey wake off the dark grey water.

'At least this one is mechanised,' said O'Toole. 'He's probably a Communist.'

The girl laughed.

'I suppose I have a sore spot,' said O'Toole, as they resumed their anti-clockwise walk. 'Let's try this for size. Have you ever had a broken rib? Football, boxing, anything like that?'

'No.'

'Well, if you ever do, you'll find you don't notice it if you keep perfectly still. You can even flex it about a bit, experimentally. It's when you've forgotten all about it a sudden twist will stab you with it and you'll realise it was there all the time, waiting for your attention to wander. Not bad, eh?'

'You'd rather be here with someone else, you mean. Why not say so?'

'Now you're really stabbing me,' said O'Toole. 'It's not as easy as that. I'm a professional word-spinner who has had an armchair ride through life, more or less. I suspect something real has happened to me.

For once, I'm the victim whispering his name, address and measurements to the reporters. But I'm not sure. I mean, it seems such a corny, ridiculous thing. You can buy those syndicated short stories for a guinea a thousand words if you've got a hole to fill up on the women's page. What could be a weaker lead than "Discarded Swain Spills It to Sympathetic Girl round Round Pond"? We'd have to break the line between those two "Rounds", but even then we'd get it back to write it more brightly.'

'You're just making it all sound ridiculous to give the knife another twist.'

'That's me. Masochist, picks his nose on the quiet, tries to get away with dirty socks. I'm guilty, guilty, guilty.'

'There's no need to wallow in it.'

'You're right. Dignity. As a matter of fact, there are a lot of aspects of this I can't figure out myself. It always seemed to me that nothing much could go wrong with people if they were kind and decent to one another and knew when to make the unobtrusive exit. Bondage and possession and that sort of thing seemed to me to cause most of the trouble in the world.'

'And doesn't it?'

'I'm not sure any more. How does a rational individual like me get himself involved in a slushy woman's supplement situation? The obvious answer is, because he likes it, just like these microscopic Nelsons here with their boats. But we have to look deeper, don't we, seeing this is the middle of the twentieth century? When you cover your first passionate axe murder you get a suspicion you're dealing with emotions which go deeper than "I was an innocent mill-girl". But you've got to get back to the office and write your story. When it happens to you, however, you don't have to write it, and you don't quite know how to handle it. You ask the questions you never have to ask on the job, like: How did I get involved in this in the first place?'

'Well, how do you?'

'The same way anyone else does, of course. I'm starting to see it as a camouflage for the feelings those kind, decent people never allow themselves to have. You know, meanness, joy in personal property, class and race pride, going one better than everyone else, private and exclusive possessions and clubs marked Members Only. No decent person can permit these feelings. But if you wrap them all up in a bundle called Sue or Sid or whatever the name of the illusion happens to be, you can have a licensed wallow in them. Then the bubble bursts, or graduation day arrives as a friend of mine says. The victim is left with his principles, which he now sees were a lot of balls all along. He gets mean, or rather he sees how mean he always was. He lashes out. The bystanders get it across the chops.'

'That's a very complicated explanation for a simple situation,' said the girl. She's really very pretty when she frowns, thought O'Toole. Frowning is really man's work. The attractive thing about women frowning is that they do it differently, like wearing trousers.

'That's as far as I've got with it,' said O'Toole. 'Another interesting symptom is that you figure several new explanations every day, depending on what books you happen to be reading. Would you like to see another essay on the subject?'

The girl nodded, and O'Toole handed over the blue air-letter.

'Go ahead, read it,' he said. 'It's in English.'

The girl read, smiling once or twice and exhibiting a pointedly blank expression through the rest.

'He's very free with his advice,' she said. 'Is his name really Jowls?'

'It's another of those functional names, like Crapper,' said O'Toole. 'Jowls is a heavily built thinker who has shared a lot of easy living with me in the past, and looks to share some more in the future.'

'He's a journalist, too?'

'Naturally. We're a pretty clanny crowd, you know. Like hangmen. After a while no one else will talk to us. You'll notice Jowls somewhat misinterprets how I'm getting along here.'

'Jenny, I suppose, is... '

'Exactly. Another name for the human predicament.'

'I don't know whether that's praise for her or not,' said the girl. 'I see we're going to have Jowls over here shortly as well. What does he want?'

'Same as me,' said O'Toole. 'The big time.'

'Why does he have to come here for success and money? Can't he find them in Australia?'

'Success and money are only the outward and visible signs,' said O'Toole. 'Of course Jowls and I want to be surrounded by rich, sincere men and generous, beautiful women, just like anyone else, but what we're really after is more of a mystical experience. I'll have to tell you a parable to make it clear.'

'No more blasphemy, please.'

'This is really on God's side, if you grasp the message. Once upon a time I had to go along to the BBC. I was holding the coat of someone who was doing a turn – who, doesn't matter in this connection. Well, after the broadcast we were milling around in a big room, the technicians, the BBC people and the odds and sods who had been trying to turn an honest guinea by saying something bright into the camera.'

'Like "In Town Tonight".'

'That's it. We were all in town that night. Well, suddenly a seedy little somebody appeared out of a closet and dived into the crowd like a sheepdog, sorting us all out into a big group and a smaller group. The big group he steered towards tea and buns set out on trestle tables. The others present he steered towards an inner room, where I could see white-jacketed waiters serving ham sandwiches and Scotch on the rocks. You know what principle he was using?'

'To separate them, you mean?'

'Exactly. It took me a little while to work it out. He was acknowledging VIP status. The people being steered to the Scotch included an individual who said he was the king of the London underworld, a crummy person in a midnight-blue dinner jacket who does TV research, whatever that is, and a whole lot of horrible people. The tea-drinkers, I should say, were hard-working, noble, industrious, generous and sweet-tempered. In fact, the salt of the earth. Wonderful people, lapping down the free tea and the buns made out of some new kind of waterproof plastic and really enjoying themselves.'

'What happened to you?'

'I saw the sheepdog coming at me, his muzzle aimed at the tea. I stood my ground. He stopped and stared. I started off on my own accord toward the Scotch and as I passed I whispered the word "Press". I was out of work at the time, but I meant my personality, not my job. Slowly, deliberately, I kept going, expecting a row of sharp little teeth in my heel any minute. I couldn't relax until I had a glass tinkling in my hand. Then I spotted a door leading into an even more inner room. I never got in there, but I suspect there was inner room beyond inner room, with God sitting alone in the final room drinking Scotch straight out of the bottle. But I don't suppose I'll ever make it.'

'I had no idea you were so obsessed with drink, James.'

'Actually, I like a dish of tea,' said O'Toole. 'At home. Not in the outer room.'

'It sounds horribly snobbish and class-conscious,' said the girl. 'I thought you were all for equality.'

'I know it,' said O'Toole. 'But a man has to live for something. Mind you, I don't hold with people being born in the inner room with their mouths glued to the bottle. Gets too crowded in there in no time. It's not really a class matter, anyway, because God knows the muzzles I saw thrust into the Scotch weren't out of the top drawer. The point is, they'd passed through the closed door; through and beyond, room after room, with the carpets getting thicker all the time so you think you're walking uphill. Don't ask me what happens when you get to the real holy of holies, because I've never been there, and neither has anyone else. You can go far enough you can't hear the spoons rattling in the teacups, though.'

'You just want to be famous, James, and by the sound of it all you need is your picture in the paper often enough.'

'But how do you get them there? Don't give me that stuff about hard work: that's just a vulgar commercial transaction that takes all the exhilaration away. What I want is VIP status the easy way, just for being myself, just for being around. That's the only magical kind. The trouble is, ever since you could get somewhere by your own efforts – how long would that be, a hundred years perhaps? – all the bright kids with an IQ of 120 or better have caught the disease. Most of us don't want to do anything about it, though, we just want a handwritten note from God to all doormen saying: Let him in. He's got what it takes.'

'Well, you still haven't told me why you and Jowls come all the way over here to do this.'

'More doors, more doormen,' said O'Toole. 'What sort of a club is it when everybody's a member?'

'How will you know when you've made it?'

'I don't know what I want,' said O'Toole. 'I'm not going to get it, anyway, whatever it is.'

'You took an awful lot of words to say that.'

'Your fault, you're a good listener,' said O'Toole. 'You know, you're much too agreeable a person to get saddled up with my disappointments.'

'I thought I was a bystander getting it in the chops.'

'Come a bit closer,' said O'Toole. 'In fact, let's go home to the inner room and have a cup of tea.'

Elizabeth was sitting on the bus seat with her back against the wall. O'Toole lay on his back with his head in her lap, looking up past her bosom, her round chin and a curl on her forehead at the ceiling, and smoking. A motherly teapot squatted on the bare floor between its twin cups and saucers. The only light was the red glow of an electric fire, like hell, O'Toole phrase-made, seen through a Venetian blind. Nice line for the *Catholic Herald.*

He moved his head, exploring with the back of his neck the Platonic form of pillows.

'Don't wriggle,' said the girl.

'The head-rest is the best feature of this crummy set-up,' said O'Toole.

'Oh, it's not all that bad,' said the girl. 'It depends on who you're with, doesn't it?'

'I suppose so.'

'Anyway, you'll be able to move out of here soon, if you keep going with your job. But it doesn't matter if you don't, I don't mind simple furniture.'

'Or none,' said O'Toole. 'That's the trouble with one-night standing. The conditions are never right and it doesn't give people a chance to give of their best. One can't expect much from boat-decks, bus seats and the nephews of Remus at alleyways and cross-roads, can you?' He felt the girl move uneasily and explained, 'The last bit is strictly for local colour.'

The girl laughed and relaxed. 'I'm more interested in people than in places,' she said. 'But I know what you mean – you like someone and you worry about disappointing them.'

'Don't worry about me,' said O'Toole. 'I only...'

'And don't you, idiot,' said the girl, tugging a strand of O'Toole's hair.

'That's not the worst feature, either,' said O'Toole. 'It's such an impersonal business, isn't it? Now and again you meet someone you really like, but you can't get off the merry-go-round to follow it up. But I take it you don't select all your... er... accomplices out of the red wine in garrets crowd. You don't seem that sort of girl to me.'

'I haven't had all that many accomplices,' said the girl. 'You just came along at a particular moment. You had a good word for it yourself – what was it, sprain liniment. I'm surprised I like the treatment.'

'I suppose Henry Something is the big-money man in your life,' said O'Toole. 'How does he fit into the picture?'

'He really has a lot to offer, and I think I can make him happy. I have to get married some time, you know.'

'You're playing with fire and you know it,' said O'Toole. 'But you do it with a lot of courage and dignity.'

'That doesn't sound like you.'

'Sorry,' said O'Toole, laughing. 'It just slipped out. You know, the men I've met here haven't impressed me all that much, except for one or two odd cases. It's the women who are bringing me round. Now and again I get a glimpse of that island breed stuff.'

'Speaking of women,' said the girl, after a pause, 'what's the story about Jenny?'

O'Toole felt a guilty pang: the old irrational feeling of disloyalty.

'Ah, the time bomb in Jowls' letter finally went off,' he said. 'An old accomplice, yesterday's newspaper now glimpsed when you unwrap the fish.'

'A painful case?'

'Sort of. I don't know if you have any experience of show business types. They can be fascinating if you happen to find one with any brains. But that doesn't mean they haven't got the same psychological twist as the lowliest chorus girl. Pretty well without exception, they come out of screwed-up backgrounds, and sooner or later they sink back into them. But they think they've found a lover who will always be young, always be loyal, never criticise or complain.'

'The public?'

'Clever girl. The big love of their lives is that warm, grateful monster out there in the dark, who will wash all their troubles away with a hot, sweet, sticky gush of applause.'

But show business people have private lives, too, don't they? You read enough about them.'

'Oh, they sleep around a bit with real people. It hardly ever lasts. Just one man, or one woman, can clap away like hell for years, but sooner or later the entertainer sees them not as a person any more but as a pitifully poor house. I ought to know, I'm a bit show business myself.'

'How did it finish? Nasty?'

'It all sordid itself out in the end,' said O'Toole.

'What do you want me to do, clap?' asked the girl.

'I've got a million of 'em,' said O'Toole. 'This is a crazy world, isn't it? Thanks to the chain chemists, the act of passion which people worried about for centuries is turning into a sort of horizontal handshake. Then, slowly, tentatively, just like they always did, people get to know one another. Or they never do, just like always. The chemist can't help you there.'

'I don't want to inflate your ego, which is monumental enough already, James,' said the girl, in a teasing voice. 'But it's people like you who make life hard for tea-planters.'

'Where would the word-spinners be without people like you?' asked O'Toole tenderly, and he reached his arm behind her yielding back in the cosy half-dark.

Elizabeth had gone, finally, but only because of the impossible size of the bus seat. O'Toole squirmed restlessly on it, his feet freezing, locked in a loop of emotions. He began, and in a few minutes came back to, a longing for his own kind, for the world he had thought was his: Jenny, what have you done to me, what am I doing to this girl, Jenny, Jenny, Jenny.

XV

SLEEPING badly, O'Toole was late to the office. A picture in the *Express,* with a caption about 'rising young Australian actress, Jennifer Taylor' didn't help. She was smiling at the world in an empty and oddly meretricious way. Going up in the *Sun*'s lift, O'Toole felt poor, obscure and impotent.

Norman Knight looked up with a grin from a typewriter. His blazer was, as ever, lintless and well-pressed, the handkerchief peeping from his sleeve aggressively white. The more O'Toole saw of his ruddy, broken-nosed good looks, the more he liked him.

'Sit down and have a cup of char, Digger,' said Knight. 'I liked the way you handled the Green golf murder story. Couldn't have done better myself, if you'll pardon the comparison.'

'Coming from you that's real praise, Norman,' said O'Toole, sitting and pouring a cup from the teapot at Knight's elbow. 'Is this leading up to something?'

'I've borrowed you for the day,' said Knight. 'We've got a hard day on the vice ahead of us. I want you to get your exes sheet in as soon as possible and we'll hit the road. This might be the most important interview of this whole series, so I particularly want you along.'

'Who are we seeing?'

'We need a vice czar to hang this present lot on. Sort of arch villain of the piece. I think I've flushed him.'

'The North South Trading Company?'

'Bullseye. While you were up in Liverpool I dropped in up the road at

Bush House and started digging in the company files. There's a whole spider's web of shady little companies woven round this North-South operation. Not only do they own the massage joint, but a lot of slum property elsewhere, all in the Soho and Bayswater Road areas. The spider in the middle of all this appears to be a man named Hawkesley. John Hawkesley. He seems to have a respectable business too, making cigarette lighters, of all things. That will be his front. Our first job is to try him on for size as the emperor of London vice.'

'How do we know him, Norman? By a birthmark?'

Knight grinned. 'It will depend on getting an admission, or series of admissions, out of him. Barr won't wear a direct accusation unless we get Hawkesley to admit to us that he's a big vice operator. That's why I need you along. Get your swindle sheet in and we'll go round and have a chat with him.'

The Churchill Lighter Company had a registered office over a snack-bar in a narrow street in Soho. The firm's name was painted on a peeling board, indicating a narrow entry and a steep stair. O'Toole followed Knight past a barrier of stinking dustbins up the stairs to an ante-room. An angular woman sat at a stained desk.

'Mr Hawkesley,' said Knight.

'What is it about, please,' asked the woman, lowering a copy of *The Queen.*

'Just tell him we're close personal friends,' said Knight. 'Very important.' There was no doubt in his voice.

'I'll see what I can do,' said the woman, rising to disclose an optically flat chest. She knocked timidly on the door, and after a moment came out and said, 'Mr Hawkesley can only spare a minute.'

'That will be plenty,' said Mr Knight, going in.

Mr Hawkesley's office had once been painted with some cheap concoction, in a medical shade of yellow, which had never dried properly. A desk, chairs and an impractical-looking filing cabinet were the only furniture. Mr Hawkesley was a middle-aged man, short, stout and thinning on top, who would clearly never know why one tie went better than another with a striped brown suit. He had a fugitive air of authority, like a man promoted sergeant in the Pay Corps early in 1945.

'John Hawkesley?' asked Knight.

'That's me,' said Hawkesley. 'What's this all about?'

'My name is Knight and this is my colleague, Mr O'Toole,' said Knight, sitting down. 'I believe you make cigarette lighters, Mr

Hawkesley.'

'That's correct. What's the trouble, purchase tax?'

'Not as far as I know,' said Knight. 'You're also the owner of premises in Elizabeth Street, off the Tottenham Court Road, through a concern called the North South Trading Company of which you are the only shareholder.'

'What business is it of yours?'

'I'm only asking you to confirm the facts, Mr Hawkesley,' said Knight. 'They're all on record.'

'What if I am?'

'You also own properties in the Bayswater Road area, through different flimsy companies.'

'Well?'

'All these premises are brothels, Mr Hawkesley, and what's more they are brothels catering to obnoxious perversions.'

'Oh, I get it,' said Mr Hawkesley, relieved. 'You want a cut, eh?'

'Certainly not,' said Knight. 'I represent the *Sunday Sun* newspaper, and I intend to publish the fact that you are the owner of these premises and that you are living on immoral earnings. My colleague here has heard your admissions.'

'My God,' said Mr Hawkesley, gripping the edge of his desk. 'Ronson's have sent you to smash me.'

'What do you mean, Ronson's?' asked Knight.

'The small man hasn't got a hope in hell,' said Mr Hawkesley bitterly. 'You start a little business, and as soon as you cut into the big concerns' territory, they smash you.'

'I've got nothing to do with Ronson's or any other manufacturer of cigarette lighters,' said Knight. 'Mr Hawkesley, I'm here to stamp out your evil business. Why not give up and get out?'

'Look, boys, give me a break,' said Mr Hawkesley, whining. 'Give me the chance you'd give a mangy dog. At least let me get rid of my stock. Only a few dozen gross, I swear it. Then you can have the field to yourselves.'

'Can't you understand we have nothing to do with cigarette lighters?' asked Knight. 'My colleague here will tell you that we're not interested in the manufacturing side of your activities.'

'That's right,' said O'Toole, clearing his throat. 'We're reporters. Forget the lighters and tell us about your corrective massage business.'

'I can't afford a big ad, but I might be able to manage a monkey's worth,' said Mr Hawkesley. 'Next week, honest.'

'We're not soliciting advertisements,' said Knight, losing patience. 'We just want the truth.'

'In God's name what is this about?' squealed Mr Hawkesley. 'You're in business, aren't you? You'd take an ad from Ronson's, wouldn't you?'

'Let's get back to the place in Elizabeth Street,' said Knight. 'You own it, don't you?'

'Course I do,' said Mr Hawkesley. 'Anybody can find that out.'

'You know what it's being used for, don't you.'

'Nobody would want to live there, would they?'

'Just answer my questions, Mr Hawkesley.'

'You're crucifying me,' said Mr Hawkesley. 'Yes, I let it to a couple of girls. They're not doing anyone any harm, are they?'

'They tell me you charge fifty pounds a week rent,' said Knight, casually.

'Well, they're bloody liars. Twenty-five and I pay the light and gas bills.'

'So you know they're using the place for immoral purposes, if no one would live there.'

'Look, boys, I'll close it up straight away,' said Mr Hawkesley. 'As a matter of fact, I was thinking of it. Leave my name and the Churchill lighter out of it and I'll see you're all right.'

'What do you mean, you'll see we're all right?' asked Knight, bristling.

'I don't expect you to go away empty-handed,' said Mr Hawkesley. 'I can manage two hundred and you can chop it up between you. That way, we're all sweet, eh?'

'You heard this man offer us a bribe,' said Knight, turning to O'Toole.

'I heard him,' said O'Toole.

'Jesus, what's up with you people?' asked Mr Hawkesley. 'We're all in business, aren't we? You can find plenty of other things to write about. Why pick on me? In fact, I'll give you an article on my new lighters. Latest thing from the States. I'm offering you a decent cut, and all the work you've done is look me up at Bush House, which any mug can do. If you didn't like my place, no one asked you to go there, now did they?'

'We're fighting vice and the rats like you who run it,' said Knight.

'What do you mean, fighting vice. You're selling it, same as me. Don't give me any of that high-and-mighty talk.'

'That's a nasty accusation, Mr Hawkesley, and I'll remind you I have a witness here,' said Knight.

'How much are Dunhills paying you?' asked Mr Hawkesley, cunningly.

'I don't take bribes from anyone,' said Knight.

'Well, it beats me,' said Mr Hawkesley. 'If we can't do business, why did you come here?'

'We've heard all we want,' said Knight. 'We're going.'

'Look, three hundred,' said Mr Hawkesley. 'You'll ruin me.'

'It's useless offering bribes,' said Knight. 'You'll have to take what's coming to you, and in my opinion it's overdue.'

'Won't you let a man live?' asked Mr Hawkesley, grabbing Knight's sleeve. 'I always knew lighters were a tough game, but I never expected anything like this.'

'I advise you to get into a decent business before you go to prison,' said Knight from the door.

'Thanks for nothing,' said Mr Hawkesley, slumping behind his desk. Then he stiffened in a fury. 'The same to you,' he shouted at the departing reporters. 'All right, I might be a bit bent, but at least I've got a heart, not like you poncing sticky-beaks.'

Knight was laughing as Mr Hawkesley's voice faded down the stairs. 'Now we've heard everything, Digger,' he said. 'Ronson's have sent us to smash him. That's really the limit.'

'I can see his point of view,' said O'Toole as they walked down the alley in search of a cup of tea. 'He figures one business is much like another, and basically we're all trying to make an honest shilling. He made us a pretty handsome offer, and we unaccountably came over high-and-mighty on him. As he sees it, there can only be one explanation. We've already got a better offer elsewhere. By the way, don't you have any use for an easy hundred?'

'When I go off the rails, Digger, it will be for something big,' said Knight good-humouredly. 'I might look at fifty thousand. I'm certainly not taking any hundreds off Tottenham Court Road ponces.'

'But you can be bought if the price is right.'

'Everyone can.'

'You're just agreeing with Mr Hawkesley,' said O'Toole. 'To tell the truth I just can't see you taking a back-hander, no matter how big. You have to believe you can be bought, because you share the common feeling that a man who won't sell out for money is anti-social.'

'Maybe you're right. No one has offered me fifty thousand, anyway.'

'By the way,' said O'Toole. 'Ronson's haven't got shares in the *Sun*, have they?'

'They might have one or two,' said Knight. 'There are thousands of shareholders. It wouldn't help them if they did in a case like this.'

'Now there's a funny thing,' said O'Toole. 'I never asked anyone before. Who does own the *Sun*? Who's the big top man?'

'There isn't one,' said Knight. 'There's a board responsible to the shareholders. Mostly lawyers and accountants. The shareholders don't care what goes in the papers as long as they pay dividends. Neither do the board. All they do is appoint the editors of the various papers, and they – Cam Barr, for instance, with the *Sun* – they run them how they please.'

'To make money.'

'That's it.'

'You know, poor blundering Hawkesley might have been on to something,' said O'Toole.

'Don't let it worry you,' said Knight. 'In many ways, it's a better set-up than having some Lord stick his nose into everything.'

'You disappoint me,' said O'Toole. 'I had an idea in the back of my mind there was a belted earl somewhere round the place grubbing through the pin-up pictures with blue-veined shaking old hands.'

'That went out in the thirties,' said Knight. 'There won't be any more Press Lords. Too big a business these days.'

'And I suppose the people who made them lords in the old days never read the papers these boyos owned.'

'Probably not,' said Knight. 'Let's find that cuppa, Digger.'

Over tea and sweet biscuits, Knight explained the next job.

'You're going to enjoy this one, Digger,' he promised. 'I've been in touch with a girl named Eileen and she's laying on another one for you – a bit of young stuff, I gather. This one is over in Knightsbridge.'

'I'm getting sick of the wrong side of town,' said O'Toole.

The entrance was beside an expensive Knightsbridge milliner's. Knight and O'Toole paused outside, the stream of lacquered women on their way to Harrods dividing to swirl around them.

'I used Commander Williams again when I phoned, Digger,' said Knight. 'You'd better be your pal McNaughton. All you need to keep in mind is that we're here for a bang-up afternoon's fun. I've got great hopes of this one: the Knightsbridge angle alone makes it good. Let me make the running for a bit, just turn on your bushwhacker charm and find out as much as you can. And remember, don't expose the old person, eh?'

O'Toole ran his hand over his fly, then carried two fingers to his forehead in salute. 'Aye, aye, Commander,' he said.

Knight led the way up three flights of stairs and knocked briskly on a cream-painted door, triggering off giggling inside.

'It's not locked,' said a woman's voice.

Knight pushed the door open, and over his shoulder O'Toole saw a thirtyish woman in a black-based floral housegown.

'Hullo, m'darling,' said Knight. 'Williams. Remember, I phoned this morning. This is Commander McNaughton, over from Australia to freshen up on torpedoes, y'know. Secret stuff, of course. Hullo, who's this pretty little thing?'

O'Toole saw another, much younger girl by the window. She might have been nineteen, anyway inside the age-group when any face is pretty, even with this one's too prominent teeth.

'I'm Eileen,' said the older woman to O'Toole. 'This is Kathleen,' she said to both men. Kathleen simpered.

'Well, we've got the ingredients here for a cosy little party, eh, girls?' said Knight, rubbing his hands together. 'Got anything to wet the whistle, m'darling?'

'Oh, you men,' said Eileen coyly. 'If it's not the other thing, it's the drink.'

'I'll tell you what,' said Knight. 'Kathleen and I will slip over to the boozer and get something to liven the party up a bit. Dave, you can entertain Eileen while we're away. Won't be long'

'A pleasure,' said O'Toole, sounding clumsy and provincial to himself. He hadn't expected such chumminess from Knight. He tried a jolly party-goer's smile.

'Oh, I won't eat him,' said Eileen, half-motherly.

'He'll melt in the mouth,' promised Knight. There was general laughter in which O'Toole played a token part. Then Knight and the girl left, hand in hand.

'Now tell me about yourself,' said Eileen, moving her chair closer to O'Toole's and allowing the housegown to part enough to show a sagging triangle of breast.

'Well, I'm regular Navy, you know,' said O'Toole.

'What did you say your name was?'

'Dave,' said O'Toole, expecting disbelief. 'I just love the way you say that,' said Eileen brightly. 'As a matter of fact, my husband's a

Canadian, you know.'

'Oh?' said O'Toole.

'You've been there?'

'Not exactly,' said O'Toole. Studying his answer, he decided it was a clear-cut yes-or-no proposition. You've either been in Canada or you haven't. Eileen didn't seem to notice.

'You'd like him. He's a dear,' said Eileen.

'He's not around?'

'On tour,' said Eileen. 'Not very practical if you know what I mean. He's a singer. I hope you don't mind me mentioning him.'

'Oh, not at all,' said O'Toole. 'Very free and easy, show business people, aren't they?'

'I'm in show business myself,' said Eileen. 'I suppose you guessed.' She leaned closer.

'Tom is a great fellow,' said O'Toole. 'Commander Williams. He's showing me round London.'

'I suppose you're pretty gay in Australia,' said Eileen. 'All those sheep-farmers.'

'My word. Have a great time. Like Canada.'

'We must keep the Commonwealth together,' said Eileen.

'You're right,' said O'Toole. There was no sign of Knight and the girl.

'I'm sure Don – that's my husband – would like you,' said Eileen. 'He likes a good listener.'

'Sounds a broad-minded type.'

'Silly boy, of course he is,' said Eileen. 'I wondered why you were so nervous, particularly being Navy.'

'Oh, don't mind me,' said O'Toole, trying to imitate Knight's open-hearted manner. 'We're a bit slow, we country boys, y'know.'

'I'd rather have a man like that than the other way, if you know what I mean,' said Eileen, flapping the front of her housegown. She had nothing on underneath, all the way down. 'Rather warm in here, isn't it?'

'I hadn't noticed,' said O'Toole. This sounded uncooperative, so he added, 'Come from a hot climate, y'know.'

At this moment, O'Toole heard Knight and the girl come laughing up the stairs.

'Ah, there you are, children,' said Eileen. 'I was just trying to persuade Dave here to be a devil and take his coat off.'

O'Toole looked to Knight for help. 'Come along, Dave, get into the spirit of the party,' said Knight, tormenting him. O'Toole slowly took his jacket off, catching a hand in a sleeve. Eileen helped. He had a sweater on underneath.

'I'll put it inside,' said Eileen, going through a door.

'Care for a snort, Dave, to get you relaxed?' asked Knight, with a careful wink.

'Thanks, Commander,' said O'Toole.

Knight poured four shots of gin from the bottle he had brought back with him. Then Eileen came back.

'Oh, thanks, darling,' she said. 'Are you two infants going into the other room?' O'Toole noticed uneasily that something about the way she spoke reminded him of Elizabeth.

'We certainly are,' said Knight. 'Be careful now, Digger.'

'What's that he calls you?' asked Eileen, when the others had gone.

'Digger,' said O'Toole, with a harsh laugh. 'It's what we Australians call one another. Comes from the Army. Or we sometimes call each other "sport". Not in the biological sense, of course.' Eileen looked blank. She's not as bright as Elizabeth, anyway, thought O'Toole. 'Tom's a great one for a laugh,' he added. The gap in the housegown was widening again.

'All the better for it,' said Eileen. 'I think people ought to let themselves go now and again, don't you?'

'Why not?' said O'Toole. 'Within reasonable limits, of course.'

'What do you mean by that?' asked Eileen. The gap closed suddenly.

'Nothing, just a figure of speech,' said O'Toole. 'Pay no attention.'

'By the way, dear, there's something I should have mentioned to Tom,' said Eileen. The gap oozed open again. 'We have to pay the rent here, you know.'

'Of course,' said O'Toole. 'Actually Tom's the captain as you might say. Why not nip in and check with him?'

'I'll do that small thing,' said Eileen.

O'Toole took a deep gulp of his gin as soon as he was alone. With his foot, he pushed Eileen's chair away from his own as far as his leg would reach. She just missed catching him on her return.

'They're really having a ball in there,' she said. 'But your friend Tom says he's left his wallet down in his car,' she added accusingly.

'Oh, he's a terribly honest chap,' said O'Toole hastily. 'He got a bit twisted out in the East, you know. No reflection on you, don't think that for a second. I'm sure he'll pop down in a minute or two and do the right thing.'

'He'd better,' said Eileen. There was a sudden muffled burst of giggling from the inner room. 'I do like to be business-like, don't you, dear?' she added.

'Oh yes,' said O'Toole. 'Cash on the nail, the only way to do business.'

'A girl can't be too careful, really, these days,' said Eileen, moving her chair closer and annihilating all the distance O'Toole had gained while she was out. 'There are a lot of very mean men around, really mean.'

'I know what you have in mind,' said O'Toole. 'Times are tough.' He wrenched his eyes away from the front of her housegown.

'My husband's not like that, thank goodness,' she said. 'Don is the soul of generosity, when he has something to be generous with, poor dear. There I go talking about him again.'

'Feel absolutely free,' said O'Toole.

'Oh no, you must be bored with him,' said Eileen. 'Let's you and I get more friendly, shall we?'

'Let us indeed,' said O'Toole. This sounded strained so he forced a smile. Eileen put her hand on his knee. He stifled a violent virginal twitch.

'No, you haven't got a thing to worry about with dear old Tom,' he said quickly. 'Terribly honest.'

'I'll get angry with you in a minute if you keep on and on about Tom,' said Eileen crossly. 'Aren't I more interesting?'

O'Toole seemed to have exhausted every possible avenue of conversation. He steeled himself to slip a chaste hand under the housegown, to buy time. Then it occurred to him that Eileen might take this as an invitation to throw it off altogether. With a tepid kiss, he thought, there would be less immediate danger, although even this was a long way to go for a newspaper story – and at that moment Knight came running through the inner door, his collar hanging from the stud, his jacket over his arm and a smear of lipstick on his face.

'Let's get the hell out of here, Digger, quick,' he said to O'Toole as he passed.

O'Toole jumped to his feet. 'My coat,' he said to no one in particular, then remembered it was in the inner room and went for it.

There was a bed, a cupboard and some chairs. On the bed, in a pool of light from a reading-lamp, Kathleen lay stark naked. Her face showed a mixture of bewilderment, voluptuousness when she spotted O'Toole, and buck teeth. Probably thought he was Knight returning. She really hasn't a bad figure at all, thought O'Toole as he grabbed his coat from a chair. He turned for a second look, then felt foolish. 'Good evening,' he said, moving toward the door. It seemed the polite thing to say.

Eileen seized his arm outside.

'What on earth's going on?' she asked.

'It's my mate, not me,' improvised O'Toole. 'One of his queer turns. Malaria. Just gone for a breath of fresh air. I'll fetch him back, never fear.'

'Come back yourself,' said Eileen.

'Of course,' said O'Toole, plunging down the stairs.

Knight was waiting in the street, his coat on, fiddling with his collar. 'Into the pub, quick, Digger, before we're spotted,' he said.

They got their breaths back in the saloon bar. Knight seemed pleased.

'We're on to a hot one here, Aussie,' he said. 'Sorry I had to drag you away like that just when you were getting better acquainted with Eileen, the cunning old sow. She came bursting in just when Kathleen was telling me everything.'

'She was worried about her money?' said O'Toole.

'Not half as worried as she's going to be,' said Knight. 'Did you notice Kathleen had stripped off? It was her idea. I let her peel down to get her confidence.'

'Did you expose your person?' asked O'Toole.

'It was a very near thing,' said Knight. 'That's why I had to scarper like that. Kathleen was getting impatient. Sexy little bitch. Any idea how old she is?'

'Oh, about nineteen, I'd say.'

'Fifteen. What's more, this is her first job. We'll put it right on Eileen, procuration. She could fetch five years for it.'

'Kathleen didn't look too unwilling to me,' said O'Toole.

'Oh, she knows what it's for, all right,' said Knight. 'Randy as they come. Wait until her father reads the paper. He'll tan the hide off her.'

'You're going to put her in the story? How about this protection of juveniles stuff?'

'Doesn't affect us. She gave me her address and phone number. I told her I was a prospective regular, but there was no need to cut Eileen in. I said you were more Eileen's type.'

'Thanks.'

'She lives out Kennington way somewhere. Respectable family by the sound of it. That makes it all the better, of course. Eileen, the vampire of Knightsbridge, preys on suburban maidenhood. We'll nip straight out and see Dad before Kathleen discovers her new boyfriend isn't coming back.'

Knight and O'Toole sped through the heavy breeding districts of South London to the girl's address, a house like a hundred others in a Victorian concertina terrace.

Knight knocked, and the door opened six inches. A man in shirt-sleeves peered round. He looked as if he had done outdoor work and lots of it.

'We've come about your daughter, Kathleen,' said Knight.

'Police?'

'No. I'm Norman Knight of the *Sunday Sun*. This is my colleague, Mr O'Toole.'

'Oh, you are, are you. What do you want?'

'I'm afraid I've got bad news about your girl. She's in serious moral danger,' said Knight.

'Nothing doing, mate,' said the man. 'I've got an idea what you're after and I don't want any part of it, see? Of course, if the price is right, that might be different.'

'That's a callous attitude, I must say,' said Knight.

'Call it what you like,' said the man. 'I know you lot. You'll get nothing here for nothing.'

'There's no call to be rude,' said Knight. 'We're here in your daughter's interests.'

'Pigs might fly,' said the man. 'When I want your help I'll ask for it. And that will be never.'

The door slammed, rattling sheets of stained glass. A chain grated behind it.

'Come on, Digger,' said Knight. They went back to the car.

'The news that we are a commercial outfit seems to be spreading around,' said O'Toole.

'Money is all these people think of,' said Knight bitterly. 'No wonder his daughter has gone on the game. We can hang about and wait for her to come home, but Dad is bound to get to her first and that will be that. I can't swear I wouldn't do the same in his position, of course.'

'I wonder why she took it up.'

'Only sort of work she could find in the West End, I expect.'

'We've had a funny day,' said O'Toole. 'First Hawkesley wants to pay us, then this bloke wants us to pay him.'

'Keeps the money circulating,' said Knight.

XVI

'THIS IS really not good enough, O'Toole,' said Barr, glancing at the clock on the newsroom wall. 'Half an hour late. Your work seems to be shaping all right, but the spirit is missing. I want men who are dead keen to get on.'

'I had a late night on the vice,' said O'Toole.

'Well, just remember who is paying who around here,' said Barr. 'We have to keep some sort of discipline in the office. Are you a music-lover, by the way?'

'As much as the next man,' said O'Toole.

'Good enough,' said Barr. 'Here's a quickie for you. Have you heard of Ricky Rogers, the crooner?'

'Vaguely.'

'I've been tipped off he's selling his life-story to the *Graphic*. Selling, if you please. It will be a load of old bollocks concocted by some publicity man, but it means a lot to the rock-and-roll crowd. I'm not going to let them get away with it. All we need is a bit of diplomacy. I want you to go and see him and con him along. Tell him we're doing a series on the top singing stars and he can't afford to be left out. In fact, say we'll start the series off with him, if he's agreeable.'

'Will he ask for money?'

'Probably. Look terribly hurt. It's enough to have to publicise these dead-beats without paying them for the privilege. Don't mention the life-story angle; just explain you're assembling a few personal details. A few meaningless scraps, that's the line to use. You might have to explain what "meaningless" means. Get a line on his life-story from the cuttings and add a few things he tells you – his favourite colour and that sort of thing. Basically they all have the same life-story, anyway. We'll run the lot on Sunday as "My Life by Ricky Rogers" with a seven-point line somewhere "as told to James O'Toole". That will cover us and kill the *Graphic*'s series stone dead.'

'And the other singing stars?'

'We'll forget them. I want the story in good shape by this afternoon, so you'd better get going straight away. His agent is a woman, by the way – she's expecting you. If he cooperates we might mention the feature in an ad during the week, which will snooker the *Graphic* completely. Go to it, boy.'

The office was in Regent Street, decorated with moulded plastic chairs in clanging colours. There was a dusty pot plant growing from a mixture of earth and cigarette stubs in a tub in the waiting-room. The agent, busty and bright, said her name was Mary Lou. She walked O'Toole into an office where Ricky Rogers in person sat sulking on a foam-rubber divan. His face was boyish and podgy, his skin blotched as if he had just started using an electric razor. He might have been twenty-five, or he might have been the original chubby youth amenable to discipline.

'Ricky, this is Mr O'Toole, from the *Sun*, a good friend of ours,' said Mary Lou.

'Hi,' said Ricky, offering a plump hand.

'Glad to know you,' lied O'Toole briskly.

'I've prepared you a summary of the facts about Ricky,' said Mary Lou. 'I'm afraid we can't give you his life story just at the moment. We've... promised.' She handed O'Toole a duplicated handout headed 'His Deep Purple Voice Plucked a Million Heartstrings'. O'Toole skimmed through it. He had read it a few minutes before, in a clipping from the *Sun* library.

'I just want a few background details,' said O'Toole.

'My favourite food is steak,' said Ricky.

'Well, that's interesting,' said O'Toole. 'You were a bellhop before you took up crooning, weren't you, Mr Rogers?'

'I never done a regular job like,' said Ricky.

'Please don't use the word "crooner", it's terribly out of date,' said Mary Lou to O'Toole. 'I don't think you should say bell-hop, either, that's not the sort of publicity we want, is it, Ricky?'

'You know best,' said Ricky.

'How about head waiter?' suggested O'Toole.

'Let's say he worked in the catering industry?' said Mary Lou.

'Did you dream of being a big star as a boy, Mr Rogers?' asked O'Toole.

'I wanted to run me own barrow,' said Ricky. 'Couldn't do it, though, with me bad ankles.'

'That's just our little joke,' explained Mary Lou. 'You used to save your pennies to buy Bing Crosby's records, didn't you, Ricky?'

Ricky nodded.

'Did your parents encourage you?' asked O'Toole.

'Of course they did,' said Mary Lou. 'Your mother was your inspiration during the years of struggle, wasn't she, Ricky?'

116

'Mum used to say she didn't mind what I did as long as I kept out of trouble,' said Ricky. 'Me Dad didn't really get interested until I landed me first big job. Fifty nicker a week. He's me manager now.'

'You've shot right to the top,' said O'Toole.

'I'm knocking out a thousand a week now,' said Ricky. 'Of course, there's a few people get a cut out of that.'

'That's not very nice publicity, is it?' asked Mary Lou. 'Tell Mr O'Toole how loyal your fans are.'

'Yes, I'd be nowhere without them,' said Ricky. 'They're entitled to me very best and they'll always get it, so help me. I'm spending twenty-five nicker a week just on stamps and photos but I don't grudge a penny of it.'

'Ricky's terribly generous,' said Mary Lou. 'Terribly loyal to his fans.'

'They worship the ground I walk on, like,' said Ricky. 'But I'm the first to admit I owe everything I am today to them.'

'It says here your favourite colour is blue,' said O'Toole, consulting the handout.

'Yes, and me favourite classical music is Tchaikovsky. The fans love those little personal details.'

'Do you expect to stay right on top forever?' asked O'Toole.

'Why not?' said Ricky. 'I'm not just a singer, I'm an entertainer, see? That's where the others fall down. They've just got one gimmick, like a guitar or a hearing aid. I'm an all-round entertainer, and I'm ready to give of me best all the time. So why should I worry?'

'Why, indeed?' said O'Toole. 'These facts will just about do me. I'll take the handout along and write the story from that.'

'Sorry we couldn't give you Ricky's full life-story,' said Mary Lou. 'It's grand stuff, I can tell you. But perhaps some other time.'

'If you've promised, you've promised,' said O'Toole. 'But I think I've got all I need.'

'Any time, I'm always glad to meet the reporters,' said Ricky.

O'Toole nerved himself for another handshake but none was offered.

'Ricky is no mental ball of fire, Mr Barr,' said O'Toole, handing over his copy. 'He told me his fans loved him and he loved them.'

'Was the agent any help?' asked Barr.

'She's a hard, sly piece of work, I should judge,' said O'Toole. 'She's brighter than poor old Ricky, of course, but she seemed to swallow the story about the big series of singing stars all right.'

Barr frowned as he read the crooner's life-story. O'Toole detected a hint of reprimand for himself, probably because he had too loosely implied that he and Barr were in the relationship of fellow-conspirators. 'The series sounds a good idea, by the way,' O'Toole added.

'We'll see,' said Barr. 'What's this crapology about working in the catering industry? What did the lout actually do?'

'Bell-hop,' said O'Toole.

'That's more like it,' said Barr, altering the copy with a pencil. He read on to the end. 'Seems okay,' he said. 'It's not what you'd call a thrilling read, but in the circumstances it's good tactics. Norman Knight tells me he's dug up a tasty little procuress.'

'A real monster,' said O'Toole.

'Sounds first-class,' said Barr. 'I'd like you to learn as much as you can from Norman, we can always use a second string to him. I think he wants to see you, by the way. And try and improve that time-keeping, there's a good lad.'

'I'll watch it,' said O'Toole.

As he left Barr's office he spotted Knight with a big, bright, fair-haired man holding a camera.

'This is Sam Jensen, our photographer, Digger,' said Knight.

'Any pal of Norman's is a pal of mine, Aussie,' said the giant, holding out a massive hypo-tanned paw. O'Toole liked the look of him.

'Same here,' he said, shaking the lump of muscle.

'How would you like to see Eileen, the love of your life, in daylight?' asked Knight.

'Not a bit,' said O'Toole. 'Must we?'

'We're moving in for the kill,' said Knight. 'Sam is going to take her portrait and we're going to tell her what's going on. After all, we didn't actually pay her anything. We need her admissions to clinch the story. Barr always wants me to confront the clients and reveal my identity, mainly to keep on the right side of the Press Council. It makes sense, too, I've got to give him that. Generally speaking, he's got a cautious streak. If it ever came to a court case, we've heard what she has to say together and we've given her a chance to put her side of the case, if she has one.'

'Very right and proper,' said O'Toole.

O'Toole enjoyed the ride down Piccadilly to Eileen's place with his two hefty and congenial colleagues. The trip had the flavour of a fishing expedition in good company. Knight explained the assignment to the photographer as they went.

'I'll knock on the door, Sam,' he said. 'O'Toole will be right behind me and that will just about block you from sight until she gets the door open. Then I'll step aside and you've got your shot. You'd better leave then, just in case she's got company. Go and sit in the car. We won't be long.'

'I've heard that before,' said the photographer. 'But I'll wait.'

The front door of the building stood ajar. They climbed past the door marked 'Private' to Eileen's apartment, and Knight knocked. A chain clattered out of the way and Eileen, tousled, looked out, frowning as she recognised Knight and O'Toole.

'You can't do this to me, boys, running out and then coming back in the middle of the day,' she said, running a hand through her hair. 'Please go away.'

'We're just here for a cuppa, m'darling,' said Knight.

Eileen opened the door some more. 'Oh well, perhaps…' she said. In the middle of her sentence Knight stepped aside and O'Toole followed suit. There was a harsh, dry blink of electronic flash and the click of a shutter. Jensen was turned and clumping down the stairs before Eileen quite knew what had happened. 'What on earth…' she said, cringing back. Knight was over the doorstep into the room before she had recovered her balance. O'Toole followed close behind, nodding an unsmiling greeting.

'You won't want the neighbours to hear this,' said Knight. 'I am Norman Knight of the *Sunday Sun* and this is my colleague, O'Toole.'

'My picture,' Eileen gasped. 'What…' O'Toole noticed she was wearing the same floral housegown.

We have discovered that these premises are being used for immoral purposes,' said Knight. 'We are going to put your name and this address in the paper.'

'And my picture?' asked Eileen, ashen. Knight nodded.

'But why, why?' asked Eileen. 'Is it a crime to have a bit of fun?'

'How old was the girl who was here yesterday?' asked Knight.

The woman flinched.

'I don't know,' she said. 'I didn't… ask her.'

'She's fifteen,' said Knight.

'You're not going… going to say I brought her into this, are you?'

'Yes. You did.'

'But please, please. I didn't know how old she was. She might be lying, trying to get your sympathy or something.'

'She's not.'

'I swear I didn't know. I swear it, I...'

"You should have known,' said Knight. 'If you bring young girls up here for prostitution you ought to find out how old they are.'

'But she wanted to come,' pleaded Eileen. 'All I said was she could meet some nice people, and perhaps make a few pounds, and she wanted to come. I swear I was going to give her half. After all...'

'That's not the point,' said Knight. 'You procured her for immorality for the purpose of gain and I'm going to put your name and address in the paper.' Knight sounded like a magistrate, rolling off the pompous legal phrases.

O'Toole noticed that the woman looked older in daylight, forty, perhaps, or forty-five. The geisha's professional veneer she had worn the night before had gone, and Eileen was a sagging middle-aged terrified housewife on the point of tears. Then her face twisted and she sobbed desperately.

'Norman, Norman, you just can't do this to me,' she choked out. 'It doesn't matter about me so much, but think of my poor husband. All his friends know this address. You'll ruin him. You'll kill him. I know I've done wrong but it didn't seem so bad at the time, I swear it didn't. I'll stop. I'll get a job, I'll take in washing, I'll do anything. Please, Norman, you look a kind man, please, please...' and then sobbing stopped her.

'You should have thought of that before,' said Knight. 'I'll quote you in the story saying you didn't know how old the girl was, if that's any comfort. I'll tell my editor about your husband. The decision is up to him.'

'Oh please, Norman, please,' the woman moaned. 'And that picture,' she said, to herself.

'Come on, Digger, let's go,' said Knight. 'We've got all we want.'

Eileen's face was buried in her hands as they left. Her uncombed black hair showed streaks of grey.

Knight and O'Toole went down the stairs and got into the car in silence. 'Sticky time?' asked the photographer.

'You know, I feel sorry for the poor bitch,' said Knight, staring straight ahead.

'So do I,' said O'Toole, softly.

'She should have thought of this before she took to whoring,' said Knight.

'And we wanted to be Fleet Street men,' said O'Toole. 'Don't take that the wrong way, Norman.'

'I know what you mean,' said Knight. 'There are parts of this job I don't like, either, Digger.'

The office was deserted when they got back. O'Toole didn't feel much like lunch so he got on with the mill-girl's confession. He had reached the part where the Marquis plied her with champagne and she escaped from his penthouse in the nick of time.

Not very enthusiastically, he wrote:

'My head was swimming from his expensive wine, but when he whispered a disgusting suggestion, I saw through his SLY TRICKS.

' "You may be a Lord, but you're no gentleman," I said, and he flinched when he saw my Yorkshire determination.

'He flinched even more when I said: "Let me go this minute or I'll dial 999."

'I could see he wasn't used to girls who stood up to him, who weren't a bit impressed by his money and his title and his smarmy hand-kissing manners.

'He knew when he was beaten. He touched a bell, and a silver-haired butler came in with a soft tread that made my flesh creep. Yes, he had plenty of servants and important connections, but what he didn't have was... '

At this point O'Toole stalled. What on earth didn't he have? If this boy wasn't nicely fixed, no one was. He didn't have a bluff Yorkshire manner with accent to match, but hardly any of the aristocracy have, if you can believe the *Evening Standard*. O'Toole was getting bored with the mill-girl's struggle to preserve her virtue, especially as he knew she would. Her imaginary personality was getting tangled up with Kathleen's, who had just had a much more real escape from disaster at the hands of the *Sun*. Unable to recover his sincere interest in the story for the moment, O'Toole phoned Elizabeth and arranged to meet her that evening. But that didn't seem a very thrilling prospect, either.

O'Toole walked up the crooked length of Fleet Street, the detour by St Clement Danes and the depressing straight cut of the Strand, with its fake railway lost property shops, rubber goods stores and shop-fitter's Minoan style hotels on the way to his date. By Aldwych Tube a newspaper poster

PROMINENT ACTRESS CRITICAL

trapped him for an unwary tuppence ha'penny. It wasn't Jenny, of course, but some museum-piece who had wowed them in the nineties and who now made her last newspaper appearance, thanks to a malignant carcinoma and the unaccountable failure of Krushchev to do anything newsworthy in time for the six o'clock West End Final editions. The poor old duck rated two paragraphs in eight point low down on the front page, which they'd probably held open hoping for better things. The dirty, confidence-tricking, bad-apple-polishing bastards, thought O'Toole. If I fall for it, what chance have the public got?

Wondering how long misleading posters about obscure show business people would continue to stab him at unexpected moments, O'Toole slid into a dangerous nostalgia for the flat overlooking the harbour, the bulging balloon sails of the eighteen-footers, the green gelatinous heave of the water behind the ferries, Sydney rock oysters for two and the bright, clean world of no problems. It was only a few months ago, cut off forever by the armoured glass shutter which separates us from the past.

Elizabeth was waiting, dimpled, real and present, in a coffee-house in Leicester Square. Her voice really was quite like Eileen's. They talked about nothing special, and went to a movie which took a long time to end. O'Toole didn't ask her back to South Kensington, and she didn't suggest it, and for the first time there was no real contact between them at all.

XVII

'LATE AGAIN, Old Tool, you brothel of a boy,' greeted Jacobs. He had rehearsed it somewhere. 'You'll miss half the fun if you're not here early on Saturdays.'

The newsroom was jammed with the Saturday crowd of unknown faces, noisy with the rattle of typewriters, lively with the flicker of telephone lights.

'It's hysterical, Tom,' said O'Toole. 'I don't really want to be here at all. I want to be punished. What's on, anyway?'

'Knight and a client are waiting to see you. They're in the waiting-room. Some sort of trouble over one of your whorehouses.'

O'Toole found Knight and a thin-nosed little man with horn-rimmed spectacles glaring at one another. The little man was clutching a seedy briefcase.

'Hello, James,' said Knight. 'This is Mr Ifor Morgan, a solicitor. He tells me he represents Eileen, the lady we saw yesterday. This is my colleague, Mr O'Toole.'

'Are you an Australian of some sort?' asked the lawyer fiercely. O'Toole nodded.

'I believe you go by the alias of McNaughton. You are a party to the conspiracy against my client.'

'Am I?' asked O'Toole.

'Just a moment, Mr Morgan,' said Knight. 'Let's get to the point. What do you want, exactly?'

'Certainly. I am here to give you a solemn warning.'

'Oh, yes,' said Knight. 'What about?'

The lawyer cleared his throat. 'I have reason to believe that you intend to publish a criminal libel on my client,' he said. 'I don't suppose you have more than a layman's acquaintance with the law, Mr Knight, so let me inform you of the punishment for criminal libel. Imprisonment, Mr Knight. A severe term of imprisonment. Your colleague will naturally join you in Wormwood Scrubs.'

'Indeed,' said Knight. 'Do you happen to know what this libel is that we intend to publish?'

'I do,' said the lawyer. 'I am instructed that you intend to brand my client as a woman of loose morals. That is clearly a criminal libel of the gravest sort, you can take my authority for that.'

'But it's true,' said Knight.

'You are aggravating your offence, Mr Knight. All this will go to the question of damages. An impudent perseveration in the libel.'

'Did she tell you what we were doing in her flat?' asked Knight.

'I believe she was ill-advised enough to admit you into her home,' said the lawyer. 'You claimed to be close friends of her husband's.'

'She told you that?'

'Those are the facts, Mr Knight. I will not be called a liar to my face by your type of person.'

'Why were we there for more than an hour?' asked Knight. 'We have ample evidence of the time we spent on the premises.'

'I am afraid that my client was taken in by your glib talk,' said Mr Morgan. 'She allowed you to stay a few minutes. A grave mistake on her part, clearly, but no basis for a foul defamation.'

'Why did she disrobe, then?'

'An outrageous suggestion,' said the lawyer. 'Of course, this will increase the damages.'

'Why was the younger girl naked?'

'I believe my client has a respectable young lady friend who visits her from time to time. I cannot accept for a second that she was improperly dressed.'

'Why did this respectable young lady come with me to a public house to buy a bottle of gin?'

'There is only your word for that, and you are hardly a person of credit.'

'There were a dozen people in the bar, including my chauffeur and photographer.'

'Perjury is cheaply bought, but easily exposed,' said Mr Morgan.

'Let me tell you something, Mr Morgan,' said Knight. 'We are publishing nothing about your client tomorrow. You might get an injunction over the week-end, but you will merely be stopping something which isn't going to happen yet, anyway. If you apply for your injunction on Monday, we shall bring evidence to support our accusations. Your client will be spread over all the newspapers, not just this one. You won't get your injunction, and we will get some nice publicity for our exposure. The best thing you can do in your client's interests is to refund your fee and go back to collecting small debts.'

'Don't you dare to threaten me,' bristled Mr Morgan. 'I am a professional man.'

'I'm just telling you what will happen if you go ahead with this,' said Knight.

'You will regret this foul, wanton attack on the honour of a respectable woman, Mr Knight,' said the lawyer. 'Your newspaper will be compelled by the courts to publish the fullest retraction and apology for your disgusting allegations. My client is not interested in money, of course, but I shall be compelled to ask the court for nominal damages – say, ten thousand pounds. You will find the British bench has a quick way with irresponsible, criminal defamation, Mr Knight.'

'Is this your first libel case, Mr Morgan?' asked Knight.

'Are you disparaging my professional reputation?' asked the lawyer, in a furious squeak. 'I advise you to watch your tongue, sir, or you will find yourself in even more serious trouble.'

'I have heard some amateurish approaches in my time,' said Knight, amused, 'but this business about your professional reputation is the silliest one I've heard yet. I've crossed swords with the best libel men in London and you're certainly not one of them. Do you imagine we are frightened of you just because you've scraped through articles somewhere?'

'This is outrageous, Knight,' shrieked the lawyer. 'You can't adopt this tone with me. I am an officer of the court. This is a grave contempt.'

'Rubbish,' said Knight. 'You are a pompous idiot, Mr Morgan, and if you don't like the sound of that I advise you to leave before you hear more.'

'You'll regret this, Knight, and so will your accomplice, whatever his real name is.'

'O'Toole,' said O'Toole. 'James O'Toole.'

'You'll regret this, both of you. I shall increase the damages to twenty-five thousand pounds, at least, and your employers have only themselves to blame. I'll see both of you in the dock before I am finished.'

'Good morning, Mr Morgan,' said Knight. 'If I was ever in two minds about your client, I certainly am not now.'

The lawyer snatched his brief-case from the table and stamped out. Knight lit his pipe.

'Well, that settles Eileen, Digger,' he said. 'If we let this snide little bastard get away with it, we'll have every whore and ponce in London sending someone in here to ask for twenty-five thousand nominal damages. The silliest thing she could have done was to go to some cheap lawyer with a sketchy knowledge of the libel law and then lie to him about what really happened.'

'When does the series start?' asked O'Toole.

'Next Sunday, I think, with an announcement tomorrow,' said Knight. 'After this, I think we might lead off with Eileen.'

O'Toole had barely got back to his desk when Jacobs came up with another man, a stranger.

'You did a story about Ricky Rogers, didn't you, Mr O'Toole?' he asked, with unexpected formality.

'I did, Mr Jacobs,' said O'Toole. 'This looks like visiting day.'

'This gentleman wants to tell us something about it,' said Jacobs, with a wink. 'Would you attend to him?'

'Surely, Tom,' said O'Toole. 'Better step into the waiting-room,' he said to the visitor.

The newcomer was short and fat, around fifty. He had horny hands and a good suit, like a man who has done well in the motor trade. His blood pressure looked high.

'I'm James O'Toole,' said O'Toole.

'Glad to know you,' said the man. 'I'm Ricky's father. His real father, that is.'

'Oh yes, I heard about you from your son,' said O'Toole. 'You encouraged him in his early struggles. You're in the transport business, aren't you?'

'You're mixing me up with that ponce who is living off Ricky now,' said the man.

'Let's get this straight,' said O'Toole. 'Mr Rogers told me his father used to be a lorry-driver and was now his manager. Is that you?'

'No, I'm his real father,' said the visitor. 'The man you're talking about married his mother while I was away.'

'Let's start from the beginning, Mr...' said O'Toole.

'Saunders. That's his real name, Ricky Saunders. Of course, he's ashamed of his old Dad now he's in the money.'

'How does that come about, Mr Saunders?'

'It's like this. I wasn't exactly married to his mother, like. Just before Ricky was born I got seven years.'

"What for, if that's not too personal?"

'GBH. That's Grievous Bodily Harm. A dirty frame-up, of course.'

'Of course, a frame-up. Where does Mr Rogers Senior fit into the picture?'

'Prendergast's his real name. I suppose Ricky didn't think that sounded too well on the stage, so he called himself Rogers. Well, this twot Prendergast... you'll have to excuse the language but my feelings are pretty deeply hurt, like...'

'Don't worry about me,' said O'Toole. 'Go on.'

'This Prendergast got on to the sweet side of Ricky's mother while I was away. She'd promised to wait for me, too, but you know what women are. When I came out she wouldn't have nothing to do with me. I let her keep the kid, of course, and this Prendergast brought him up. As a matter of fact, I more or less lost touch with them until Ricky started singing and I recognised his picture in the papers. He'd changed his name by then, but I knew him at once – regular chip off the old block.'

There was, O'Toole noticed, a distinct resemblance. It was exactly the hint of this soured podginess to come which ruined Ricky's present chances of being a handsome young man.

'You saw him again?' he asked the visitor.

'Well, not right away, like. I was doing another three years at the time. They framed me for immoral earnings. I'll be level with you, Mr O'Toole, I haven't been as good as I might have been. But I'm straight now, straight as a die. I've gone straight for Ricky's sake. For my boy's sake.'

'I'll bet he's proud of you.'

'That's the trouble. Would you believe it, he treats me, his own father, like common dirt. It's not right, is it? Oh, he's slung me a few quid now and again, like, but I've had to go down on my hands and knees to get it. Once he even grudged me a lousy hundred nicker to get me out of a spot of bother with some cheques. Just a loan, that's all I needed to tide me over. He wouldn't come across until I said I'd send the cheques to the papers with a note saying who I was – just to scare him, of course, I'd never have dreamed of doing it. What makes my blood boil, he was making a thousand nicker a week at the time and this ponce Prendergast was getting plenty of it, I'll bet. What do you think of a boy who treats his own father like that?'

O'Toole looked suitably scandalised. 'Was that the time he was topping the bill at the Palladium?' he asked.

'No, I was in the nick then,' said the visitor. 'It must have been a few months later – he was in the Royal Command show and the papers were full of him. I can tell you, the kid's rolling in it. Mind you, he can sing, and no mistake. Gets it from me. The girls used to be at me all the time in my young days to give them a tune. That wasn't all I gave them, either.'

Mr Saunders winked obscenely and O'Toole joined him in a laugh.

'Often thought of doing a round of the halls myself as Ricky Roger's Dad,' he went on. 'Just for a bit of publicity to get me started off, like.'

'Well, that's a most interesting story,' said O'Toole. 'What do you want us to do about it?'

'Print it,' said the visitor. 'The story of a father's love that his son's got no use for. I want you to bring the kid to his senses. Make him realise how shockingly he's treated his old Dad.'

'It mightn't do Ricky any good,' suggested O'Toole.

'Of course it will,' said Mr Saunders. 'I'll write it myself, but you can touch it up here and there. It's a warm, human story, and I know how you can dish it up, make it real inspiring. His fans will love every word of it.'

'We could write it to save you the trouble,' suggested O'Toole.

'I'll do it myself,' said Mr Saunders. 'It's my own life-story and I'm the man to do justice to it. When I sell my life-story, I want it treated right.'

'Did you have any price in mind for your reminiscences, Mr Saunders?'

'Well, it's worth something, you've got to admit. I'm not after money, of course, but I can't let it go buckshee. Say, hundred and fifty nick?'

'I'm not the man to decide,' said O'Toole. 'I suppose you can prove all this? Not that I doubt your word, of course.'

'Dead easy. I've got Ricky's birth certificate here – I treasured it over the years, like – and you can easily check up on me with the law.'

'Good enough,' said O'Toole. 'Hang on here for a minute and I'll put your idea up to the editor.'

'You're not going to ring Ricky, are you? I want to surprise him.'

'I know how you feel,' said O'Toole. 'No, I'm not going to ring anyone, just have a word with the governor.'

O'Toole crossed the busy office and found Starsh correcting a proof, a long filament of chewing-gum stretching from his mouth.

'Nick, we've had a visit from Ricky Rogers' father,' he said. 'He's told me a lot more about the lad's early troubles. A whiff straight off the sewer.'

'We've got enough rubbish in the paper about him already,' said Starsh.

'This is different. This is a story, for a change.'

'Oh?'

'It appears Ricky is a bastard, technically speaking. He's probably not the only bastard in show business, of course, but he's a special kind of bastard. It appears his father was in prison when he was born and, oddly enough, was in stir again when Ricky was topping the bill at the Palladium and doing his act for the Queen a few months back. Seems the old man's been blackmailing him for years by threatening to tell all.'

'Nice type.'

'He even makes Ricky look good,' said O'Toole. 'His Dad's a peg-legged, hump-backed, bad-breathed bastard of the old school.'

'Will he co-operate?'

'Ricky's been getting stingy, and there's some jealousy there about his *de jure* Dad, who's usurped the paternal spot on the payroll. He's ready to tell us everything for one-fifty. According to him all he wants

128

is recognition as the man who sired the wonder boy.'

'Cam ought to hear this,' said Starsh. 'Sounds like an interesting sidelight.'

Barr, too, was writing when they went into his office.

'O'Toole has something new on Ricky Rogers, Cam,' said Starsh.

'We're not wasting more time on that pissology, are we?' said Barr, annoyed at the interruption. 'This might be worth it,' said Starsh. 'Tell Mr Barr about it, James.'

O'Toole told his story.

'I can see how we can handle it,' said Barr. 'We give this individual his hundred and fifty for a signed story. Then we run something like this: "Get out of London, you beast, Saunders. Haven't you done enough harm already? Drop dead. Ricky doesn't want to know you and you're not fit to mingle with decent people. Slink back to the slums, you gaolbird." Then we tell the story, finishing up with how this vulture has blackmailed and bloodsucked the singing idol of millions of British teenagers. Then we round it off like this: "Now your spell is broken, you evil monster. The *Sun* has told your shameful story and the people of Britain know you for what you are. Never again can you profit from your shabby secret." We might say this heartless father has even tried to hawk his son's shame for money. Of course we put a line in somewhere to the effect that it's not Ricky's fault he's illegitimate and his Dad's an old lag. How does it sound, Nick?'

'Neat,' said Starsh. 'Pity about the one-fifty, we can easily check this ourselves.'

"We'll have to pay him something to tie him up,' said Barr. 'What's he like, O'Toole? Think you could con him into taking a fiver?'

'He's a hard man, I'd say, Mr Barr,' said O'Toole. 'I might beat him down a bit.'

'Give it a try,' said Barr. 'You two work on it, I'm busy here with the leader.'

O'Toole rejoined the anguished father.

'The editor is very sympathetic, Mr Saunders,' he said, "But I'm afraid our budget won't go to more than fifty pounds. After all, we're doing you a service by revealing the treatment you've suffered.'

'Seventy-five,' said Saunders.

'I think I might be able to get that through for you,' said O'Toole. 'Can you type?'

'Never got round to it, like.'

'Well, it doesn't matter,' said O'Toole. 'You tell me your story and

I'll type it out for you.'

'Now, like I said, I admit I'm no clean potato, but I got a father's natural feelings. Got that?'

O'Toole began typing.

Mr Saunders took nearly an hour to tell his story, of which perhaps ten lines were usable. Then he left the office in high good humour.

O'Toole sent out for a sandwich which he munched as he composed the exposure. He found the work agreeable, and particularly enjoyed the balance of his peroration:

Saunders, you worthless blackmailer, your evil spell is broken. You have done this innocent boy your last injury. Get out of London, out of Britain, out of sight of decent people.

Ricky, you are free at last. It is no fault of yours that your gaolbird father has fastened the shame of illegitimacy on you. To the broad-minded people of modern Britain, it is no shame. Now the *Sunday Sun* has exposed this callous monster for what he is, you have nothing more to fear. Now, thanks to this newspaper, you can get on with your real job – the job of bringing joy to millions of British teenagers!'

O'Toole was re-reading his piece when, painted, perfumed, varnished, lacquered, bulging, bare and cloven in the chest, Mary Lou swept into the office. She spotted O'Toole at his typewriter and altered course majestically in his direction.

'James,' she said. 'You've been terribly, terribly naughty.'

'Have I?' said O'Toole.

'I just heard from that nasty little man who says he's Ricky's father,' said Mary Lou. 'Of course he wanted money again and we're sick of paying all the time. He says you have promised to print his disgusting article about Ricky.'

'Does he now,' said O'Toole.

'I thought no decent newspaper would publish his lies,' said Mary Lou. 'You've met Ricky – you know what a marvellous person he is. This would ruin his career.'

'His Dad says his fans will love every word of it,' said O'Toole. 'I thought it was his human warmth they went for. Now they'll know where he gets it.'

'You know that's not true,' said Mary Lou. 'If this is published, every time he gets up to sing they will shout a horrible word at him – you know what I mean.'

'Bastard,' said O'Toole. 'A true word, for once.'

'That's not the publicity we want. You can't give us publicity like that. After all, it's not Ricky's fault, is it?'

'Look, Mary Lou,' said O'Toole. 'We're not in the business of giving Ricky good publicity. This is supposed to be a newspaper. We print what we think people will be interested in. For years you have been feeding us your cooked-up rubbish about Ricky's ties and his favourite dishes and we published it because deluded editors thought it was interesting. Ricky got rich in the process and you seem to be doing all right yourself. Now we've got something which is even more interesting. Maybe Ricky's income will go down but that's no concern of ours. We're not here to build him up in the first place. Those who live by publicity can't squeal if they die by publicity, can they?'

'That's blasphemous and horrible,' said Mary Lou. 'You must have a mind like a sewer. I'm not going to waste any more time with you, I'm going straight in to see the editor.'

'Good luck,' said O'Toole, but Mary Lou had stormed out of earshot. Sure enough, she went into Barr's outer office.

O'Toole left his typewriter and found Starsh.

'There's something odd going on here, Nick,' he said. 'That dame who just steamed in is Ricky Rogers' agent or publicity woman, something like that. She's the one who gave me the priceless load of crap about Ricky's favourite classical composer. She seems to know we're going to tip the bucket on her meal-ticket, and she's gone in to talk Barr out of it. What I don't like is, she's still in there, and she seemed to know exactly where his office is.'

'She probably knows him already,' said Starsh. 'Newspaper editors get about a bit, you know. Could the father have got at her in the meantime?'

'Easily. He would have had time to get to her office, and there's always the phone. He's obviously trying a double-cross.'

'I don't think she'll get far with Cam,' said Starsh.

'When will we know?'

'Perhaps never. Cam isn't obliged to explain himself.'

'We don't want to have this heart-warming story of a father's love tampered with, do we?'

'I'll nip in and see if I can find out what's going on,' said Starsh.

O'Toole sat on the edge of his desk as Starsh scurried into the editor's office. Above the clatter of the office, O'Toole thought he heard a woman's voice raised inside, perhaps even a muffled scream. But there was too much going on in the newsroom to be sure.

The sub-editors had already started work around the big horse-shoe table a few feet from him, trimming and shaping the smaller stories for the news pages. There were twenty of them, in shirt-sleeves, heads bowed and pencils flying over piles of copy-paper. The bare arms and furrowed foreheads, the unbuttoned collars and loosened ties made them look like ageing schoolboys doing a gruelling Eng. Lit. paper. The chief sub-editor, a one-eyed elderly man who looked after the answers to readers' queries during the week, presided at the centre of the outer curve of the table. He was working through a pile of stories from the basket at his elbow, reading the first few paragraphs of each, marking a spot on a clipped bundle of page schemes and throwing the document to one of the labourers with his order, 'Five pars with a single-column staggered two-line head in eighteen' or 'Two-par fill, early page.' For more complicated prescriptions, he wrote directions on the copy and sometimes drew the shape of headline he wanted.

As the sub-editors worked, O'Toole noticed that their left hands were periodically busy on the table, the fingers thumping in order like practising pianists'. They were counting letters, reducing political turmoil in far-off republics to

RED GRAB BID

because eighteen-point Roman Ultra-Bodoni makes nineteen units (including spaces) in a twenty-four em line over a shallow double, and even the Russians haven't developed rubber type faces yet.

Barr came out of the office first. He was patting Mary Lou on the shoulder, comfortingly, and smiling a polite social smile O'Toole had never seen before. Mary Lou looked a little tear-bruised around the eyes, which went effectively with her expression of sun shining through the rain. Starsh looked glum.

As Mary Lou passed O'Toole, she let him have a silent broadside of venomous triumph.

'Take this bravely, dear boy,' said Starsh, breaking station to join O'Toole. 'The idea's been killed.'

O'Toole saw Barr's back as he led Mary Lou to the lift.

'Dad's right out?' asked O'Toole.

'Except where he figures in Ricky's struggle to the top. She looked through your original version and said it was okay. She didn't seem to notice we've pinched his life history.'

'But what about the dirt?' asked O'Toole. 'What happens to the real story? It's right out?'

'Afraid so.'

'How on earth did she do it?'

'It was a great performance,' said Starsh. 'I only caught the tail end of it, but it was brilliant. First she cried, then said her career was finished and so was Ricky's. Finally she pulled out a bottle of pills and threatened to commit suicide right in the office, on Cam's good carpet.'

'This is fantastic,' said O'Toole. 'What do we care about Ricky's career, or hers either for that matter? Who ever heard of an agent committing suicide because the lunch coupons were in danger? I thought we were here to tell the truth without fear or favour.'

'We can't assist this blackmailer in his filthy tricks.'

'We were going to break his evil spell forever,' said O'Toole. 'What happened to that?'

'I'm surprised, James,' said Starsh. 'I know you're disappointed over your story, but you seem to be getting personally involved in this. You're always pleading for mercy, aren't you?'

'For people who can't defend themselves, yes,' said O'Toole. 'I'm not too keen on some of these attacks on wretched insignificant women who do a bit of whoring. I accept them because they're news and we're supposed to be printing news where we can find it. I've used news value as a standard all my life. Just because this great tub of low-class lard Rogers has enough money to hire some dame with a big bust to come down here and cry for him, I don't see why he's entitled to examine what we're going to print about him and get the parts he doesn't like killed.'

'You're taking this too seriously, James,' said Starsh, smiling and shaking his head. 'We might have had all sorts of trouble on our hands if this girl had carried out her threats. Besides, Rogers is a big public figure and we have to handle him carefully.'

'We made him a big public figure,' said O'Toole heatedly. 'Here's another small point. We now know that Rogers' life-story is not only a nauseous piece of bum-sucking, it's totally untrue into the bargain. What about the paper you can rely on?'

'Don't look at it that way,' said Starsh. 'It's a good, inspiring read and it does no one any harm. Who cares if it's been touched up a bit here and there, artistically speaking?'

'I can't see Rogers and his hired bosom getting away with this,' said O'Toole. 'This is getting close to dishonesty.'

Starsh put a hand on O'Toole's shoulder.

'Look, James, we can all be guilty of rationalising our resentments, especially when there's a natural disappointment involved. You strike me as an honest man, so I'll be frank with you. Are you sure you haven't got it in for Rogers because he's making money? We have to be fair to the rich, you know, and treat them like anyone else. We're not here to conduct class war on these people.'

'All I want is for us to tell the truth,' said O'Toole, 'especially when it's a good, juicy story. I can't see why not.'

'Policy, dear boy, policy,' said Starsh. 'Is it possible you are treating Rogers as a symbol for show business in general? Do you dislike all music-hall entertainers, for some reason?'

'Why should I?' asked O'Toole, with a start.

'I don't know,' said Starsh. 'What I do know is, you're starting to sound like Norman Knight in one of his more passionate crusading moments. After all, you must have guessed by now that Cam is the editor of this paper and Norman Knight isn't because we need Norman's energy in swinging the shining sword of reform, but even more we need Cam's judgment to keep us out of bankruptcy and keep the show going. Come, come, James, you know this rock-bottomed honest pose is terribly naive. We might present a bit of fiction now and again as if it was literal truth, but what about Dickens and Dostoievski and the rest of the literary trade? They write the truth and pretend they made it up. It's all dishonest, if you are going to take this stern puritan line.'

'But look, Nick...' said O'Toole.

'I'm sorry, dear boy, but you'll really have to defer this exposition of your views to some other time. We've got a paper to get out, you know.' Starsh patted O'Toole's shoulder again, as he left.

O'Toole tore up his story in disgust and returned to his desk, boiling. He tried to imagine Ricky and Mary Lou as poor, put-upon people, but he couldn't see Mary Lou poor in any heterosexual environment.

Having for the moment nothing more to do, and unable to sit any longer at his desk, O'Toole went over to Jacobs, who happened to be between telephone calls.

'They don't want stories here, Tom,' he said. 'If anyone wants me I'm out for a drink.'

'You're entitled to your break, but why the despairing tone?' asked Jacobs. 'Spent too much time on the nest lately?'

Then the phone rang again, and Jacobs waved O'Toole away.

'I'll be in the Falcon,' said O'Toole, leaving. Norman Knight came up at that moment.

'I could do with one myself, Digger,' he said. 'Mind if I come along?'

'Of course not, Norman,' said O'Toole.

XVIII

KNIGHT and O'Toole were wedged in a corner of the bar, speaking softly because the place was full of people from the opposition papers.

'It really gets me, Norman,' said O'Toole. 'For years I've been waiting to get something good on one of these repulsive show business types, just to even up the score for all the free publicity I've given them. A story finally comes along and Barr kills it because Ricky Rogers' agent comes into the office and cries.'

'That's who she was,' said Knight. 'What have you got on Rogers? He goes with whores, or something?'

'He might, for all I know,' said O'Toole. 'The story is, he's a bastard, and his Dad was in stir when he was topping the bill at the Palladium.'

'Not bad,' said Knight. 'On the other hand, these crooning nine-day wonders are not really top-weight celebrities, are they? Barr might have smelt some sort of weird publicity stunt.

'That really would be an original one,' said O'Toole.

'They'll try anything,' said Knight. 'What did Starsh have to do with it? I saw him trailing the publicity woman out of the office.'

'Oh, nothing much,' said O'Toole. 'He found out what was going on for me. He seemed to take it pretty tamely, though, I thought.'

'I'd be a bit careful with him if I were you,' said Knight. 'He's straight enough, no question about that, but he's clever and he knows it. I suppose you've noticed he writes or rewrites just about every word that goes into the paper. You know anything about his background?'

'Nothing,' said O'Toole. 'Provincial by the voice, perhaps Jewish by the name. That's all I can guess.'

'Comes of a well-off family in Liverpool,' said Knight. 'Studied to be an accountant or economist, something like that. He's got all the degrees. Became a Communist during the war and worked in some flea-bitten little publishing house in Prague, I think it was. Then he saw the light, came back here and started doing a Saturday trick on the subs table. That would be four or five years ago. Cam took a shine to him, although he just about had the arse out of his trousers at the time.

Maybe that was why. Anyway, in no time he was Cam's right-hand man, and I suppose he's in line for the job if Cam ever turns it in.'

'What do you mean, he saw the light?' asked O'Toole. 'Not your light, by any chance?'

'Good God, no,' said Knight, laughing. 'He says he's broken with the reds. Possibly he has, you can never be certain with these people.'

'His job would tend to indicate that he has,' said O'Toole.

'Once a Communist, always a Communist, that's what they say' said Knight. 'As far as I'm concerned his politics are his own business. The thing you ought to know is that Barr takes a lot of notice of what Starsh says, and when the pair of them get together they're likely to take some fantastic risks. Starsh hasn't come up through the mill like you and I have, and he's sometimes inclined to think his degrees entitle him to get away with murder. Just keep your eyes open, that's all.'

'Thanks for the tip, Norman,' said O'Toole.

Jacobs called O'Toole to his desk when the pair returned to the office.

'Editor would like to see you, Aussie,' he said. 'No idea what about. He said as soon as you came back.'

Barr was reading a proof when O'Toole went in.

'Sit down, laddie,' he said. 'I won't be a moment with this.'

O'Toole sank into a velvet-padded easy chair, intimidated by the distance he had to lean back to keep his feet on the carpet. It was not the sort of chair you could get out of without an undignified heave. Barr's spectacles flashed in the light of his reading-lamp as he finished with the proof and put his initials in a corner. Then he raised his head and gazed at O'Toole, unsmiling and unspeaking for several seconds.

'I believe you don't like the way this paper is run,' he said after the pause.

'It's certainly not what I'm used to, Mr Barr,' he said.

'Anything in particular you object to?'

'I think you must be referring to Ricky Rogers,' said O'Toole. 'Since you ask me, I think we passed up a good story.'

'That's my decision,' said Barr.

'Of course,' said O'Toole. 'I can disagree without questioning your right to decide. I don't. It's your paper.'

'I'm glad you see that,' said Barr, with perhaps a touch of irony. 'Let me give you a word of advice, O'Toole. I'm sure you can see how I like to run a paper, as a big happy family. I took a chance when I brought you in here. After all, you're a stranger, you're not accustomed to the way we do things. But I thought I spotted the Fleet Street touch

136

in you, and I don't think I was mistaken.'

'Thank you,' nodded O'Toole.

'I may have overestimated you in other ways,' Barr went on. 'I thought you'd catch on to our methods quicker than you have. Frankly, there's something about your approach I don't like. I know you Australians have a reputation for being difficult. I'm prepared to go to a certain amount of trouble with you, because you seem to go after a story in the same aggressive way, and we can't have too much of that. But I draw the line when a reporter starts to get too big for his boots.'

'Fair enough,' said O'Toole.

'Now take this Rogers story,' said Barr. 'Considered just as news, it's good – we've both been in this business long enough to know that. But there's another side to it you mightn't see. You had a good story, you would have had a page-one by-line on it, and you've missed out. You're disappointed, and I'm prepared to understand that and make allowances for it. But when you let your anxiety for a by-line blind you to everything else in the situation, you're letting the team down.'

'It wasn't exactly the by-line, Mr Barr...' O'Toole began, but Barr cut him short.

'It's my job to see the whole picture,' he went on. 'This chappie Rogers mightn't mean much to you or me, but we mustn't forget he's the idol of millions of British teenagers.'

'He certainly is,' said O'Toole.

'Now I won't mince words about this,' said Barr. 'This is a paper with a largely working-class readership. It's those readers who pay our salaries, O'Toole, and don't you forget it. These people mightn't have as much so-called good taste as the West End snobs, but they're decent people and their hearts are in the right place. I won't have snide snobbish attacks on their heroes in my paper.'

'I would never have thought I was a snob,' said O'Toole.

'Neither would I, until this came up,' said Barr. 'I'm making allowances for the fact that you're new over here, laddie, or you wouldn't be on the staff now. It's possible that you're keeping snobbish company outside the office and you've picked up the wrong attitudes without realising it. I don't care where you get it from. The point I want to make is, I'll sack any man without a second's hesitation who tries to sneak that sort of thing into my paper. Got that?'

'Got it,' said O'Toole. He hadn't even begun to digest this accusation.

'I hope this is the last time I have to say it,' said Barr. 'It's a final warning, and I'm serious. Now that we've cleared that up, I think I might still be able to get you that by-line.'

'Oh?' said O'Toole.

'I suppose you saw the society strangling in the papers this morning?'

O'Toole had. It concerned a girl in a fur coat who had been found strangled the previous night in an alleyway near Marble Arch. She apparently came from a middle-class suburban family and had no police record for soliciting, or at least none the Press had been able to find. The location and the fur coat had lifted it out of the ruck of routine murders, and the first edition of the *Express* had christened it 'Park Lane Society Strangling'. All the other morning nationals except *The Times* and the *Guardian* had followed suit in the later editions, the *Telegraph* compromising with 'Park Lane Murder Mystery.' The *Sketch* had offered five years' free subscription to any registered reader who could produce the girl's missing handbag. The *Mirror* had a box-Brownie snapshot of the girl, evidently from some relative, headed 'She Kept Her Last Big Date – With Death.'

'I saw the story,' said O'Toole.

'You couldn't really miss it,' said Barr, smiling for the first time. 'Now this is a long-shot, but it might work. I think I told you at the time I thought your handling of the Liverpool golfing husband story was up to top-class Fleet Street standard.'

O'Toole nodded.

'Now I have an idea in the back of my mind that you've done something with Michael Macedon, haven't you?'

'I tried to buy his story,' said O'Toole.

'Of course,' said Barr. 'How did you leave him – friendly?'

'Oh, yes,' said O'Toole. 'I'd say we're quite good friends.'

'Splendid,' said Barr. 'He's one of these deb's delight Park Lane types, isn't he? He's bound to have known this girl, moving in high society circles and all.'

'It's quite possible,' said O'Toole.

'You can see the possibilities,' said Barr. 'I want you to put it right on him – get his full denial, with his alibi. Use the business about swearing on the Bible again, if you like. Saturday night he's probably at home dressing for some big shivoo. You should be able to see him and get back in an hour and a half, say. That would give us an hour to clear the story through the lawyers before the first edition. No, come to think of it, we'll hold it back till the second in case some of the others want to get in on it. That would give you a clear three hours. What I have in mind is something like "Society Playboy's Angry Denial – Peer's

138

Nephew says, I'm No Strangler". If you get it, I can promise you that front-page by-line after all.'

'But...' said O'Toole.

'Any problems?' asked Barr sharply.

'Nothing,' said O'Toole, heaving himself out of the chair. 'I'd better get going.'

'Good lad,' said Barr. 'You won't forget our little talk, will you?'

'I won't,' said O'Toole. 'Thanks for being frank.'

Barr said nothing, but began reading another proof. O'Toole, staring straight ahead, walked uncomprehending through the clatter of the newsroom to his desk and sat down.

A moment later Jacobs came up and, leaning his bare hairy forearms on the desk, pulled an anguished face at O'Toole from uncomfortably close range.

'Did Cam smack, Aussie?' he asked. 'There, there.'

O'Toole smiled. 'Not really, Tom,' he said. 'Just suggested I should be more democratic, that's all. And he's given me a top-level assignment to get on with.'

'More whores?'

'Not this time. He's dreamed up a suspect as a follow-up for the society strangling. He wants the usual denial of the vicious rumours.'

'Who's the lucky man?'

'Michael Macedon.'

Jacobs nodded appreciatively.

'Not bad at all,' he said. 'Just a minute, isn't Macedon some sort of pal of yours?'

'I know him quite well,' said O'Toole.

'That's a lucky break,' said Jacobs. 'You've got the ice broken before you start. Nice contact to have.'

'I won't have him long after this,' said O'Toole.

'Oh, I don't know,' said Jacobs. 'I exposed my uncle once for black-marketing whisky. He's still my uncle. Anyway, who cares if he isn't? The only point about having contacts is to use them when the time comes. I didn't take you for the squeamish type.'

'I'm not,' said O'Toole. 'I'm off on the job now. I expect I'll be about an hour and a half.'

'Mind, no expensive drinks,' said Jacobs. 'Beer and sincerity.'

O'Toole walked along Fleet Street and turned up Kingsway to get out of range of the office. Near Holborn Tube he found a coffee-house and sat in a far corner with his back to the door. Over a coffee he wondered what to do.

The time to refuse the assignment had passed: he'd never refused one before, and he couldn't afford to convict himself of snobbery straight after the warning.

On the other hand, he thought, you have to live somewhere.

Finally he saw a phone by the counter and rang his own number. Macedon answered.

'You know who this is,' said O'Toole.

'I do, lodger,' said Macedon. 'Are you giving notice?'

'No fear,' said O'Toole. 'Look, Michael, I'll explain what this is about later. I just want you to answer a question. You didn't know this floosie who was strangled in Park Lane last night, did you?'

'Not as far as I know,' said Macedon. 'Should I?'

'It's just a crazy idea, and not mine,' said O'Toole. 'Will you be in tonight?'

'I'm going out in a few minutes.'

'Don't answer the phone before you go.'

'This is pretty exciting stuff,' said Macedon. 'Who's after me?'

'I am,' said O'Toole. 'Just go out and forget about it. I'll fill you in later.'

'If it's that good, I'll wait up,' said Macedon.

O'Toole paid for the coffee, caught a bus up Oxford Street and slipped into a newsreel. On the screen, a man with a beard said he was going to give the news behind the news, but it turned out to be the ski-jumpers and floods in Japan, just like it always was. When the programme came round to the baby crocodiles in Florida again, O'Toole left and caught a bus back to the office.

Barr and Starsh were talking together near the subs' table.

'Did you get it, O'Toole?' asked Barr.

'I'm afraid Macedon just wouldn't play at all,' said O'Toole.

'I couldn't even get him to admit that it was possible rumours were going round about him. He was quite ready to talk to me, but I'm afraid he's a bit too bright to fall for this particular pitch. Perhaps he saw our story about Mr Green the other week.'

'Well, never mind,' said Barr. 'It was worth a try, anyway. We still need a strong lead story. Nick, could you whip me up one of your Court Correspondent pieces?'

'What about the Queen does the football pools every week?' suggested Starsh. 'Doesn't gamble, of course, just marks a coupon and then checks the results for fun. It'll never be denied.'

'Thursday night at Buckingham Palace is just like your home, with pools and telly,' said Barr. 'It'll do. A close friend of the Royal Family told us, eh? Perhaps we could have a crown drawn with ones twos and x's.'

'Home and away with Royalty,' suggested Starsh.

'Let me see it,' said Barr.

Turning to O'Toole, Barr dismissed him with 'Better luck next time, laddie,' and went back into his office.

The rest of the night was quiet. When the first edition came up and was distributed, a copy to each man present, by an evil-looking copy-boy, O'Toole flipped through the paper and found the spurious life-story of Ricky Rogers on the first feature-page.

Sure enough, there was no reference to Ricky's loving father, but the piece was now boldly by-lined 'by Ricky Rogers'. The tiny eye-straining line, 'as told to James O'Toole', had disappeared too. No doubt, thought O'Toole, Mary Lou had given Barr the green light to use Ricky's byline, as a sort of tip. Or perhaps Barr had just picked up the small change.

On the front page the *Sun* Court Correspondent broke the news about Thursday nights at the Palace. It appeared that 'a trusted Royal servant' wrote off for the pools coupons.

By eleven o'clock the subs' table was down to one late-stop sub-editor who was settling down with a Western for the long haul to four a.m. Jacobs was playing dice with a group of Saturday-casual reporters. Barring the Second Coming, the only changes likely to be made in the paper for the four million copies still to be printed were late darts tournament results from pubs in outlying parts of the country.

Starsh came up, wearing an overcoat and scarf.

'I believe you live near me, James,' he said. 'Like to share a cab?'

'Good idea,' said O'Toole.

Starsh gave the driver an address in Knightsbridge. It turned out to be a small block of, evidently, big flats.

'You can walk from here, James,' he said. 'I usually have a nightcap after the big rush on Saturday. Care to join me?'

'Very cosy,' said O'Toole.

Starsh led him through a vestibule along a carpeted corridor lined with orange-toned mirrors with engraved nymphs and waterfalls and up a broad stair to the first floor. He let them in with a key. The light was on inside.

The room was furnished with dark wooden table and chairs and some glass-fronted cupboards, all in phoney Elizabethan style. It didn't look as if Starsh, or anyone else, lived there.

A neat, dark, early middle-aged woman came through another door. She was wearing a housegown, slippers and a bright lipstick.

'Oh!' she said, seeing O'Toole.

'Dear, this is Mr O'Toole from the office,' said Starsh. 'I've brought him in for a nightcap.' Turning to O'Toole, he added, 'This is Mrs Starsh.'

'I've heard so much about you, Mr O'Toole,' said the woman, offering a cold hand. 'Nick's often talked about you.'

O'Toole mumbled a polite greeting.

'I'll leave you men to it,' she said, smiling brightly.

'Won't be long, dear,' said Starsh.

He took off his overcoat, unlocked one of the glass-fronted cupboards and brought out a bottle of whisky and glasses.

'Could I have one of your cigarettes, dear boy?' he asked O'Toole, pouring out drinks.

'I thought you were tapering off,' said O'Toole.

'Weakness,' said Starsh, lighting the cigarette and puffing it timidly, as if he was learning to smoke.

'Now,' he said, after sipping his drink. 'You're angry with us.'

'Storm in a teacup,' said O'Toole. 'You know how we are in this business, like greyhounds on the leash. As soon as I got out after Macedon I was all right. That was an odd idea of Cam's, wasn't it?'

'I suggested it,' said Starsh, with a wicked grin. 'Aren't you living with Macedon?'

'Does Barr know that?' asked O'Toole.

'Not as far as I know. Tell me, just how hard did you try to get his denial?'

'Hard enough,' said O'Toole, feeling guilty.

'This is completely off the record, of course,' said Starsh. 'I'm only mentioning this because of the little ethical problems we've discussed. And, of course, I'm not saying for a moment that anyone could have got Macedon to deny the murder. But equally, you've got to admit, this could be a case of a man who's not prepared to do to a friend something which he'll do to a stranger without a moment's compunction – and do very competently, too. I thought you'd enjoy the possible paradox involved here.'

'Obviously, I can make no comment,' said O'Toole. 'You wouldn't have suggested it to Barr in the first place to make some sort of point, would you?'

'Of course not,' said Starsh, grinning again. 'Purely on its merits as a news story, that's all.'

'I'm glad to hear it,' said O'Toole. 'Now that we're talking so close to home, Nick, is it true you used to be a Communist?'

'That's right,' said Starsh.

'You mean you used to believe all that stuff?' asked O'Toole. 'About the thesis being negated by the antithesis and the bread turning into flesh and the wine coming out as blood and all that?'

'At least I never believed *that,*' said Starsh, smiling again. 'You're thinking of Norman Knight.'

'Nothing to be ashamed of,' said O'Toole. 'Everyone has some scruffy little belief in the background he doesn't want people to know about. Look at me, for instance. I used to believe in cub's honour.' He raised two fingers to the side of his head.

'Sometimes I think you still do,' said Starsh.

'This is turning into a hate session,' said O'Toole. 'What are you trying to do – give me notice?'

'Not a bit of it, dear boy,' said Starsh. 'We can certainly use you, or at any rate someone with your peculiar combination of talents. But I wonder whether you need us.'

'I have to eat,' said O'Toole.

'Come, come,' said Starsh. 'You're young and unmarried, and there are a thousand other things you could do for a living. You don't strike me as a vagabond, so I suppose there was some serious purpose which brought you all the way over here. I am just wondering whether you are going to achieve it with us. You have the necessary ability to hold the job you have now, certainly. Your attack and aggressiveness might even qualify you for an editor's chair one day, on the right kind of paper. But, to be quite frank with you, I doubt that you have the suppleness to slip under the barriers which lie between.'

'Not slippery enough?' asked O'Toole, uncertain if he was being flattered or asked for his resignation.

'That's not my choice of word,' said Starsh. 'Perhaps it's a kind of sensitivity I have in mind. Your puritanical outbursts, for example. Strictly speaking, it's not your place to have them at all, or at least show them. But ours is not an authoritarian organisation, and we are prepared to overlook a great deal in a promising man settling in. However, beyond a certain point, they impose an unwanted strain on those who are unlucky enough to be your superiors. A man who is going to succeed must sense these tensions, and desist before it is too late.'

'Or not have puritanical outbursts at all,' suggested O'Toole.

'Not in the least,' said Starsh. 'Simply to do what you are told will never qualify you to give orders to others. That is the outlook of the hack, and the place for hacks is on the bottom rung. They must be changed frequently, too, before they have a chance to make themselves indispensable – rather as barnacles are periodically scraped off ships.'

'You can't win,' said O'Toole. 'You mustn't do what you're told, and you mustn't annoy the boss by objecting to what you're told to do.'

'There is a narrow path between,' said Starsh. 'Those who want power in an organisation like ours must pass along it.'

'What sort of work do you suggest I should take up?' asked O'Toole.

'Now don't misunderstand me, James,' said Starsh. 'This is in no sense an ultimatum. If you're happy where you are, by all means stay with us for as long as you need to find your feet. Perhaps your future is with us: I do not mean to be dogmatic either way. But, since you ask me, I rather see you with a pile of yellowing manuscript. Perhaps you may be able to resolve some of your problems that way. Certainly, you will first have to accept the way we do things before you can hope to impose your own ideas on us, and you don't seem to me to show any signs of doing so.'

O'Toole took a long sip of his drink. 'There's a funny thing, Nick,' he said at length. 'Just the other day I was telling someone that you don't have to be sincere in the newspaper game.'

'Not sincere about the day-to-day stories, of course not,' said Starsh. 'But ours is a small organisation, and we cannot function without teamwork. On that level we must have sincerity, or at least mutual loyalty. If one of us has secret reservations about the others, the organisation will soon begin to suffer. Every man we have is valuable to us, but none is invaluable.'

O'Toole finished his drink saying nothing. Starsh rose. 'Now, dear boy,' he said, yawning, 'we have had a wearing day.

'Of course,' said O'Toole. 'Thanks for the drink, Nick. I enjoyed the straight-from-the-shoulder stuff, and there's really only one thing I can add to it: I still think Ricky Rogers is a bastard.'

'Now you're being sincere,' said Starsh, laughing and helping him into his coat.

Walking home by Cromwell Road and the locked-up South Kensington Tube, O'Toole wondered about Starsh. The oblique, intricate reprimand – if it was a reprimand – sounded like the higher grades of the Civil Service, ludicrously out of place in relation to an enterprise like the *Sunday Sun*. It sounded even more ludicrous delivered in Starsh's voice, with its ample tint of Lancashire. The only other person O'Toole had ever heard speak that way was Stanley Holloway, on a comical gramophone record, but Starsh was evidently making some sort of serious point. There was no one up at the flat as he crept to bed.

XIX

'Quite by accident, the name of Michael Macedon was tossed into a very complicated situation which really had nothing to do with you,' O'Toole explained. 'Mind if I fry myself one of your eggs?'

The pair were breakfasting in the kitchen of Macedon's flat: O'Toole in a turtle-necked sweater and crushed trousers in which he had taken to sleeping, Macedon in a frayed but once magnificent silk dressing-gown. The inhabitants and assorted itinerants who lived in the flat with any permanence each had a personal stock of food in an agreed nook or corner of the pantry, but O'Toole was down to a piece of salami and a mouldy packet of pre-sliced bread, neither of which he fancied for breakfast.

'We'll have to make a note of it,' said Macedon. 'This is Liberty Hall, of course, old boy, but we're not exactly all mucking in together, you know. We have to cling to a minimal landlord and lodger relationship to preserve our dignity, yours as well as mine. On second thoughts, let's say I'm inviting you to breakfast, to cut down on the book-keeping.'

'This is the old civilisation of Europe,' said O'Toole, cracking an egg into the frying-pan. 'People who have lived together a long time, and all that stuff.'

'Let's get back to the mystery phone call,' said Macedon, munching a slice of toast with honey. 'Did this involve another of your attractive cash offers? It may have been rather presumptuous of you to turn it down on my behalf, James. At the moment I would be prepared to go quite some distance for a little ready money to buy the furniture back, as you well know.'

'No money had been mentioned at the point where I rang you,' said O'Toole. 'The management of my paper live pretty sheltered lives, and they believe what they read in the other papers. This wretched girl who was strangled is supposed to be straight out of *Debrett,* and so are you. As a matter of fact you are, aren't you?'

'I'm somebody's issue living, if you call this living,' said Macedon. 'You know, one s, one d, I'm an s. But go on.'

'Well the big boss got the idea of getting me to get you to deny you strangled her.'

'Willingly,' said Macedon. 'I didn't.'

'There's a bit more to it than that,' said O'Toole. 'You were supposed to deny it with plenty of picturesque detail, if possible with your hand on the Bible, so as to convey the impression you did it.'

'Great fun,' said Macedon. 'Why me?'

'Your name was actually suggested by an organisation man from Manchester we have round the office,' said O'Toole. 'He doesn't know you, any more than he knows any of the other unfortunates who get written up in our paper. But he does seem to know that I know you, and he was giving me my Boy Scout fire-lighting test. It's not easy to explain this to anyone who's not in the business.'

'Did you pass?' asked Macedon. 'I hope you're in no danger of unemployment. Can't afford that now.'

'I failed,' said O'Toole. 'They failed, too, in a way. I think I can ride out the storm by good work and sincerity, so the rent is safe for the time being.'

'That's the main thing,' said Macedon. 'Tea?'

'Just the way it comes,' said O'Toole, pushing his teacup over. 'I must say you're taking this very calmly, Michael. You were nearly branded as the society strangler.'

Macedon laughed.

'Really, old boy, no one takes your paper seriously, do they? I'm sure no one I know does.'

'Maybe not,' said O'Toole. 'Why didn't you take the money for your love-life, the first time I came round here?'

'That was different,' said Macedon. 'Getting mixed up with Czech actresses isn't really the thing, is it? Beside, it would have led to complications with my authentic love-life at the time. On the other hand, I'm sure no one I know would really think I was the society strangler, and I don't think they'd care, either. I mean, we all know what sort of tricks you chaps get up to on Sundays. Still, if my not denying I'm the culprit scores some sort of victory for you, I'm prepared to overlook the cash I've missed.'

'Very decent of you,' said O'Toole.

'You've given me an idea, though,' said Macedon. 'I do a bit of scribbling myself now and again. I had some interesting war experiences – I don't mean hero stuff, of course, but some rather funny things happened in the prison-camp I was in. The Germans had some very peculiar ideas about who was important and who wasn't, and they picked some of us out for special treatment. Had some notion about bartering us off. Perhaps your paper might be interested in some articles? Strictly cash basis, of course.'

'Let me see some of it and I could give you some sort of verdict myself,' said O'Toole. 'Not much sex, eh, but some big names?'

'There were some quite well-known people there,' said Macedon.

'Give me a week or two until your strangling exploits blow over,' said O'Toole. 'Could I have another cup?'

Elizabeth phoned later in the day and told O'Toole she knew about a party in Hampstead, and they met in the coffee-house with the string and the pot-plants, and then bought a bottle of Spanish Beaujolais and went along.

It was a furnished-flat type of flat, yellow paint and Portobello Road furniture, with amusing slogans like MUST YOU? drawn on pieces of paper stuck on the walls. The guests were men who had gone to school with Dylan Thomas and Stephen Spender, with woollen neckties and one wing of the collars of their woollen shirts turned up to prove it.

A girl in red stockings and a black dress was dancing with British abandon, a heavy frown creasing her round, chubby and pretty-when-young face, the kind you see behind a tea-urn at the WVS. Her partner, improbably, was a pale young man in a waistcoat. Because she looked a little like Elizabeth, O'Toole turned quickly away and spoke to a blond man with a creased face who turned out to be a South African.

O'Toole had hardly opened his mouth when the South African challenged him on the White Australia Policy. O'Toole tried to explain that it was not racialist, but had actually begun with the determination of the infant Australian working-class movement to prevent Australia becoming a race-exploitation society like South Africa, the explanation he had learnt at school but had never quite accepted. He said to the South African that you had to understand the historical preconditions, and the South African began to say that if you took a sympathetic

147

enough view of the historical pre-conditions you could defend anything, when a woman in a sari who had been leaning forward in a chair with glazed eyes suddenly vomited on the South African's suede shoes.

As the South African was stamping about the room like a man just come in out of the snow, an Indian hurried up with a towel and said to O'Toole in passing: 'She isn't an Indian, you know, she's a German in a sari.'

'Whatever she is she probably got interested in what was going on and missed the inner signal,' said O'Toole to Elizabeth. 'It could happen to anyone.'

But the South African seemed to hold O'Toole responsible, and it was hardly the sort of thing you could argue about, so O'Toole and Elizabeth finished their drinks and left. There seemed nothing else to do but go back to O'Toole's room.

Elizabeth made tea and they sat down.

'Well?' said O'Toole. 'Where do we go from here?'

'Don't be so restless, James,' said Elizabeth. 'What happened at the party was a pity, but they'd had a lot to drink and it was just one of those things.'

'They were a pretty crummy bunch, taken all in all,' said O'Toole

'Now really,' said the girl with a tolerant smile, 'look who's talking.'

'I know,' said O'Toole, 'I go round tricking people like a door-to-door salesman, or worse, and here's a new development – I've just taken to double-crossing my employers, even according to their tilted lights.'

'I've asked you this before,' said the girl. 'Why do you do it?'

'It's my trade,' said O'Toole. 'I'm too old to start ballet-dancing, heavyweight wrestling or lyric poetry. It's my only chance to make the grade.'

'But surely, James, you're too intelligent to regard this dreadful paper business as making the grade, aren't you?'

'I might get a column of my own,' said O'Toole. 'I might even get to be top vice man.'

'And?'

'No "and" about it. Naturally I'd prefer to get into the big time in a light, clean, interesting line of work, but this is better than nothing. At least there's no heavy lifting.'

'Whenever the subject of your job comes up, you get into this funny, bitter mood,' said Elizabeth. 'I don't like you because of what you do, you know.'

'I don't know what you can make of me,' said O'Toole. 'For that matter, I can never really get the hang of people like you. I used to think once the world was split up into successes and people who'd like to be, but it's slowly coming through to me that most of the faces in the crowd don't even know they're faces in the crowd – they just want to stay alive, and be happy, and not get into too much trouble, and so the world goes on from one dull day to another.'

'I suppose I'm a face in the crowd,' said Elizabeth. 'I never really thought of it. At least I'm not a face in the paper.'

'I can recognise it intellectually,' said O'Toole. 'Of course there's a clean, decent world outside the rat-race. The ordinary world isn't a mouse-race, either, it just isn't any race at all. Now and again I meet normal members of the public in the line of duty, you know. The trouble with me is, I can't recognise it emotionally. Unless people want to fight me, or put me down, they just seem dull.'

'Women, too?'

'I'm afraid so. I keep hankering after an edge of ambition in a woman, and if there isn't one there already I try to sharpen her up. Before we know where we are, we're at it with straight razors, cutting each other down to size.'

'That isn't love, it isn't even friendliness.'

'I know it,' said O'Toole. 'Ultimately it is completely destructive. But while it lasts, it has an excitement about it which is difficult to explain if you haven't felt it yourself.'

'It's terrifying,' said the girl.

'So is being a face in the crowd,' said O'Toole.

There was a pause, and then O'Toole put his arm round the girl. 'I'm sorry, I was mostly talking to myself,' he said. 'I suspect all this is some sort of national thing I'm trying to shake off. I'm really envious of you under all the bluster.'

The girl turned toward O'Toole, smiling through mist.

'Good girl,' said O'Toole. 'You're better than the British Council.'

Later on they made love, fiercely, but on O'Toole's side with certain reservations. If you make love unless you absolutely want to, you're really making something else and you wind up hating the whole human race, he thought.

Later, full of guilt and gratitude, he slept.

XX

NEXT morning the air-letter from Australia O'Toole had been expecting arrived. The first few lines confirmed his guess:

Dear Shoulders:

Just a few more weeks and we'll be rolling in luxury together, mate.

I've thrown in the job and I've got a booking by P & O for the 21st, which is a bit over a fortnight. They're giving me a cut rate on a single cabin for writing a couple of publicity handouts.

I don't want my old cobbers to be ashamed of me so I'm getting a new suit made. It will cost sixty quid, but they tell me it's the only way to get a decent job in London. I don't want to get so desperate I have to take yours.

I guess I'll be putting up with you in your West End luxury flat, for the first few weeks, months or years. I'm scared of the cold, so lay in a few extra bags of coal. There's hardly anybody left in Sydney now – I'll be lucky if I can raise a dozen to see me off. Even that unemployed lurk-man Don Clarke left for Lunnon last week, taking the knock on most of the bookmakers in town in the process. I dare say he'll be on your back before I get a chance to, so brush him off like a man.

If you can think of anything I need bring, this is your last chance to let me know. You can get enough to eat over there, can't you? Someone told me to take a case of soap and razor blades, but the war's been over for fifteen years, hasn't it?

Jennifer's getting a big play in the papers here on the local girl makes good theme. Don't be bitter.

Won't be long now, Cobber,

Jowls.

On the way to the office O'Toole wondered how Jowls would react to the bus seats, and how he would react to Jowls' reaction, and how many people would live to a ripe old age if you had to do some positive thing every night when you went to sleep to make sure you woke up in the morning.

Norman Knight, pipe, blazer, handkerchief up the sleeve, didn't look like that at all.

'Get that exes sheet in as quick as you can, Digger,' he said. 'I've got you for the morning, and we've just got one little angle to clear up.'

'No writs yet?'

'Touch wood, nothing,' said Knight. 'The series starts on Sunday, and Starsh wants copy for the first three instalments by Thursday latest. That's to give him a day to rewrite the whole thing, on his usual form.'

'Where to?'

'Soho. We're going to get to the bottom of these cards.'

O'Toole typed up his expense claim, not forgetting twenty-five shillings he had not spent on drinks for Macedon. The office was in the normal Tuesday morning doldrum and there was no sign of Jacobs, Barr or Starsh, so he left his sheet on Jacobs' desk. Then he walked with Knight up the Strand to Soho and the dubious bookseller-cum-stationer's from which the vice inquiry had begun.

'You'll notice they've changed around a bit,' said Knight, consulting notes. 'Miss Maria is now giving relaxing treatment and Miss Raymonde appears to have moved to the other side of town and got into the corrective game. Notice anything else about them?'

'Handwriting,' suggested O'Toole.

'All the same,' said Knight. 'Master-mind of vice at work, eh?'

'Could be,' said O'Toole. 'Maybe they all went to the same school.'

'Let's find out,' said Knight. 'Here's the drill. This Charley is bound to sell dirty books and pictures – they all do. You go in and ask him for something special. Get him to spread the gear out, and I'll come in and jump him.'

'How long do I get?'

'Five minutes will be plenty,' said Knight. 'On your way.'

O'Toole took a deep breath and walked into the shop. For a bookshop, there were hardly any books in it. Tattered American magazines dealing with body-building, gun collecting and similar Freudian topics hung by bulldog clips from hooks on the wall. The one bookcase, a shoulder-high affair full of paperbacks, formed a defensive screen for the door at the back. O'Toole was studying the titles when a middle-aged man with rimless glasses and a printed hand-painted tie came out behind the counter.

'Got any interesting books?' O'Toole asked him.

'You mean... interesting?' the man asked.

'That's it. Interesting,' said O'Toole. 'You know what I mean?'

'I might,' said the man. 'Do I know you?'

'Doubt it,' said O'Toole. 'Straight off the boat. I'm in wool.'

'I suppose you're all right,' said the man.

'Safe as the bank,' said O'Toole. 'I'm interested in pictures, too.'

'Come inside,' said the man. I'm getting bloody good at this, thought O'Toole.

The inner room had nothing in it at all except a trestle table and some filing cabinets. O'Toole sat down.

The man went through another door and came back with some books, green and white paperbacks. 'The Whip', 'White Thighs', 'The Enormous Bed', O'Toole read off the titles. The man stood watching him as he flipped the pages. By the look of the fat paragraphs and sparse dialogue someone had been dirtying up John Galsworthy.

'I'm not much of a reader, mate, if you know what I mean,' he told the man. 'Have you got something different?'

The man went out again and came back with an armload of comic-books. O'Toole opened one. It was badly-drawn and poorly-printed, but good enough to see that it was an obscene space-age comic-strip. Males in space helmets and oxygen cylinders, with subtly streamlined phalluses, were engaged in metallic *soixante-neuf* with Martian maids dressed mostly in zip-fasteners. In the distance there was flagellation by atomic power. O'Toole fought down a smile.

'We have to move with the times,' he said.

The man smiled faintly.

'I'll take a dozen,' said O'Toole. 'How about some pictures?'

The man went out again and came back with a shoe-box. O'Toole dipped in it and brought out a packet of photographs fastened by a rubber band.

The first one gave him the time-freezing shock you always get from a dirty picture, like a flashbulb fired in your face. It showed a man with a moustache who might have been a second-hand car salesman and a schoolgirl in dark tunic, white shirt, necktie, and black stockings. She even appeared to have navy-blue bloomers on or, rather, half-off. But on a second look at her face, she was no schoolgirl. Badly needing a rational approach, O'Toole decided for no particular reason that the pair were Germans: the room in the background put him in mind of a set he'd seen in a film: 'The Blue Angel', was it?

The next photograph hit him, too, but less. It was the same pair, a different position and not so much on. He flipped through the set and by the time he'd reached the twelfth, he could feel the photographer getting desperate for a new angle. Saying nothing, he spread the first set out on the table and dipped into the shoebox for another.

This was more familiar territory, French personnel on the job. A couple of women went through the permutations, the most memorable thing about them being the strange expressions on their faces, as if they were holding their breaths. O'Toole put that set down and took out another: he'd seen enough now to achieve a life-class, anatomy lecture detachment. This time the photographer used a very big, very black and by his looks very good-natured Negro to liven up his limited subject: a topical touch but it got tedious, too, after a few pictures. In the next set the man and woman shown copulating were each missing a leg, to cater, presumably, for some obscure specialised market. I myself have only used women as crutches, thought O'Toole, and he must have smiled.

The shopkeeper took it for approval and said, 'Nice little lot, eh?'

'Very tasty,' said O'Toole. 'How much?'

'Flat rate, five bob each, two quid the set,' said the shopkeeper. 'How many do you want?'

O'Toole didn't get a chance to answer, for at that point Norman Knight walked in, glanced quickly over the pictures scattered along the table, and turned on the petrified shopkeeper.

'A disgusting collection of filth,' said Knight in his most magisterial manner. 'How long has this been going on, eh?'

'This is Norman Knight of the *Sunday Sun,*' O'Toole cut into the pause. 'I'm James O'Toole from the *Sun.*'

'It's a frame-up,' said the shopkeeper, getting an outraged tone functioning.

'Rubbish,' said Knight. 'You've been caught red-handed. I interrupted you trying to sell my colleague a load of degenerate filth.'

The shopkeeper, spurred, perhaps, by the words, made a dive at the table, got the shoe-box under his arm and began frenziedly clawing the photos together. Knight and O'Toole each grabbed the nearest handful, stuffed them into their coat pockets and stood back. The shopkeeper kept on gathering, slowing down and finally stopping like a switched-off gramophone. Then he turned toward them and said, in a new, tired voice: 'All right. What do you want?'

'That's more like it,' said Knight, pulling out his pipe. 'We're going to put you out of business.'

'How?'

'Everything goes into the paper. Your picture, your name, your address, the sort of stuff you carry, everything.'

'Might do me a lot of good.'

'Maybe. You'll be raided, of course, the day after the story comes out. Coppers have to cover themselves, even if they are on the take round here. Be nothing here, of course. Then we'll send someone else in and do you again. Then they'll raid you again. How long do you think your customers will run the risk of being pinched on the premises with the gear in their pockets?'

'I paid three thousand for this business,' said the shopkeeper. 'Why pick on me? I'm not doing anyone any harm, am I? There's hundreds of businesses like this. What's so special about this stuff?' He waved deprecatingly at his stock.

'We're cleaning up London and we've got to start somewhere,' said Knight.

'That's a good one, cleaning up London,' said the shopkeeper. 'I'll lose the little bit I've scraped up to put into this place and someone will open up next door. You couldn't even clean up a public lavatory. You make me sick.'

'There might be another way,' said Knight. 'You help us, we help you. As you say, you're nothing special.'

'I get it,' said the shopkeeper. 'How much?'

Knight didn't bristle in his usual style.

'Nothing,' he said. 'Just some information.'

'If it's where I get the stuff, nothing doing,' said the shopkeeper. 'They'd have my blood.'

'We might settle for less,' said Knight. 'I'll have no mercy on ponces, but after all, this is not so bad. Tell us how those cards get in your window and we might be able to arrange something.'

'People bring them in,' said the shopkeeper. 'Anyone can.'

Knight turned to O'Toole. 'Go and call the nearest copper, Digger,' he said. 'We'll start the campaign right here. He can cart this lot down to the station.'

O'Toole started out of the room.

'Oh, all right, all right,' said the shopkeeper. 'I rent the whole board out for a fiver a week. Geezer comes round and puts his own cards up. I know nothing about it and I don't want to know, see? I only have it there to attract my own customers.'

'Who is he?' asked Knight.

'Dunno.'

Knight glanced at O'Toole, who turned again for the door. 'Got a card here somewhere,' said the shopkeeper. 'Perhaps I could look for it.'

'Strictly confidential,' said Knight. 'No one will know where we got it. The shopkeeper raked through a drawer and brought out a grubby card:

OLIVER DAWSON ASSOCIATES
Advertising
221, Damascus Road
Camden Town

'We appreciate your help,' said Knight. 'If Dawson doesn't know we're coming, we'll know you're sincere. Otherwise we might have to come and see you again.'

'He won't,' said the shopkeeper. 'Always glad to oblige.'

As they left, he resumed the frenzied collection of his pictures. O'Toole felt his pocket: he still had a handful of them.

On the way, they passed Russell Square, and O'Toole wondered who was suffocating down in his basement now. Just round the corner was the pub where he had last seen Jenny, presumably forever, unless she took to posing for dirty pictures. O'Toole was still wondering what made a dirty picture dirty, considering that when you'd seen one you'd seen them all, when they arrived at Dawson's office.

It was over a tobacconist's, in a seedy shopping block. By opening doors which weren't locked, Knight penetrated to a first-floor room looking over the street, O'Toole following. A man about thirty, with a long, thin nose and slicked-down fair hair was working at a desk. He seemed not at all put out by the interruption.

'Sit down, boys,' he said, waving them to chairs. 'Won't be a jiffy.'

Sure enough, he was working over a pile of blank visiting-cards with a fountain-pen, consulting a big notebook beside him before each card. There was a ginger-coloured brief-case with tarnished brass buckles on the desk, open and gaping towards him. He blotted the last card, stacked them and slipped them into the case, then looked up hospitably.

'Oliver Dawson?' asked Knight.

'At your service,' said Dawson, with a wide smile. 'You've come to the right place. What's your line, massage?'

'I'm Norman Knight of the *Sun* and this is my colleague James O'Toole,' said Knight, and paused for a reaction.

'Well, this is a surprise,' said Dawson. 'I'm always real glad to meet the Press. Looking for a story?' There was no trace of alarm.

'What's your business exactly, Dawson?' Knight asked.

'Well, it used to be called publicity,' said Dawson. 'We've only recently reached the status of a profession if you know what I mean. The proper term is public relations.'

Even O'Toole could hear that there was something wrong with the accent, but Dawson used the jargon with a glibness he could have learnt only in pubs around Bond Street. Ex-barman, perhaps.

'Many clients?' asked Knight.

'We're in a fairly small way, so far,' said Dawson. 'Mainly the medical and theatrical professions.'

'Whores, ponces, brothels?' asked Knight.

'Now, now, that's dreadfully old-fashioned talk,' said Dawson. 'No one uses those words these days, you know. Let's say my clients are broadminded people, shall we?' His face lit up again with that neon smile, and O'Toole noticed he had long gums and short crooked teeth, like broken glass on top of a wall.

'You're living on immoral earnings,' said Knight.

Dawson laid his hands palms down on the table, but made no attempt to rise.

'There are many misunderstandings in the public mind,' he said. 'We are shaking off the bad old legacy from the past, you know. Don't confuse us with the vaudeville advance men of former times. We work creatively, not to plug our clients indiscriminately, but to mould and guide the attitude of the public, to influence, in a straightforward way, of course, the editors of the mass media...'

'Where are you getting this rubbish from?' Knight cut in.

'Patience, patience,' said Dawson, with another pink flash. 'Perhaps I have not found the right words to get my point across. I know there has been hostility toward us on the part of the working press, but you must remember that our interests do not basically conflict. We must work together to educate, to shape...'

'Let's get down to brass tacks,' said Knight. 'How many girls are on your books?'

'Like I said, we are beginning in a small way,' said Dawson. 'I haven't the precise figures at my finger-tips, but I should say we have a couple of hundred accounts.'

'How much each?' asked Knight.

'It depends, of course, on the service,' said Dawson. 'As a rough guide, I should say a guinea a week.'

'You write all the cards yourself?' asked Knight.

'Now that's an interesting point,' said Dawson, 'you would really be surprised at the selling power of those small window displays. Not the coverage of the mass media, of course, but the basic reader rate works out quite phenomenally low.'

'What it says on the cards – do you think that up?' asked Knight.

'Of course, part of our service,' said Dawson. 'We aim at a balanced coverage of the various reader interests.'

'Do the girls tell you exactly what they do?' asked Knight.

Dawson smirked. 'Have to be diplomatic, you know,' he said. 'Actually it's nobody's business but their own, is it now? My job is to get the customer to the point of sale, if you understand me. From there, my clients take over.'

'Now that's very interesting,' said Knight. 'You seem to be pioneering new techniques here, Mr Dawson. I'm sure my editor will want to publish this story.' O'Toole looked at him sharply, then at Dawson: Knight's expression hadn't changed and Dawson hadn't noticed the switch in tone.

'There's no room for the old hit-or-miss methods,' said Dawson with a modest shake of the head.

'Our readers will want to know what you look like, of course,' said Knight. 'I wonder if you could spare the time to stop by at the office for a photograph?'

'Of course,' said Dawson.

'We're going back now,' said Knight. 'No time like the present, is there?'

'That would be quite convenient, I could begin my rounds from the Fleet Street area,' said Dawson. 'I think it's very important to establish the right relations with the news media, don't you?'

They parked Dawson, brief-case under his arm, clearly enjoying the bustle of the office, in the waiting-room, and sent Jensen to take his picture. Then they went to Knight's desk at the other side of the newsroom.

'Nobody can be that simple-minded,' said O'Toole.

'Oh, I don't know,' said Knight. 'You can just never tell about people in advance. There are always surprises waiting for you in this business. If he's silly enough to come into the office and pose for his portrait, why do it the hard way?'

'I have a sudden temptation to explain things to him,' said O'Toole.

'Fight it,' said Knight. 'Anyway, I don't think you could. He's convinced himself that this is public relations and you'll never shake him off it. It probably is, at that. What the hell is public relations, anyway?'

'It means getting stories into the papers without paying for them,' said O'Toole. 'He's certainly doing that.'

'Good luck to him,' said Knight. 'Now, I think the time's come to put all this stuff together. If you'd like to give a hand, I'll be glad of your help. Not that I can't do it myself, of course.'

'I'll type and you can dictate,' said O'Toole, pulling over a typewriter and winding in three sheets of paper and two carbons. 'What's this called?'

'Call it first vice,' said Knight. 'We'll write it in one long story to begin with and put an overall lead on later. I think we might kick off with Hawkesley, the vice czar of Soho. How about: "Today, after weeks of painstaking investigation, I can name the man who controls the vice web of London"?'

'You're flattering him,' said O'Toole.

'Be realistic,' said Knight. 'Is some other ponce going to sue us for libel because he's really the man who controls London vice? Hawkesley would like to control it, even if he doesn't.'

'Just a suggestion, Norman,' said O'Toole. 'This might be better: "Today I can name the fat, ugly spider who sits at the centre of London's web of vice – Henry Horsecollar Hawkesley" or whatever his middle name is.'

'Nice swing to it, Digger,' said Knight, 'Get it down.'

O'Tooled typed. 'Now how about this, Norman?' he asked, and went on typing:

This man is evil. He reaps the profits of the trade in shame while running none of the risks himself, and when the searchlight of the *Sun's* investigation was turned on him, this rat tried to buy his way out with his tainted money!

'Perhaps we ought to leave that last bit out about buying his way out,' said Knight. 'The readers might think he didn't offer enough.'

'Suspicious minds they've got, eh?' said O'Toole, xxxing out the reference to the bribe.

'Now I think we might work Eileen into the lead, too,' said Knight. 'What about this: "Hawkesley is not alone in his filthy trade. My probe has uncovered..." – well, what?'

'A fit companion to him, a woman who has led an innocent young girl into the LOWEST PIT OF DEGRADATION,' O'Toole suggested on the typewriter.

Knight read over his shoulder. 'Pretty racy style you're developing

158

there, Digger,' he said. 'Innocent young girl is perhaps stretching it a bit, but no one will sue us for it.'

'With all respect to you, this seems to be the way they want it written, Norman,' said O'Toole.

'If we don't jazz it up, Starsh will do it for us,' said Knight, 'and I don't suppose he's ever spoken to a whore in his life. Now, can we get friend Dawson in pretty high up? How about this: "My survey of the seamy world of London vice has turned up an army of parasites who are growing fat on the shame of fallen women: even a man who has debased the profession of public relations by cynically advertising every kind of perversion and vice".'

'It's long for the fourth par of the lead,' said O'Toole. 'Let's break it up into two sentences. We've got one "fat" already so let's say they're growing rich on the shame of et cetera.'

'The filthy ponces,' said Knight. 'Get it down.'

As O'Toole was typing Knight nudged him. He looked up and saw Dawson, smiling, mincing across the office.

'Well, it didn't hurt, eh, Mr Dawson?' said Knight.

'I just have a small favour to ask, boys,' said Dawson. O'Toole was unobtrusively winding the sheet out of the typewriter, but Dawson didn't notice. 'Could I pop in and see the photos? I'd like the best one to go in, you know.'

'Of course,' said Knight. 'Come back tomorrow, around the same time if you can.'

'I could manage that,' said Dawson. 'Be good now.'

As soon as he was out of earshot O'Toole wound the sheets back into the typewriter.

'Now, let's see, Digger,' said Knight. 'What about this: "It was a public-spirited informant who put me on to the track of Eileen, the vampire of Knightsbridge". Might encourage some more readers to grass on these procuresses.'

'Fair enough,' said O'Toole, typing.

O'Toole stood modestly a half-pace back at Knight's elbow as he gave the first instalment of the series to Starsh,

Starsh read the opening paragraphs.

'Ah, there's that old reforming zeal, Norman,' said Starsh. 'I'll go through this and send it down to the Judge. You'd better go and see him this afternoon, and take James along. I take it James is your corroboration for most of this.'

'He gave me some useful ideas on the story, too,' said Knight loyally.

'He's quite a find, for a bushwhacker.'

'We can always use a good man,' said Starsh. O'Toole, uneasy, put his hands in his pockets and encountered, and identified, the dirty pictures.

'I'll let you have the next piece tomorrow,' said Knight, turning to go.

'Got a moment, James?' Starsh said to O'Toole.

O'Toole stepped forward.

'You've made quite a hit there,' said Starsh confidentially. 'Norman usually keeps a wary eye on his assistants, in case they get ideas about taking over.'

'Never noticed it,' said O'Toole, resenting something: perhaps a buried guilt. 'Here's something that will interest you, Nick.' He opened the front of his coat, put a dirty picture into the gap and showed it, bending over, to Starsh.

Starsh leaned forward, smiling, saw what it was, and swallowed hard at the air. O'Toole thought he was going to be sick. Then he leaned out a hand to the corner of his desk and clutched his stomach with the other.

O'Toole, triumphant, patted his thin shoulder.

'Really, James,' said Starsh helplessly.

'I'm surprised, Nick,' said O'Toole. 'It's the raw material of this industry, isn't it? The shame of big-hearted Britain.'

Starsh was getting hold of himself. 'That's not very funny,' he said. 'We've all got work to do, you know. In particular, I've got a little job for you.'

O'Toole, reproved, stuffed the picture back in his pocket.

'You've seen the letters to the editor feature,' said Starsh.

'Bright little snippets of everyday life, the trials and tribulations of ordinary folk.'

'Five guineas for the best laugh of the week,' said O'Toole. 'I never miss them.'

'The quality's poor this week,' said Starsh. 'You can look at these letters from readers if you like, but I can tell you now there's nothing there for us. There hardly ever is. All they can think of is a variation on the letters we published last week, which is just what we don't want. Now, you bring your formidable intellect to bear on the problem and let me have a dozen bright, interesting letters, will you?'

'What about?' asked O'Toole.

'You must have some grudges to get off your chest,' said Starsh. 'Here's your chance. I don't want subtle undergraduate stuff, of course:

just a dozen honest-to-God heart-warming rib-ticklers, and get right off the sort of subjects these idiots have been writing in about.' He handed O'Toole a parti-coloured bundle of handwritten letters.

O'Toole nodded and took the letters back to his desk. They were, indeed, pretty uninspiring: a tedious string of moans about gossiping neighbours, surly doctors, bullying foremen: 'Something I read in your paper last week reminded me of the time...' and so on. There was a basic fallacy in the whole idea. The sort of people who read the *Sun* weren't likely to interest each other, or anyone else, in their views of life.

Bright little snippets of everyday life, thought O'Toole. Now let's see. I'm bustling about my little kitchen in Bradford stewing a cow's udder or whatever they eat up there waiting for hubby to come home from the mill. A woman's life is hard, especially at certain times. Our Jack's been done for GBH and daughter's up the pole. Make a catchy rhumba. Still, I can face life with a grin because there are always those heart-warming rib-ticklers, so have a basinful of laughs with us, chums, in your family paper, the *Sunday Sun.*

For a second, O'Toole wondered what the lives of the faceless millions could be like: whether they bled for what Jennies had done to them, or what they might have to do to Elizabeths; whether they raged against Barrs and Rogers and Mary Lous and, deceiving them, cut the ground from under their own feet and felt themselves sinking into the slime; then he wrenched himself out of this mood with the thought that these were only his own problems, not life in modern Britain, and he flicked through his mind the stock subjects for Brighter Letters to the Editor. Babies, bottoms, bloomers, wife's cold feet and Hubby's pay packet, the landlord, the lodger and the mother-in-law. Twelve twists on the old themes and we're in business.

My mother-in-law makes me give her my unopened pay envelope every week... he began in desperation, studied the possible permutations of this situation for several minutes and then wrenched the sheet of paper out of the typewriter and crumpled it up.

My husband's feet are so cold in bed that I make him... he began again, but this opened such a field of painful reminiscence that he tore it up, too.

Jesus, Franz Kafka used to knock himself on the head just like this to produce real writing, O'Toole thought. But then, he got nothing out of it, either.

Then a more promising line occurred to him:

My dear old Mum has just passed on and in her will she asks me to have her ashes scattered over the beautiful rose garden in our public park. But my husband says I can't do this because they've passed a law against it. He says it's called the Litter Act. Is this really true? (Mrs) Elsie Shaw, Huddersfield.

O'Toole re-read his effort. It might tickle some particularly thick ribs, but it's not really heart-warming, he decided. It might do for a filler, especially as I'm not going to win any five guineas, anyway. Now, what else. There's only one place to go for the real stuff about the family situation, and his Mum called him Sigmund.

My daughter says the strangest things. The other day she remarked, 'When I grow up I'm going to marry Daddy' and when I told her that Daddy couldn't have two wives, she said, 'Oh, that's all right, you'll be dead long before that. I'll be his second wife.' I wonder who could have put this funny idea into her head? (Mrs) Shirley Roberts, Idle, Yorks.

That one really smells of the Public Library, thought O'Toole. Starsh will pick it up for certain. Still, it might just scrape by as heart-warming. Now, mum, dad, the kids and the milkman, and what have we got? I was advised to give my husband plenty of rope, and now he's skipped. No, that's really too old, and anyway it's the wrong dialect. What about
I have become involved with a girl I met at a party... but this was real, and O'Toole quickly shut it out of mind. Perhaps there's a twist on My husband got a job at the iceworks, and now he's grown cold...
So, wrestling with his own griefs and the intractibilities of everyday life, O'Toole doggedly piled word on word, letter on letter.

XXI

'THE APPROACH of these letters is okay, James, but they somehow seem to lack sparkle,' said Starsh. It was Saturday morning, and O'Toole was looking over Starsh's thin shoulder as he checked a damp proof of the second feature page on a corner of the big subs' table.

O'Toole's letters to the editor filled a shallow three-column box at the foot of the page, headed

THEY'RE LIVELY... THEY'RE LAUGHS... THEY'RE LIFE.

'We all have our off days, Nick,' said O'Toole. 'What do you expect for twenty-five quid a week – Lord Chesterfield? By the way, who gets the five guineas that Mrs Elsie Shaw of Huddersfield has won for the brightest letter?'

'Dear boy, you are storing up treasure in Heaven,' said Starsh, smiling. 'Have you checked through the copy of Norman Knight's exposure?'

'I saw the galley-pulls,' said O'Toole. 'Has the page come up?'

'We'll lead with it, of course,' said Starsh. 'I can't get the heads and intro cast yet, and it's far too early to get the blocks made or the captions set. In the meantime, Cam asked to see you as soon as you came in. If you will excuse me for just a second, I'll come along.'

Starsh bowed over the proof, his lips moving as he read the headlines letter by letter for a final check. Then, with a sigh, he initialled the page, his green ball-pointed-pen ploughing deeply into the wet paper, and signalled to a copy-boy.

'It's not the perfection we want, but it's an early page and it will have to do,' he said. 'I trust you are not offended at the dispassionate criticism of a brother craftsman, James?'

'Not at all,' said O'Toole. 'What does Barr want?'

'I believe he wants you to handle an exclusive which will go very nicely with the vice exposure,' said Starsh. 'Come and we'll see.'

Barr scowled at the clock on his wall as O'Toole and Starsh came in. 'You're slipping into your old habits, laddie,' he said to O'Toole. O'Toole felt it was too early to debate the point.

Starsh said 'I'm afraid I held O'Toole up.'

'Oh, never mind,' said Barr. 'O'Toole, I've got a really shattering story for you, but you'll have to extract the digit and sew up the facts in a few hours, or it's no go. Get me?'

'Right,' said O'Toole.

'Well, here's the score,' said Barr. 'During the week, some filthy little chemist from Victoria way was put up for trial at West London for supplying dope for abortions. It seems the police could only get the girls to give evidence against him by promising they'd try to keep their names out of the papers. Nice respect for the freedom of the Press, eh?'

O'Toole managed a faint look of disgust at this interference with fundamental democratic liberties.

'We know a trick worth two of those,' said Barr. 'They rushed the case on after the normal hearing time when the local court man wasn't around, and they won't release the transcript of the evidence. The clerk of the court gave me some cock-and-bull story about the papers being with the Director of Public Prosecutions. He actually had the nerve to suggest that we'd be helping the police by keeping the story quiet... I told him we'd be well on the way to the police state if we let them get away with a fast one like that, but he wouldn't budge. However, a chappie in the court office has done the decent thing and flogged us the names and addresses of the girls, which as I see it is the important end of the story. The court hearing doesn't matter, really, and the chemist needn't come into it, either – there's always the risk of a contempt action. But we're on perfectly safe ground with the girls, and they're the human interest in the story. Agreed?'

O'Toole and Starsh nodded.

'Now the angle is quite straightforward,' said Barr. 'Take Jensen along and snatch a picture of each girl on her doorstep. We want them to say something like this: "I sinned, and now I realise the awful crime I committed. I beg forgiveness from the broad-minded people of Britain." If you happen to strike a Catholic, get her to say she's going straight into a nunnery – they'll love that in Ireland. These girls are all top society debutantes and models, of course, and we want to play that angle up: something like "I now realise how heartless and cruel the world of high society is." It would be a bit risky to run the names of the men who got them into trouble, but I want you to emphasise that they are public school boys with titles. You see, O'Toole, we are not afraid to hit out at the snobs and the toffs when the story justifies it.'

O'Toole nodded.

'I think you're just the man for the job,' Barr went on. 'Give them some line about signing them up for Australian television: that ought to get you in without difficulty. If any of them have got pictures of themselves in bikinis among the nobs in the South of France, that would really be first-class. I'll want at least half a dozen of these girls for a decent spread, and I want them in a hurry. Luckily all the addresses seem to be around Earls Court and Fulham, so you ought to be able to knock them off one after another. In the interests of speed, I'd say you were justified in taking a cab, wouldn't you, Nick?'

'There's just one thing, Mr Barr...' began O'Toole.

'I can't spare any more time,' said Barr. 'Nick will answer any queries and give you the list of names and addresses. On your way, laddie.'

O'Toole followed Starsh out of Barr's office. Starsh went to his desk and handed O'Toole a list of names and addresses, inaccurately typed on court stationery. O'Toole studied it glumly.

'Models and debutantes my arse,' said O'Toole. 'A baby would know that top society snobs don't live in basements in Fulham, and they don't go to chemists in Victoria. These girls are typists and shop-girls, I can tell you that for a start. What does Barr expect them to do? Use knitting needles?'

'It's very unprofessional of you to be so perverse on a Saturday, James, you know it's our production day,' said Starsh. 'From the viewpoint of our readers in Bradford, anyone who lives within feasible walking distance of Harrods is society. We're not responsible for the condition of these young women.'

'I don't know about you and Barr, but I might easily be,' said O'Toole.

'Your morals are no concern of ours,' said Starsh. 'Now don't get difficult just now, there's a good chap. Come and see me on Tuesday and we'll discuss it at length, if you are still interested.'

Dismissed, O'Toole went to the art room to find the photographer, Jensen. He was reading the *Express,* or, rather, looking at the pictures.

'We've got a job on, Sam,' said O'Toole.

'Snatch?' asked the photographer.

'How often do we get a willing sitter?'

'Doorstep?'

'As usual. It would be better if they weren't too sure they had been photographed.'

'Sounds like a Leica job,' said the photographer. 'Are they likely to get tough?'

'I shouldn't think so,' said O'Toole, smiling. 'We take a cab all the way to Fulham, so you can see this is front-page stuff. Grab your gadgets and we'll be off.'

In the cab, Jensen didn't ask about the nature of the story and O'Toole didn't volunteer the information, apart from telling him that they were going to knock on a series of doors and Jensen was to stand behind O'Toole and photograph whoever answered, over his shoulder.

The first address turned out to be a basement in Trebovir Road. The name that went with it on his list was Virginia Bradshaw (23). O'Toole, still annoyed at his unsatisfactory conversation with Starsh and uncertain about his own attitude, neglected to rehearse what he was going to say, and the photographer, knowing nothing of this and concerned with his aperture and his distances, unconsciously led him to the door. O'Toole found himself pushing the bell-press.

It was opened almost at once by a girl in jeans and a sweater. She was pale and pulpy under the eyes, and obviously very young.

'Miss Bradshaw?' asked O'Toole, hearing the camera shutter click behind him as he spoke.

The girl nodded. 'Pol... police?' she said timidly.

She was terrified. So, after a second, was O'Toole, the same fear which is transmitted to the hunter by the screams and struggles of a small, wounded animal. He searched and found that he had nothing prepared to follow the identification, and a good part of his mind was busy with the discovery that the girl looked a bit like Elizabeth, a bit like Jenny, a bit like all his women.

The girl stared at him miserably, as if she expected to be arrested, but in no way questioning his authority.

'No, we're the... Gas Company,' O'Toole improvised. He pretended to stare at her, as if comparing her face with one he'd seen before, but this merely increased his alarm. 'You're... you're not the right Miss Bradshaw. I'm looking for a much older woman,' he said. 'Sorry.' And he turned and went up the area steps, Jensen following, and walked quickly down the street.

'No need to talk to her, eh?' said Jensen, busy with the levers and dials on his camera.

'Look, Sam, I'm sorry to involve you in this,' said O'Toole. 'It's no concern of yours. These girls have been to some abortionist and Barr wants to cook up one of his so-called human interest stories about them. For some reason I just don't want to do it. The picture will be okay if he can get someone else to handle it.'

'I'll back you up in anything you want to say,' said Jensen. 'You can rely on me, Digger.'

'Thanks, Sam, but it's better to leave it to me,' said O'Toole. 'I'm supposed to be in charge of the job. All you know is, I suddenly told you to come back to the office.'

'If it means a row, tell Norman Knight about it,' suggested the photographer. 'Whatever the story is, I'm pretty sure you can count on him.'

'I'll keep that in mind,' said O'Toole. 'What are you doing?' Jensen was twiddling with the knobs on his camera.

'Fogging the film,' said Jensen.

166

They caught a cab to the office. O'Toole considered the situation. It was highly unlikely that all of the girls could have been out, or entirely uncooperative. He had not laid even the minimum groundwork for a sudden attack of illness. Because of the photographer, he could not simply get lost for the day. There was nothing for it but to face it out.

Starsh, busy with a proof, was the first person in authority O'Toole encountered in the newsroom.

'Barr in?' he asked.

'Busy,' said Starsh. 'What's the trouble?'

'I can't handle this one,' said O'Toole.

'You approve of abortionists?' asked Starsh.

'I don't know,' said O'Toole. 'Who cares what I approve of? I'm just telling you, I can't handle the job. Where do I get my cards?'

'That's premature,' said Starsh. 'I'll have to tell Mr Barr what's happened, naturally. Is this the situation: you refuse the assignment?'

'If you like. Can't, won't, comes to the same thing.'

'It's serious, of course,' said Starsh. 'It means, among other things, that you're not as tough as you look. Still, you have other qualities, I suppose. I can't promise anything, but I'll do what I can.'

'In the meantime?' asked O'Toole.

'Oh, take it quietly,' said Starsh. 'A story is only a story, after all. Don't consider yourself suspended, or anything like that. Go and get on with your normal work, and I'll see what I can do.'

'Thanks, Nick,' said O'Toole. 'Is Norman Knight about?'

'I believe he's out for the day, tying up some loose ends,' said Starsh. 'If I were you I'd be inconspicuous.'

O'Toole reported to Jacobs, who gave him the weather and some run-of-the-mill wills and follow-ups. Barr appeared once or twice in the newsroom, but said nothing to O'Toole. He could not decide if Starsh had told him anything.

The first edition was a few minutes late coming up from the machine-room, toward nine p.m. O'Toole took the front page in at a glance. The abortion story had been done: it was the second lead. They had been able to photograph and interview one, two, three girls. The story, headed THEY SINNED, THEY ARE SORRY was by-lined VINCENT HOWARD, a name O'Toole had not encountered before in the office. After the first few words of the lead paragraph, 'Dazzled by the FALSE VALUES of High Society...' O'Toole could not bring himself to read any more. The vice exposure led the paper. The main head was

167

LONDON'S SHAME EXPOSED, and beside it, in a box, was Knight's by-line and his picture, looking, without his glasses, like a movie version of a Scotland Yard inspector, and not at all like himself.

The story was illustrated with the snatched photos of Eileen, described as 'The Vampire of Knightsbridge', and Hawkesley, 'The Czar of London's Vice Cesspool'. Lower on the page was the bland face of Oliver Dawson, captioned 'Publicist of Prostitutes', smiling out of the paper with the limitless self-satisfaction of the great reformers.

Below Eileen's picture was one O'Toole had not seen before. It showed a young girl, with the lower part of her face concealed by a drawn-on mask. It was headed 'Here is another of the vampire's teenage victims...' O'Toole studied it, putting his hand over the mask. Whoever it was, it couldn't be the girl he had met with Knight in Eileen's flat. Nor did the story make any reference to more than one of Eileen's victims, if anyone so eager could be described as a victim. Knight, thought O'Toole, must have dug up some more dirt on the vampire of SW1.

O'Toole strolled over to Jacobs, also busy with the newly-printed paper.

'Vice came up nicely, Aussie,' said Jacobs. 'I believe you did good work on it.'

'I helped,' said O'Toole. 'Who is Vincent Howard?'

'We had a lot of trouble with that story,' said Jacobs. 'I had four Saturday casuals on it in the finish, and then we only got three of these sows. Howard, in case you don't know, is the most famous reporter on this paper. Norman Knights come and go, but Howard has been here for twenty-five years or more. He doesn't exist. He's the office phoney by-line we use on anything we've got too many names for, or none at all as in this case. He often gets invitations to address women's clubs and so on, but he's always on holiday when anybody wants to see him. You can have a handful of his visiting cards if you like, to go with your dud cheques.'

'I don't know that I'll be needing them,' said O'Toole.

The rest of the night passed quietly. O'Toole was reading a book when Barr, hat in hand, tapped him on the shoulder.

'I've got a train to catch now, but I'll be wanting to see you on Tuesday, laddie,' he said severely. 'Come and see me as soon as you come in, before you do anything.'

O'Toole nodded and Barr was gone. On his way home, he tried to analyse the nervousness he had felt for most of the day, but whether it was the recollection of the girl's fright, or the realisation that he would have to do something about Elizabeth, or the prospect of unemployment, he could not decide.

XXII

THE NEXT day was a cold grey Sunday; Macedon and his girlfriend had gone away for the week-end, and O'Toole was alone in the all-but-unfurnished flat. So, when Elizabeth telephoned, O'Toole asked her to come over. It was dusk when she arrived, bright-eyed, cold-nosed, a warm and fragile place which was new to O'Toole, because women only seem like that in cold climates.

'This place is like a morgue,' she said. 'Can you take me out and buy me a drink?'

'I haven't been in a pub for months, but I'm game,' said O'Toole.

They went to the Three Elms, just around the corner. O'Toole inspected some small trees, growing in tubs by the pub door. For all he knew, they could have been elms. The place was crowded with the usual collection of extras from British films, but the people were in colour, whereas the films were generally in black-and-white, before the main feature. Life beats art again.

'You can have anything but pear juice. I've had bad experiences with it,' he proposed. She said gin, and O'Toole had one too, to cut down on the decisions.

'You're very jumpy tonight, James,' the girl offered. 'Troubles?'

'Oh, things are a bit sticky at the office,' he said. 'I refused to do a story and there might be repercussions.'

'Good for you,' said the girl.

'There you go,' said O'Toole. 'I should never have mentioned it. It's hard to con people into making nitwits of themselves if you're not in the mood, that's all. You can't force it.'

'Might you lose your job?'

'I might.'

'That would be wonderful.'

'For me? Out of work?'

'Well, I thought you might, perhaps, be considering sort of settling down here, really using your abilities, doing something you were proud of, something constructive...'

169

'Have a heart,' said O'Toole, wearily. 'This is my trade, you know, like a man might work in a bank. I just can't afford to start telling the boss how to run his business. You don't ask the man behind the grille if he's considered the implications of the capitalist system when you go to the bank to change a pound for the gas meter.'

'You seem to have more imagination than the run of bank clerks,' said Elizabeth. 'That's why I like you.'

'That's my trouble,' said O'Toole. 'Here I've got a good job, not too badly paid for unskilled clerical work, and I look like losing it just because I let my guard down for a moment and the implications sneaked up on me. Where's this going to end? The lucky people just can't see the implications of anything, or they can deceive themselves to order, like my boss. If you follow up all the implications, you're finished. You'll have me winding up as some crummy out-of-work saint in a coffee house, martyred to absolutely no principle at all except that the world is a jungle and you can either fight it or go with it.'

'And you're going with it.'

'I'm confused,' said O'Toole. 'Which way is going with it? Do you think, for instance, that I should consider the implications of this set-up – of being here with you?'

He wasn't very pleased with the clumsy style of this change of subject, but there it was – he'd brought it out.

After a few seconds, the girl said in a low voice: 'Are you trying to say that we've come to the end of our time?'

O'Toole was caught off-balance. He found himself trying to remember what Jenny had said to him the last time he'd seen her: wanting to improve on her performance, to come out of it better: knowing, he thought, exactly what he was letting Elizabeth in for: restraining an impulse to minimise her hurt, because it would suit him very well to do so, and so he could not be sure if it were true: feeling that it was better, on balance, to receive the axe than to give it, because it was the executioner who had to select the time and place. Thinking this, he had not even nodded.

'Does the silence mean yes?' asked Elizabeth, fearfully, but not unkindly.

'It means nothing,' said O'Toole. 'I'm just the man from the Gas Company. In your position, if I wanted to hang on, I would, as long as I could. In fact, I did.'

'I suppose I want to,' said the girl.

'Go with it,' said O'Toole. Then, after a pause, 'Do you think we should get a bottle and go back to the flat?'

'I don't think so, tonight,' said the girl. 'I'll have another drink and then I'd better be getting along. I've got the smalls to wash.'

Leaving, she said she would call O'Toole during the week.

Walking home alone through the chilling London mist, O'Toole thought about the symmetry of the situation, like a game of chasings. The only way you can stop being *it* yourself – is to make someone else *it*, and it goes on forever: there is no all in, the whippy's taken.

He decided he had found something new to admire in Elizabeth. She wasn't very fast with the cracks, but she had seen that he was floundering, and had tried to help him. But her kindness didn't affect the situation; it only made it more difficult to rationalise what he had to do, anyway. People select their sexual partners on a yellow, goat-eyed basis: the whole thing was a psychological disease, the coupling and decoupling merely the symptoms, and the only cure to be born adult. In every pair, thought O'Toole, one party is getting out more than they put in, and the exploiters and exploited are sorted out in the cradle. The shame of big-hearted Britain.

The way to get by is to learn your piece off by heart and say it when the time comes, irrespective of the audience reaction.

Deciding this, O'Toole felt a mood in himself he had not previously experienced: not despairing, but sombre. He put it down to London being cold, and himself getting older and losing his nerve. In fact, it was just that he had never thought seriously before, even about such a simple subject.

On Tuesday morning there was a postcard from Ceylon: a picture of the liner *Himalaya* on the front, and on the back the message, 'Better start teeing up that job for me. Money running low. Jowls.'

On his way to the office, O'Toole wondered how his friend would take the news that he, too, was out of work... He decided that he would have to improvise the interview with Barr, who was bound to have devised some contorted and unpredictable reason for sacking him without notice. It might be better, he thought, to snatch the initiative by implying that he was a Catholic with strong views about abortionists: he wondered if he could get away with claiming that they didn't have them in Australia and he was too embarrassed to ask just exactly what they did.

Norman Knight, ruddy and masculine in a blazer with a Navy crest was the first person to greet him: he seemed to have been waiting for O'Toole to come in, took him by the arm and steered him to the waiting-room.

'We've got to get our lines right or we might be in trouble Digger,' he said.

'I am already, Norman,' said O'Toole. 'I'm supposed to go and see Barr and get the sack.'

Knight laughed. 'You've got the safest job in Fleet Street this morning,' he said. 'Ifor Morgan – you remember, that cheap snide lawyer that Eileen sent in here to get nasty with us – he's been as good as his word. His writ arrived promptly yesterday afternoon. Morgan must have been working like a maniac to get it out.'

'How much does he want?'

'That hasn't come up yet,' said Knight. 'Technically, this is an imputation against the chastity of a married woman, so he doesn't have to prove special damage or put any figure to it. Unless we can prove what we say, he can ask for the earth and get it.'

'How do we stand?'

'It comes down to who the jury believes, of course, but as far as the story goes you and I can swing it between us, I should say. The trouble is in the headlines and the pictures.'

'Oh?'

'Like an idiot I wasn't here on Saturday night,' said Knight. 'I suppose you saw that childish masked picture and the line on top of it, "Here is another of the vampire's victims"?'

'I wondered how you got that,' said O'Toole.

'I didn't,' said Knight. 'Either Barr or Starsh – or, more likely, Starsh egging Barr on – thought that the story needed a sexy picture to pep it up. Eileen certainly looked a fright in her dressing-gown. So they've dug some doll's picture out of the files and had that mask painted on it, and then put the line about "another victim" over it, although we haven't got a scrap of evidence that there's ever been another victim. The office lawyer looked over the copy but of course he's never seen the blocks or the heads. Eileen has told Ifor Morgan that the picture doesn't look at all like her young friend, and naturally he's fastened on to it in his pleadings. If he can show that we've faked the picture, the whole of our case sounds fishy and it might be enough to sway the jury against us.'

'I'm sorry I didn't know more about it,' said O'Toole, 'although I doubt they would have listened to any more protests from me on Saturday night.'

'You were in no position to know,' said Knight. 'I don't care if the

172

case costs the paper a million, but I can't afford to have one of my series knocked down. Not that the business over the picture really affects the issue, of course: Eileen is a cow and a procuress and we both know it. But it was lunacy to risk the whole series for the sake of a silly ornamental frill like that.'

'It's just a matter of someone saying the picture shows Eileen's victim, is it?' asked O'Toole. 'Won't the girl be called in?'

'I doubt it,' said Knight. 'Eileen won't be very keen to call her for fear she breaks down in the witness-box and spills her lot, and we can't now, because she looks nothing like the picture.'

'You didn't take it, did you, Norman?' asked O'Toole mischievously.

'You know damn well I didn't,' said Knight. 'The day I start lying on oath to save Cameron Barr's money for him will be the day I turn this job in... Barr and Starsh got us into this, let them get us out.'

'I said I'd go and see Barr first thing,' said O'Toole.

'Don't let him con you into anything,' said Knight.

O'Toole put his head round the door of Barr's office and was greeted by a warm smile.

'Come in, James,' said Barr. 'I have something to discuss with you.'

'About that business on Saturday, Mr Barr...' said O'Toole, plunging into the subject.

'Oh, just a misunderstanding, laddie,' said Barr. 'Water under the bridge. What I want to see you about is this impudent writ we've had from this whore that you and Mr Knight exposed. I suppose you've heard about it?'

O'Toole nodded.

'Nothing to be alarmed about, of course,' said Barr. 'We get them every day of the week. Naturally, we think all the more highly of a man who can defend the paper in court, and I believe you might make a good impression. You were present at all Knight's interviews, were you not?'

'As far as I know.'

'You read the copy, of course, and you will be able to confirm that every word we published was absolutely accurate, the plain unvarnished truth?'

O'Toole considered this a moment.

'The story was fair enough,' said O'Toole. 'I didn't write the heads.'

'No one said you did,' said Barr sharply. 'That's no part of your job. Now let's see what your memory is like. Do you remember snapping the girl this woman had with her?'

'I understood that reporters didn't take pictures in Britain,' said O'Toole. 'I wouldn't know one end of a camera from another.'

'Must have been someone else,' said Barr. 'It's the girl, all right, isn't it?'

'No,' said O'Toole.

'Oh, come now,' said Barr. 'Jog your memory a little. You're not going to let us down when we need you, are you? You can't see her face in the paper. Women can do wonders with corsets and so on. No doubt you're more up to date on that than I am.'

Barr smiled chummily and O'Toole produced a faint echo. 'It could easily be her, couldn't it?'

'It could be, I suppose,' said O'Toole. 'It could be a million girls.'

'Of course it could,' said Barr. 'You think it over. You need a good memory to do well in this business. While your recollection is fresh, I want you to go straight down to the lawyer with Knight and let him have a statement.'

'You know the Judge, don't you, Digger?' Knight asked on the way down in the lift. O'Toole must have looked blank. 'He's the office lawyer. You must have seen him going over the proofs on Saturday afternoons.'

'Bald, skinny chap?' asked O'Toole. 'Striped pants? I wondered who he was.'

'You'll find he's a decent type,' said Knight. 'A bit on the slow side for those monkeys upstairs, but he knows his libel.'

'He slipped up on this one, didn't he?'

'Probably never saw it,' said Knight. 'He's supposed to be responsible for keeping the libels out, but of course the paper's one long libel from end to end and they don't show him any of the fancy heads or pictures they slide in at the last minute. He can't do much about it because Barr is the boss, and if the lawyers propped at every potential libel they'd be out of the job inside a week. So what it comes down to is, they're paid for worrying.'

'Some job.'

'It's regular work,' said Knight. 'Any lawyer would appreciate a client who averages a writ a week.'

They had arrived on the second floor and Knight tapped on an unmarked door. A deep radio-announcer's voice said 'Come in, please.'

O'Toole thought he had walked into a film set. The public parts of the *Sun* building were all chrome and black marble, slightly tatty, like an

174

oil company headquarters run on the cheap, but the lawyer's room belonged to some different part of town, some other century. The door through which they passed was glossy paint on the outside, carved oak on the inside. The room was half-panelled in oak with a quiet wallpaper above. Most of the walls were lined with books; row upon row of legal reports bound in scuffed red leather, darkening back through the decades, the Victorian ones bearing the marks of apparently genuine bookworms. One clear space featured the framed portrait of some long-dead, bearded Justice, perhaps, thought O'Toole, the very one who sent great-granddad away.

The lawyer sat behind a heavy leather-topped desk. As O'Toole had seen him before, he wore a black jacket, high starched collar and discreetly black and white checked tie, with a tiny pearl pin. On a nose thin as a knife blade, crimson and bulging with blood-pressure perched a pair of gold-rimmed spectacles, anchored to his lapel by a black ribbon. Neatly arranged round the desk were briefs tied with red tape, more books with places marked by scraps of paper, and an ebony-handled letter-opener. Lying on a leather-bound blotter, wildly incongruous, was a copy of last Sunday's *Sun*.

'Do you know O'Toole, Mr Firebrace?' Knight asked.

'I believe I have not had the pleasure,' said the lawyer, in that rich, expensive voice. 'Do be seated, gentlemen.'

The lawyer resumed reading the paper for a few seconds, came to the end of the story, and looked up. O'Toole noticed that a red circle had been drawn about the photograph of Eileen's victim.

'Excuse me,' said the lawyer. 'This has come upon us rather suddenly, as you might say, and I had not read the article as it actually appeared.' He smiled apologetically. 'I'm afraid that I must confess that the *Sun is* not my family paper. We take the *Observer,* as it happens. The children like to see it when they are home from school.'

'How does the story seem?' asked Knight.

'I have read your reports, of course, and those of your colleague, before the article was passed into the paper,' said the lawyer. 'In the pleadings' – he consulted a vast file of documents typed on broad brief-paper, and found a place – 'our opponent makes great play with the headlines, and I see that he has cast aspersions on the photograph of the... er... young lady whom you found with the other woman. I don't suppose either of you know anything about it?'

Knight and O'Toole shook their heads.

'I thought not,' said the lawyer. 'It is, as a matter of fact – what shall I say – new to me, too. No matter, I shall, no doubt, learn its history in due course. As to the rest of the article, it is beyond doubt defamatory to a very high, I might say un-matchable, degree, and we have no alternative but to plead truth. However, the stories of you two gentlemen appear to tally perfectly, and I notice that our opponents concede' – he consulted his file again – 'that you were in the lady's premises for some considerable time, although perfect strangers to her. That is very damning, very damning indeed. What do you think a jury might make of her, Mr Knight?'

'She's gone a million when she opens her mouth,' said Knight. 'Plummy.'

'That seems hopeful,' said the lawyer. Turning to O'Toole, he smiled and added, 'Mr Knight is an old hand in the witness-box. I suppose this is your first legal action in this country, Mr O'Toole?'

'Or anywhere else, on the business end,' said O'Toole. 'Well, nothing to worry about,' said the lawyer. 'We might take the liberty of coaching you a little beforehand, as you might say. Now, I think we should get your evidence into proper shape as soon as possible, so that you may have the opportunity of studying it.'

He touched a bell, and a grey-haired, elderly woman in a clerical-grey dress came in. She, too, wore gold-rimmed glasses, and carried a dictation pad.

'My secretary, Miss Flynn, gentlemen,' said the lawyer as they rose. 'Now, Mr O'Toole, your name and occupation, please.'

'James O'Toole, reporter,' said O'Toole.

'Journalist,' the lawyer said to the secretary. 'Now did you, Mr O'Toole, as part of your editorial duties...'

As the gamier details emerged, the lawyer chuckled, like a broad-minded clergyman listening to a dirty joke. 'My, what you chaps get up to,' he said several times. The grey head of his secretary was steady as a rock.

They finished dictating the statements, a straightforward account of the investigation, but in cooler language than the paper had used, and Knight and O'Toole left the lawyer to return to the editorial room.

'I know who he is, Norman,' said O'Toole. 'He's a character actor hired by Barr to give the place tone.'

'Not a bit of it,' said Knight. 'Firebrace is a lawyer of the old school. I can tell you, he's drawing a very fancy salary, too.'

'Why the fantastic decor?' O'Toole asked.

'He wants to feel at home,' said Knight. 'Most of these cases are settled out of court, and the money is discussed right in the Judge's office. He needs the right atmosphere to impress people that the *Sun* is no fly-by-night outfit and he's ready to go to the House of Lords if they won't see reason.'

'I suppose it makes sense,' said O'Toole. 'I don't know what I expected – someone with a barrow full of nylons, perhaps. But, after all, the law is a business, and whatever this enterprise is, it's certainly a business, too. Still, I must say I got a shock to find that you can hire one of these leather-bound boys, law-books and all, and keep him on ice till you need him. It's like Al Capone hiring a priest to give him absolution.'

'No knuckle-crushing propaganda here, you black Protestant,' said Knight, jogging O'Toole with his elbow and laughing as they got into the lift.

'One more thing, Norman,' said O'Toole. 'I may be dense, but why doesn't Barr himself get into the witness-box and say he was out with his Brownie and happened to run into Eileen's girl-friend? His human drama act should go down great.'

'Don't be silly,' said Knight. 'Look at it from Barr's point of view. Even if we lose the case, it's only the shareholders' money and we're covered to a certain extent by insurance against libel actions, anyway. But Barr himself can't afford to get involved in it. He's pulling down one of the biggest salaries in this country with a fabulous expense account, to begin with. Then, next year, there's a vacant seat on the Press Council, and if he makes a few speeches in the right places about the responsibilities of a free Press he'll breeze into it. Very handy if someone goes squealing to them about his paper. Do you see him risking all that with a silly story about a box Brownie? The other side might ask him where you put the film into it and Barr would be back selling second-hand cars.'

'How about Starsh?' said O'Toole.

'Not likely,' said Knight. 'He's got principles.'

As O'Toole walked into the newsroom behind Knight, Jacobs, busy at his desk with the morning's mail, looked up, traced an-hour glass curve in the air with his hand and jerked his thumb toward the waiting-room. O'Toole turned toward it, half expecting to see a collarless Father Sweeney waiting with his family and a new proposition for redemption. Instead, it was Elizabeth.

She was wearing a check suit, with a white hat perched on her snub-nosed, honest English head. Approaching, O'Toole saw through the glass door that her face was sombre and that she had, not all that long ago, been crying.

'Hullo, James,' she said huskily. 'I'm sorry to interrupt you at your office like this, but I had to say good-bye. I'm leaving first thing in the morning and I have a world of packing to do.'

'Where on earth are you going?' asked O'Toole, filling in until he could think of a comment.

'Ceylon,' said the girl. 'I've spoken to Henry on the phone, and explained as much of the situation to him as I thought I should, and he's been very nice about it and cabled me the air fare. We're to be married almost as soon as I arrive.'

'Isn't this rough on Henry?' O'Toole asked.

The girl twisted a glove in her hands. 'I'll do my best,' she said. 'I've been quite honest with Henry, and that is all he expects.' She looked up and smiled wanly at O'Toole. 'As you would say, I am not asking for your comment on this, just putting you in the picture.'

'Very right,' said O'Toole slowly. 'I don't suppose there is any point in saying I would like to be your friend, as if we'd met in the Navy or something.'

'We will always be that,' said the girl. 'I would like to see you again one day, when I can trust myself alone with you, that is. Please understand that I'm not reproaching you at all, James I remember you said something once about Yale keys not fitting Union locks and I know exactly what you mean, from your point of view, although I expect you know it doesn't always work the other way round.'

O'Toole nodded soundlessly.

'I'm sure you know what I want to say, James, so I won't bother with the words,' she went on. 'Would you mind if I was to write to you, some time in the future? Don't be surprised if you get a letter one day addressed to Joan O'Toole. I... I... and she bit her lip, and then suddenly stood, leaned over O'Toole and kissed him on the cheek.

'At least I found out what it can be like,' she whispered. 'I shall never forget you. Good-bye, darling.'

And, before O'Toole could say anything, she turned and, straight and brave, walked out of the office.

O'Toole sat for a long time staring at the wall of the waiting-room. The things that he wanted to say to Elizabeth rushed through his head: that he would never forget her, either: that the fact that there was no place or time for them was the same lousy deal that life gave everybody: that while he had ranted and raved at her, hour after hour, built his monstrous childish fantasies about the big time and the bleeding heart, here was someone alongside him who knew the score all the time, who could not explain it to O'Toole because it had sounded too simple and harsh and unsubtle for him to understand: that while she had learnt the names of some fashionable writers from him, and some zipped-up new opinions, she had shown him that grown-up people can grasp a painful truth, can cut their losses and start again with courage and dignity, can pity the executioner because he can no more help himself than his victim.

Then, realising that he could say nothing of this to her now, or perhaps ever, and that it was the yellow goat-eyed thing which had divided two people who liked each other very much, he walked unseeing out of the waiting-room and almost bumped into Starsh.

'Now look here, James,' said Starsh. 'Your private life may be murky, as you said on Saturday, but we really can't have you bringing your women into the office in working hours. I mean, we must maintain some sort of standards of discipline in this operation. This isn't one of your houses of assignation, you know.'

O'Toole had been silent too long: the dam burst.

'Oh, you crummy little Marxist moralist,' he said. 'You're very fast with the crooked statistics but when it comes to looking at the shabby deal life really is, all you can do is run. A man in trouble is as likely to go to you for help as he is to Stalin, and that goes for the working-class too. Norman Knight may be a mother-fixated Catholic obscurantist but at least he knows what it is to bleed. He's got something to bleed with. What the hell have you got for suffering humanity?'

Little texts of Marx
Keep girls out of parks.

'It's a good job you got tired of worrying about the starving workers before they spat you out in disgust. All your life you've wanted to suck power out of some bone-headed Beria with big boots and now you've found him. Go and help Barr play with his lying, crooked stories, you snivelling literary bootblack.'

As the tirade had begun, Starsh had jumped back as if he expected O'Toole to hit him. Pale, lower lip trembling, he heard O'Toole out and then turned on his heel, without a word, and walked to his office.

O'Toole stumbled to his desk and sat down, his head in his hands. He realised at once that he had hurt Starsh deeply, had thrown in his face a political past which had been, at least, selflessly intended, which had cost Starsh a great deal: that he had been brutal to a man who had been kind to him and had no need to be, and that Starsh's rebuke, even, had made no more than sense from Starsh's point of view, seeing that he had no way of knowing what was happening in O'Toole's life and had merely interpreted O'Toole on the data O'Toole himself had supplied.

He was ashamed of himself, but he knew, at the same time there was nothing he could do to repair the situation. Then it occurred to O'Toole that he might be merely afraid of Starsh of his power with Barr and thus over O'Toole's prospects, and that he might be looking at Starsh with a convenient and temporary fair-mindedness as phoney as the forgiveness of big-hearted Britain. Incapable, for the moment, of seeing anything certain in himself at all, O'Toole got up, called 'Something to do' to Jacobs at the other end of the newsroom, and went down into Fleet Street to walk it all into some sort of shape.

Fleet Street, bent, spurious, garish buildings, milk-bars and disposals stores, didn't help him much....

Later in the afternoon, tired of walking, he came back to the office, indifferent about the reception he might get. There was no noticeable change. He had not long sat down when Jacobs gave him a bundle of nondescript correspondents' stories to look through, asking him to watch out for angles worth following-up on the phone, but there were none. Later Norman Knight came in and O'Toole gave him a compressed account of his scene with Starsh, but Knight said such brushes were common in the office and seldom had any consequences.

In the following days O'Toole had the quietest time of his Fleet Street career. Starsh pretended that he didn't exist: Barr rather too regularly made special journeys to his desk to say such things like 'Getting along all right, laddie?' with a mechanical fatherly smile which O'Toole guessed might last until the libel action had been decided: Jacobs, apparently by direction, gave him only trivial and innocuous stories, obscure murders to be done by phone and cases of indecency and assault which had no chance of making the paper because of the *News of the World's* invincible monopoly.

During the week O'Toole saw the usual procession of evil-looking men confiding in Jacobs in the waiting-room, and sometimes shouting about money to Barr, but no one told him what villainy was being hatched. He was bothered by ingrained professional curiosity, troubled by his own distress at being left out of the know, but he was obliged by the code of the trade not to show interest in other men's stories.

The promised transcript of his evidence arrived from the legal department: it was headed 'James O'Toole will say...' and typed on brief-paper nearly as big as a page of the *Sun*. O'Toole found nothing to quarrel with in it.

That Saturday night O'Toole discovered, with an automatic shock, that for the first time since he had joined the *Sun* no story of his appeared in the paper: it was possible that one of his murders might have made a few lines in some slip edition, aimed at provincial home-town pride, but he had nothing in the main London edition, the one that counted.

Norman Knight drove him home and left him with a cheerful 'See you in court, Digger.'

O'TOOLE had often walked past the Royal Courts of Justice in the Strand, and never much liked the look of them. Of grey stone, turreted, machicolated, they seemed to bear the same relationship to justice as the nearby newspaper offices of chrome and plate glass did to Hampden and John Wilkes. O'Toole guessed that the same architect might have put up the Gothic buildings in Australia. Still, he thought, it's what the tourists want to see.

On a Tuesday morning of late autumn the great hall of the courts was cold and depressing. The place was huge, a cathedral with no altar, dedicated to nothing. Around the walls were the portraits of Lords Chief Justice, larger than life-size and indicating by their expressions that they could not conceive it possible that they had been mistaken. You're the bastards who valued a man's life below a loaf of bread, thought O'Toole idly, staring the nearest LCJ in his oil-painted eyes. Those whiskers don't fool me.

Across the hall he saw, standing in a group. Knight, Starsh and Firebrace the lawyer, improbably disguised in short wig and gown. They nodded as O'Toole came up. A dozen yards away, O'Toole spotted Eileen and Ifor Morgan: Eileen in suit, hat and pearls, like a barmaid done up for a spree. Morgan looked contemptuously at O'Toole: Eileen avoided his glance.

Firebrace consulted a gold watch with white enamelled face which he took from his waistcoat pocket. 'I think, gentlemen, we might go into court,' he said, turning to lead the way, with Starsh beside him, still avoiding O'Toole, who brought up the rear with Norman Knight.

The procession went upstairs from the main hall, along a corridor on the next floor and paused outside the heavy glassed doors of the courtroom itself, where two stunted and elderly attendants in blue uniforms cleared a way for them through the crowd of would-be spectators, the same endlessly curious English crowd of old-age pensioners, pimply typists and hero-worshipping housewives who turn up at coronations, hangings, building sites, street accidents and any other public events likely to go down in history in the newspapers or the newsreels.

Starsh, embarrassed, brushed aside an autograph-hunter who held a book out to him and said, 'Be a sport, Arthur,' and while the crowd railed at him in a good-natured way, the group passed through the doors into the calm of the courtroom.

It was like a miniature theatre, familiar to O'Toole from British movies. Above the judge's bench was a high oak canopy, unnecessarily sheltering the space beneath from the weak sunlight which filtered through the dusty glassed-in roof, and supporting a big, meticulously carved and brightly painted royal coat-of-arms. Ten or twelve feet below the Bench, in the well of the court, was a long table piled with books and papers, behind which sat the two Queen's Counsel who were to conduct the case, flanked by junior barristers and assorted helpers. From the bar table the seats for witnesses sloped up, like the stalls in a theatre, and behind them again, reaching almost to the roof, the gallery for spectators, reached by a circular cast-iron stair.

Knight and O'Toole went to the first row of witnesses' seats, from where they looked down on the curled tops of the counsels' wigs. Firebrace and Starsh were sitting at one end of the bar table, Ifor Morgan and Eileen at the other end, beside their lawyers.

'That's Godfrey Barker, QC, leading for Eileen,' Knight whispered. 'He's the top libel man in the country. She's lucky to get him. He usually appears for us.'

O'Toole identified the famous counsel, a shrivelled little old man with a pink, lined face under his wig, like an intelligent windfall apple. He was nodding, apparently half-asleep, while his junior had a whispered conversation with Ifor Morgan, suburban in a crumpled suit.

'Who's our man?' O'Toole asked, looking at the other end of the bar table, where Firebrace was conferring with a tall, handsome man with the bewildered look of well-intentioned people.

'Geoffrey Harrison,' Knight told him. 'He's more of a company law expert. I wouldn't have picked him myself for a dirty case like this: he's a very brilliant chap, but he hasn't got the killer instinct. I believe he's got something to do with the Labour Party. He's against hanging and H-bombs and all that sort of thing. Still, I suppose they had to take what they could get.'

There was a sudden murmur as the attendants opened the doors and the spectators streamed into the public gallery. The lucky ones – there were no more than a score of places – settled themselves down for a day's entertainment, waving to friends a few seats away, pointing out the people in the court and speculating on their identities, and a few of them chewing surreptitiously behind morning newspapers.

Then the judge, preceded by an official, came in from a door behind the bench. As he appeared, everyone in the court rose, a few balky ones, unaccustomed to the procedure, looking around in alarm and then imitating the general movement, and when the judge sat the assembly followed suit, collapsing fluttering like washing when the line breaks.

The judge was a dark, middle-aged man, like an older version of Starsh, incomparably more magnificent in wig and scarlet gown. He smiled in reply to the bowed greeting of the counsel, and his associate, from a table below him, formally summoned the participants in the case.

The empanelling and swearing-in of the jury took only a few minutes, as there were no challenges. O'Toole was relieved to see that the principle of a jury of one's peers hadn't been taken too literally: ten of the jurors were men in expensive suits, with waistcoats, evidently business men who could be spared from their offices, and the two women looked as if they had left maids in charge of the house. O'Toole guessed that they were not the sort of people who would read, or approve of, the *Sun*, but they were even less likely to approve of Eileen or her unmiddle-class style of life.

Barker began the case by reading the article and having copies taken to the jurors. His reading was a theatrical exercise in disgust, with long pauses between the paragraphs, during which Barker studied the jurors' faces, but whatever they thought they looked stolidly back at him. O'Toole thought that they might not be accustomed enough yet to the atmosphere of the courtroom to express their emotions, if they had any.

Then Barker put Eileen into the witness-box and conducted her through her evidence with solicitous deference, as if she was doing him an infinite favour by appearing. Eileen twisted a handkerchief between gloved hands as she told her story: do all women do that when they're up against it? O'Toole wondered. She told it as Ifor Morgan had told Knight and O'Toole in the waiting-room: the two reporters had called on her, claiming to be friends of her husband's – here she looked suitably near tears – and in courtesy she had asked them in for tea and a chat with her young friend, with whom she had been watching TV:

there had *certainly* been no disrobing, and, good heavens, no suggestion of money passing hands, and no, she had no idea why she, a respectable woman, had been selected as the subject of this foul and wanton attack.

Then, in his turn, Harrison rose to cross-examine. He was polite and gentle, a shade less phoney than Barker, O'Toole thought, but there was very little in it. He had one matter to raise, he said: was the young lady who had been present that night now in court? No, said Eileen. Why not? Eileen began to say she believed she was abroad, when Barker rose to object that he was conducting the case, and the plaintiff was not responsible for the subpoena of witnesses, and Harrison agreed urbanely and sat down.

That, said Barker, concluded the plaintiff's case, subject to the addresses: he did not propose to call evidence that the plaintiff had, in fact, been damaged by the article, as this would be self-evident. The judge nodded and turned to Harrison, who consulted a list and said to the judge's associate: 'Call Nicholas Starsh.'

Starsh had evidently been waiting for the summons and was on his feet as the official called his name. The reporters in the Press box began whispering together, and the court shorthand-writer leaned toward Harrison's end of the bar table, where his junior said in a low voice 'Starsh — S-T-A-R-S-H.' The shorthand-writer nodded his thanks.

Starsh had now reached the witness-box, the railing of which reached high on his chest. O'Toole, knowing his shyness and dread of public appearances, felt a twinge of pity for him, for his thin shoulders, ill-fitting hand-knitted sweater, his olive face set in a grim expression, with a dark stubble even this early in the morning.

The associate came toward him with a card on which the form of the oath was printed, and Starsh leaned over and whispered something to him. The associate went over to the judge and in turn whispered to him: the judge nodded and gave some instruction. The associate began rummaging among books on his desk, while a court attendant went along the bar saying softly 'A hat? Is there a hat the witness might have for a moment?'

Finally a navy-blue peaked cap was handed from somewhere to the attendant: it might have been a chauffeur's, or perhaps belonged to one of the court flunkeys. The associate took it, and a different Bible which he had found, to Starsh, who put the cap on. It was much too big for him and fell down to his ears. Starsh flushed with embarrassment as he picked up the Bible and recited the oath.

O'Toole saw the jurors whispering together, and someone near him said, 'He's a Jew.' Norman Knight, next to O'Toole, shook his head and said softly: 'All this fuss!'

Starsh took the cap off, put down the Bible and turned to face Harrison.

'You are the features editor of the *Sunday Sun*, Mr Starsh?'

'Yes.'

'And you are responsible for the final form in which this article appeared in the paper?'

'I wrote the final version, yes.'

'Where did you get the facts?'

'From the story written by Mr Knight, with, I believe, the assistance of Mr O'Toole.'

'And you then showed your version to those gentlemen?'

'Yes, and they agreed that it was a fair account of what had happened.'

'And you wrote the headlines?'

'Under the supervision of the editor, Mr Barr, yes.'

'And the pictures?'

'They were not my responsibility.'

'You had no reason to doubt the facts supplied by Knight and O'Toole?'

'None whatever. Their reports have always been completely accurate in the past.'

'Thank you,' said Harrison, and sat down. Barker rose, hunching his shoulders under his gown as if to free them, like a boxer just climbed into the ring, and said in his high-pitched, cutting old man's voice: 'You say you wrote this... er... article, Mr Stress?'

'My name is Starsh – S-T-A-R-S-H,' said Starsh, with the ghost of a smile. 'The final version, yes.'

'Oh, Starsh,' said Barker, pretending to find the name difficult to pronounce. 'But I have read this article with great care' – he picked up a copy of the *Sun* and briefly went through the motions of studying it – 'and I cannot find your name on it.'

'You won't,' said Starsh patiently. 'I merely arranged the article in its final form, subbed it, as we say in the newspaper trade, and the sub-editor does not normally have his name on the story.'

'Oh?' said Barker, apparently astonished. 'Then this attribution here – "A *Sunday Sun* Exposure by Norman Knight" – is a piece of deliberate deception?'

'It is normal newspaper practice,' said Starsh.

'I did not ask you that,' said Barker. 'We may all have our own ideas on what constitutes normal newspaper practice!' He smirked at the jury. 'Answer my question, please, is this a piece of deliberate deception?'

'No,' said Starsh.

'You admit that it is untrue? Remember, you are on oath.'

'I know I am on oath,' said Starsh. 'Mr Knight was mainly responsible for the article, and so his name is on it.'

'And you say that this is not a deliberate fraud?'

'No.'

Barker's junior handed him a scrap of paper, and Barker held it close to his face, reading.

O'Toole turned and whispered to Norman Knight, 'He doesn't know much about newspapers, does he?'

'As much as you or I do,' Knight whispered back. 'His son is an executive on the *Pic*. It's just an act for the jury's benefit.'

Barker finished his reading, and asked: 'Have you ever seen the plaintiff before?'

Starsh looked at her. 'No, never,' he said.

'You know nothing about her?'

'Only what Knight and O'Toole told me.'

'Did you instruct them to "get the dirt on her"?' Barker used the tone of a quotation for the phrase.

'Certainly not,' said Starsh. 'I have never given an instruction like that in my life.'

'You say that is not normal newspaper practice?' Again, the last phrase sounded like a quotation.

'Certainly not.'

'And that is not deliberate deception?'

'No,' said Starsh, again with the ghost of a smile.

'Thank you,' said Barker, sitting down.

Harrison was on his feet a second later.

'Mr Starsh, have you ever heard of a sub-editor getting a credit on an article?'

Before Starsh could answer, Barker jumped up. 'Surely, My Lord, we are interested in what the witness knows, not what he has heard.'

The judge smiled. 'I think Mr Starsh might qualify as an expert in this matter, Mr Barker,' he said. 'But no matter, I do not think the facts are in dispute. Have you any more questions, Mr Harrison?'

'No, My Lord,' said Harrison.

'Thank you, Mr Starsh,' said the judge, and Starsh bowed and left the witness-box. The jury followed him with their eyes as he climbed the stairs, ignored O'Toole and Knight, and sat behind them.

There was a whispered conference going on between Harrison and Firebrace. Then Firebrace followed Starsh up the stairs and bent by O'Toole's ear.

'Mr Knight is next, Mr O'Toole,' he said. 'As you will be corroborating his evidence, I think it might be politic if you left the courtroom. You will hear your name called.'

O'Toole patted Knight on the shoulder, and as he left the courtroom he heard Harrison say, 'Call Norman Knight.'

Outside in the corridor, O'Toole was accosted by a ferret-faced man he did not know. 'Jim, you'll be giving evidence, won't you? You know me, from PA pictures.'

'Yes, I will,' said O'Toole.

'The boys on the national dailies want pictures of all the witnesses,' said the man. 'Would you mind coming outside for a moment and posing?'

'Of course,' said O'Toole. He followed the man down the stairs, across the great hall and out into the Strand, where a photographer who had been leaning against the railings stubbed out a cigarette and came up oozing professional cameraderie.

'Give us a nice smile, Jim,' he said, bringing his camera up to his eye.

O'Toole found himself composing his features into a frank, winning smile, and noted with subconscious approval that passers-by looked at him with interest, taking him for someone important. This was the first time anyone had ever been interested in *him* as a news story, and O'Toole felt a momentary friendliness for the photographer and his contact man, speculating about the million breakfast-tables where he would appear the next morning.

'It's a pleasure, boys,' he said, as they thanked him. Then, returning to the corridor outside the court, he reflected that he was a minor participant in the case, had been no doubt photographed merely for the sake of a complete cover of the story, and would probably wind up as an unused picture yellowing in the photographic morgue. Still, he understood better why apparently sane people had been pleasant to *him* while he was manoeuvring them into some outrageous quotation.

For more than an hour O'Toole paced up and down outside the glass door of the court, smoking. From time to time the cutting edge of

Barker's voice penetrated the door, but O'Toole could not make out what he was saying. His thoughts kept returning to the enigma of Starsh. Here was a man who had renounced the cause of Lenin and the international working class for the cause of Cameron Barr and the shareholders of the *Sun* without any apparent regret, who had scoffed at Norman Knight and his myopic idealism, who had turned off the vague objections of principle and humanity raised by O'Toole with thoroughgoing cynicism and Jesuitical logic-chopping; a man who had seen through the nineteenth-century subtleties of Marxism, and could not possibly accept the antediluvian tribalism of Jehovah and the Chosen People; but the same man, who seemed prepared to do anything to get Barr's approval, was not willing to renounce the allegiance of a religion which he could not possibly believe, and must have known he was imperilling the paper's shabby case with the meaningless ritual of hat and Old Testament, when he might easily have sworn the ordinary oath, in which no one nowadays believed anyway, or made an affirmation which would have established him with the jury as a convinced atheist and therefore a man of honour and principle. O'Toole felt, uncomfortably, that there was nothing at all for which *he* was prepared to make even so small a gesture, whether he believed in it or not.

Warming to Starsh, O'Toole was beginning to look forward to his encounter with Barker. He had to admire the superb professionalism with which Barker had exploited the ignorance and middle-class priggish self-righteousness of the jury, but it seemed to him that a man who opened his case by contending that a reporter's by-line was a fraud on the public had departed far from the issue of truth or falsity and converted the hearing into a childish debate, with so many points for matter and so many for manner, pick your side out of the hat and to hell with the rules of argument. Barker may be good at his business, thought O'Toole, but I've had a bit of experience at hoodwinking slow-witted people with a simplified version of events myself.

Then an attendant put his head round the door of the courtroom and called 'James O'Toole' as if there had been a hundred people to choose from. O'Toole went by him into the well of the court, where Harrison motioned him into the witness-box. O'Toole, feeling every eye on him, picked up the Bible he found in front of him, and the associate handed him the printed card. O'Toole felt the momentary uneasiness he always had when he had to open his mouth for the first time in front of English strangers, the consciousness of belonging to a slightly absurd nationality, and read off the card:

'I swear by Almighty God that the evidence I shall give in this case shall be the truth, the whole truth and nothing but the truth.'

O'Toole glanced at the jury, directly across the court from him: sure enough, several were suppressing smiles. 'Provincials!' he thought, turning to Harrison.

'Your name is James O'Toole?'

'Yes.'

'I believe you are an Australian, Mr O'Toole?'

'As it happens,' said O'Toole, hearing, or imagining scattered titters.

'And you are Mr Knight's assistant?'

'That is part of my job, yes.'

'Now would you tell His Lordship and the jury what part you played in the train of events which led to the publication of this article?'

He's making it rather obvious that he's only doing this for the money, O'Toole thought, observing that Harrison was using a fatigued, almost timid tone, as if he had a headache.

'I accompanied Mr Knight to the plaintiff's flat,' said O'Toole.

'This lady?' Harrison asked, indicating the other end of the bar table.

'Yes,' said O'Toole. 'She welcomed us, and said that she had spoken to Mr Knight on the telephone. In the flat she introduced a young woman whom she said was a friend. Then Mr Knight and the young woman – I believe her name was Kathleen – left the flat to buy a bottle of gin...'

'On whose suggestion?'

'I don't remember. After Mr Knight and the plaintiff returned, the young woman stripped naked and the plaintiff asked me for money.'

'What did she say?'

'She said she had to pay the rent. Then she partly disrobed, and at that point Mr Knight and I left the flat.'

'And then?'

'We returned to the *Sun* office, where I compiled a report on the events of the inquiry, and later I assisted Mr Knight with the writing of the story.'

'And what is your view of the accuracy of the published article?'

'It squares with what I saw and heard,' said O'Toole.

'Thank you, Mr O'Toole,' said Harrison.

O'Toole turned to face Barker, who rose with that same gesture of settling his gown aggressively over his shoulders.

'What alias were you using that night, Mr O'Toole?' Barker asked.

'I said my name was David McNaughton,' said O'Toole.

'Do you often use an alias?'

'You wouldn't expect us to say we were from the *Sm*, would you?'

'I am asking the questions, if you please, Mr O'Toole. Do you often use an alias?'

'As often as I need to,' said O'Toole. It sounded weak.

'You say the plaintiff asked for money?'

'Yes.'

'She said, "Give me some money"?'

'Of course not,' said O'Toole. 'She said she had to pay the rent.'

'And how is that a demand for money?'

'I have to pay rent, too,' said O'Toole, 'but I wouldn't tell you about it unless I expected you to help me.' Keep that smart-aleck tendency under control, he thought. It's fools they trust around here.

'You say the plaintiff disrobed. What does that mean?'

'She had on a housecoat and nothing underneath. She didn't get it right off, but...'

'I think that answers the question, Mr O'Toole,' said the judge, leaning forward.

'Thank you, My Lord,' said O'Toole, enjoying the unfamiliar style of address, and wondering if it touched any ancestral memory.

'None the less, you say, on oath, that she was improperly dressed?' Barker asked.

'She was partly naked, if you call that improper,' said O'Toole. He saw that Eileen, sitting beside Barker, was making an O of outraged disbelief. Poor bitch, thought O'Toole, she's let them convince her that her story is true. Well, that's her look-out.

'Mr Knight has told us that you supplied some of the more lurid phrases of the article,' said Barker. 'Is that the case?'

O'Toole felt a surge of anger at the crude trick in the question. This is real all-in, he thought.

'Did he say they were lurid phrases? I thought they were well justified by the situation.'

'You are fencing with me, Mr O'Toole,' said Barker. And I just cut your ear off, said O'Toole to himself. 'Did you, or did you not, write a part of this article?' He held up the paper.

'Yes, I did,' said O'Toole.

'But you have not put your name to it. Were you ashamed of it?'

'No,' said O'Toole. 'I am not responsible for the credits on the stories.'

'But was it not dishonest to allow this article to be attributed solely to Mr Knight?'

'It would have been dishonest to attribute it to me,' said O'Toole. 'I am only Mr Knight's assistant. It would be most improper to credit me with the responsibility.'

Glancing at the jury, O'Toole thought he might have scored some sort of shabby point. Barker was deep in his notes. Honesty, O'Toole thought, has certainly come a long way from the primary meaning around here.

'Are you responsible for the phrase, "The Vampire of Knightsbridge"?' Barker asked, with distaste.

'I may have been,' said O'Toole. 'It emerged from discussion.'

'You think it fair to brand the plaintiff with this cheap slogan?'

'Fair enough,' said O'Toole.

'Was it not a mere sensational phrase, designed to increase the circulation of your newspaper?'

'I have no direct interest in the circulation of the paper,' said O'Toole, adding to himself, and you know it. 'We wanted a phrase to describe the plaintiff's activities and that seemed a suitable one.'

'You were not pandering to low tastes, you say?'

'No,' said O'Toole. This hardly seemed to cover the case. He wanted to add, some people like to do it, and some people like to read about it, and that's the difference between Eileen and us, but when it comes to trotting out the clichés you win hands down.

'Would you mind examining the article?' said Barker, motioning to an attendant, who passed O'Toole a copy of the paper.

'You see that photograph, ostensibly of the plaintiff's victim, as the article puts it?'

'Yes.'

'Are you responsible for it?'

'No.'

'Do you recognise it?'

'The subject is wearing a mask,' said O'Toole warily.

'It is not a picture of the young lady you say was present, then?'

The hell with you, thought O'Toole. This isn't the Boy Scouts. Eileen is lying, Barker is lying, the judge is probably wearing corsets, and I'm not going to let this hired adjuster of the truth make an idiot out of me.

'I would say it was.'

'You're not certain?'

'I can't identify a faceless figure with certainty,' said O'Toole. 'As far as I can tell, this is the plaintiff's professional assistant.'

Barker flushed. 'You are trying to be clever, Mr O'Toole,' he said angrily.

'I don't think we need pursue this, Mr Barker,' said the judge. 'Mr O'Toole, as far as you can tell, this is the young lady?'

'Yes,' said O'Toole.

'Very well,' said the judge. 'Proceed, Mr Barker.'

But Barker had sat down.

Harrison, wearing a worried frown, rose to re-examine.

'Mr O'Toole, you have a lengthy professional experience of newspapers?'

'Seven or eight years, yes.'

'Have your reports been challenged before?'

'Never.'

O'Toole saw Barker bow his head toward the bar table and shake it impotently. He was inclined to agree with him. Still, he couldn't expect to have a monopoly of low-grade arguments.

'Thank you, Mr O'Toole,' said Harrison, and O'Toole left the witness box and walked across the well of the court to sit beside Norman Knight. He noticed that his hands were hot and aching.

'How do you think it's going, Norman?' he whispered.

'You did well, Digger,' said Knight. 'Starsh didn't make much of an impression, but from that point I think we've taken most of the tricks.'

'I rather admired him sticking to his Semitic guns,' said O'Toole.

'Perhaps,' said Knight. 'He might have been afraid that Barker would pick him up on it, anyway. You can never tell.'

'Who's next?'

'That's all, I think.'

But at that moment, Harrison said, 'Call Victor Sprogg.'

'How does Sprogg come into this?' O'Toole whispered.

Knight shook his head. 'Don't know,' he said. They watched Sprogg walk timidly over the well of the court to the witness box, looking, with his protruding ears and an inappropriate fixed grin, like one of Nature's martyrs on his way to the lions' den, clearly doomed one day to dandruff, bad breath, bladder trouble, piles, rickety prostate and every other humiliating complaint known to man. This is the acid test of Barker's strategy, thought O'Toole. If he gets tough with Sprogg, the jury will believe Sprogg if he says he's Mao Tse-Tsung.

Sprogg took the oath, stumbling over the minor parts of speech, and looked desperately round, like a cornered animal, until he saw

192

Harrison.

'You are the art editor of the *Sunday Sun*, Mr Sprogg?' Harrison asked.

'Yes.'

'And part of your duties is to have charge of the paper's photographic staff?'

'Yes.'

O'Toole and Knight simultaneously turned and looked at each other, then returned their eyes to Sprogg.

'And you took the photograph which is printed with the article in question, described as a picture of the plaintiff's victim?'

'Yes.'

'Now, about this mask shown on the subject's face, what can you tell us about it, Mr Sprogg?'

'I ordered it,' said Sprogg. 'I took the view that it would be unfair that this young lady should be publicly identified as a prostitute, because she has her life ahead of her, and according to Mr Knight's information she had been lured into an act of vice by the plaintiff.'

'I see. Where is the negative?'

'It has been mislaid,' said Sprogg earnestly. 'It is our normal practice to destroy unwanted negatives after each issue of the paper, because they clutter up the office, and there is always the risk of the wrong picture being used.'

That's why we keep a negative file, thought O'Toole.

'I see,' said Harrison.

'I regret that this has happened,' said Sprogg, 'but you will understand that I had no idea this article might be the subject of an action, otherwise I should certainly have preserved the negative.'

'Thank you,' said Harrison, and Barker rose slowly to cross-examine.

'You say you took this photograph, Mr Sprogg?' he said gently. Smart boy, thought O'Toole.

'Not exactly took it,' said Sprogg. 'I accompanied the photographer.'

'Is he here today?'

'I'm afraid he's abroad on an assignment,' said Sprogg apologetically.

'I see,' said Barker. Fair enough, thought O'Toole, missing girl equals missing photographer, plus one minus one is zero.

Barker paused. 'Thank you,' he said, and sat down.

Harrison then rose to address the court. The defence, he explained, was that the allegations against the plaintiff were true: that the evidence of Knight and O'Toole, upon which the article had been based, tallied closely as to the details of this, 'I must say, rather sordid interview.' However, it would be a sad day for Britain if newspapers were not free to attack vice and corruption wherever they found it: the general policy of the paper was not on trial, and neither, he must say in fairness, were the morals of the plaintiff: the issue was whether she was a prostitute and, more serious, a procuress, for this was the paper's accusation, and in his submission her remarks to Knight and O'Toole and her conduct while they were in her flat left no doubt that, in fact, she was both. The jury were not being asked whether they approved of this manner of life, merely whether the facts were as the article contended, it not being denied that the accusation had been presented in a dramatic manner, as was customary with newspapers with a large popular circulation.

Harrison pointed out that a great deal of the evidence was common ground between the parties: the plaintiff did not deny that she had entertained the two reporters, in what was agreed to be a somewhat indiscreet manner for a respectable married woman, as the plaintiff claimed to be. There were only two possibilities: either the newspaper representatives, investigating vice in the West End, had indeed found it, or by a remarkable coincidence they had stumbled upon an extra-ordinarily broad-minded woman who thought nothing of entertaining two perfectly strange men until a late hour with a young and presumably impressionable girl in her flat. But if the plaintiff's version were the strict truth, why should Knight and O'Toole, agreed to be in search of vice, bother to concoct a false account of their interview with her, with all the attendant risk to their professional reputations, when he was sure that the jury, as men and, if he might be pardoned for saying so, women of the world, would know full well that they might easily have found the real thing in London with very little further search?

Although it distressed him to say so, Harrison felt that it was his duty to point out that the plaintiff had not produced her husband, nor given any explanation of how she was able to live in one of the most expensive districts in London. The newspaper's accusation supplied a complete explanation, and the jury might think that this was a powerful presumption for its truth.

If they disagreed with his contention, then His Lordship might permit him to have a further word with them on the subject of damages: but, for the present, while he agreed that the plaintiff, who had fallen, or perhaps even been driven, into a shameful life, presented a pitiable spectacle, none the less it was the duty of the jurors to vindicate the

194

proud British tradition of the freedom of the Press by finding for the defendants, much as it might pain their natural human sympathies to do so.

O'Toole studied the jury as Harrison concluded. They looked, indeed, warmly aware of their human sympathies, and just as determined on their duty. Nicely played, he thought, on the old banjo.

Barker came eagerly to his feet like a boxer trying to beat the bell. His style was impressionist, rather than logical: the key phrases which he had already introduced into his questions, linked by mumbled and unimportant grammatical bridges. A young married woman in the prime of life, he said, victim of a foul and wanton conspiracy to libel the first innocent person who came along, yellow gutter journalism thinking only of sensations to pander to the lowest appetites, reaching down into the mire for filth to sling at defenceless people in the incessant jungle war for higher circulations, criminal, heartless, impudent, beastly, gross, and so is your mother. Just a few too many emotive words, thought O'Toole professionally: you don't want the goose so deaf you have to say boo a hundred times to get a tremor out of her.

'In the name of British justice,' said Barker, 'I ask you to teach these conscienceless people a lesson they will never forget by a salutary, stinging award of damages, recalling that their resources are large, and no sum of money, however great, can begin to recompense my client for the foul wrong they have done her.'

The judge cleared his throat and, in a cool voice evidently intended to convey that he had not been hired by either side, began: 'Ladies and gentlemen of the jury. You have heard the evidence in this case, brilliantly marshalled and expounded by the eminent counsel at the bar.

'I shall instruct you that, as a matter of law, the article in question is capable of bearing a defamatory meaning: this is a technical matter within my province with which you need not concern yourselves.

'The defence which you have heard offered is called, by lawyers, a plea of justification. In substance, the defendant newspaper says, through its legal representatives, that the accusations it makes against this lady are true, and this is the question to which you must direct your attention.

'In the connection, the word "true" bears as the consequence of recent legislation, a slightly broader meaning than it once did. It does not mean that every word in the article must be literally true, in its strictest meaning, for the defence to succeed. All that is necessary is that an ordinary person, and you may regard yourselves as that for the purposes of your deliberations, reading the article, will gain a true impression from it, that is, an impression which is substantially in agreement with the facts.

'Now, you must ask yourselves, what are the facts? The skill of counsel has resolved this case into a direct conflict of testimony, a matter, as we say, of oath against oath. It is apparent that the accounts given by the two sides, particularly that of the plaintiff on the one hand, and the two reporters on the other, cannot be reconciled: one or the other must contain a considerable element of untruth. It is for you to decide which it is. It is proper for you to have regard to the demeanour of the witnesses as you saw them in the box: your impression of them, although not perhaps decisive, may weigh heavily in your deliberations. You may also bring your general knowledge of the world into account, in deciding which of the stories is the more probable, which, as one might say, goes more with the grain of human affairs as you have experienced them.

'I need hardly tell you that two very important principles are here involved: one is that people should not be needlessly exposed to shame and humiliation, or undue invasions of their privacy; the other is that, subject to this limitation, the Press of this country has a jealously-guarded freedom to turn its searchlight on any matter which, in the public interest, the public should know. It will be clear to you that which of these principles should govern this matter depends on your answer to this question: Did the plaintiff invite the two gentlemen from the newspaper into her home for the purposes of prostitution, or for an evening of innocent social intercourse?

'If you find for the plaintiff, I shall offer you further guidance on the matter of damages, but for the moment it is for you to consider your verdict on the question I have posed.'

Simultaneously, the judge rose, the people in the courtroom followed suit, and the jurors began filing out. Knight and O'Toole went out to the corridor outside the court and lit cigarettes, and after a moment Sprogg joined them.

'How did I go, boys?' he asked.

'Fine,' said O'Toole. 'I was wondering when the question of that picture was going to be solved.'

'It only came up yesterday,' said Sprogg, defensively. 'Got to stick by the paper, you know.'

'It might have saved me an awkward minute if I'd known,' said

O'Toole.

'It doesn't make any odds,' said Knight. 'If we lose this one there's no justice in the world. Still, you can never tell with juries...' and he launched into a reminiscence about the libel cases he had won and lost, mostly, by his account, won...

Twenty minutes later an attendant put his head round the door and said, 'They're coming back.' The three men pushed their way through the crowd squeezing against the courtroom door, and had just sat down when the judge came in and they had to bob up and sit again. The jurors were already in their places, giving nothing away by their looks.

The associate rose. 'Ladies and gentlemen of the jury, are you agreed on your verdict?' he asked.

'We are' said the foreman, rising.

'And how do you find?'

'For the defendants.'

O'Toole felt a blow on his back. 'We've won,' said Knight, exultant. The agency reporters, bowing perfunctorily, were backing out of the court to get their stories away. Knight and O'Toole followed as soon as they decently could, and they were waiting for Sprogg to join them outside when Eileen, sobbing piteously, came out leaning on Ifor Morgan's arm. The lawyer looked stonily at them and, just as he drew abreast, whispered 'Scum!' just loud enough for them to hear.

'He won't get far, he's taken the case seriously,' said Knight. 'Or perhaps he's worried about his fee. Come and have a drink, boys.'

XXIV

O'TOOLE had a thick head the next morning, having spent a good part of the night drinking with Knight. Sprogg, apparently ill at ease, had gone home early.

Arriving at the office, he went straight to Starsh's desk. 'I'm glad we won, Nick,' he said.

'Oh?' said Starsh stiffly.

'Look, Nick, about that brush the other day, I want you to know that what I said doesn't represent my considered opinion. You happened to walk into a personal crisis which you knew nothing about. I want you to know that I admired your gesture in court and...'

'Oh, never mind,' said Starsh. 'Water under Piccadilly Circus. But before you submit me to any more of this obscene breast-beating, go and see Mr Barr. He's been asking for you.'

'I get it,' said O'Toole. 'Well I may, or may not, have a chance to continue this. You get the drift of it, though.'

Starsh nodded and bent his head to his work. O'Toole went to Barr's office and found him grim and unsmiling.

'Sit down, laddie,' he said. 'I want to have a serious talk with you.'

O'Toole sat in the velvet-covered trap chair.

'I won't mince my words,' said Barr. 'Your work has been slipping lately, O'Toole, slipping badly. Something has happened to you. When you first joined, you were keen as mustard. Lately, you've been wandering in here at any old hour, arguing about unimportant details, and generally carrying on as if you didn't want the job. What's worse, when we do by some miracle succeed in getting a story out of you, it's dull and flat... You've lost your old sincerity, your human touch. I know you've got it in you, but if you won't deliver, there's nothing I can do about it. We can't afford to carry any passengers on the team here, you know.'

O'Toole nodded.

'I can tell you frankly, laddie, that I was on the point of sending you on your way. I'm deadly serious about this. On the other hand, I'm told that you didn't do a bad job for us in court yesterday, and loyalty has to count for something. Beside, Nick Starsh has put in a good word for you. He told me that he believed you had some sort of personal difficulties. I'm not interested in your private life, but I'm telling you, settle your problem, whatever it is, and settle it quick.'

'It's settled,' said O'Toole.

'I'm glad to hear it,' said Barr. 'Well, on thinking it over, I've decided to give you one more chance. I'm putting you on a month's probation... If you can get the old snap and sparkle back, we'll say bygones are bygones. There are still great chances here for you. Strictly between you and I, I'm not happy about the way Knight has been carrying on lately, either. He made a nice balls-up of this vice exposure, landing us in court through a silly mistake. Some time in the future I think I'll be needing a smart lad to take over gradually from him, and it could even be you. But first, I want that old human touch, bigger and better than before.'

O'Toole nodded again.

'Now let's delete the past from the copy, shall we, and you can make a fresh start.'

'Suits me,' said O'Toole.

'Good,' said Barr. 'I've got a story here that should be just up your alley. We've had a try-on' – he searched his desk, and produced a hand-written letter – 'from one of these sex-change queers. A medical pal of mine told me the other night that most of these people haven't changed their sex at all, they're just perverts who've had their cocks cut off for a new thrill. Got it?'

O'Toole nodded. It was a theory, anyway.

'Since the *News of the World* started it, there's a raft of this sex-change stuff going round cheap,' Barr went on. 'There's nothing in it straight, but I've got an angle which should liven this story up. This person, he, she or it, whatever it is, lives down in Gillingham. Now what I want you to do is to go down and con him or her along that we're going to use the heartrending story. Explain that we can't use a full series, but we might be able to take a oncer for, say, twenty-five. Give him that bollocks about explaining his tragic plight to the public, you know.'

O'Toole did know. He nodded.

'Now the rest depends on clever treatment,' said Barr. 'I see the angle like this: "This disgusting pervert has had himself mutilated to get money from the innocent British public. He even had the nerve to ask money for the revolting details of his sickening operation. You ought to be in prison or a mental home, you're not fit to breathe the same air as the decent people of Britain, you contemptible beast." With this twist, it ought to make a page lead. You'd better get him or her to give you a flash of the operation, just to be on the safe side, I suppose. Now, here's the address, and on your way.'

O'Toole felt suddenly tired as he left Barr's office. Across the newsroom, he saw Norman Knight, and went over to him.

'Rough night, eh, Digger?' said Knight affably. 'I've got some interesting news for you.'

'Oh?'

'Victor Sprogg is now a permanent executive, as from today.'

'Where does that get him?'

'Well, if he lasts another twenty-five years on the paper, he's eligible for the executives' pension scheme, although it's only fair to say no one has yet lived long enough to draw it. In the meantime, he gets the special tea.'

'Orange Pekoe?'

'No,' said Knight, laughing. 'You know we ordinary slaves get our tea out of a big tea-pot.'

'Twice a day,' said O'Toole.

'The executives get theirs out of a *little* pot,' said Knight. 'Just big enough to hold one cup, and they have the privilege of putting their sugar in themselves, instead of getting it already sugared. Oh, and they get the round biscuits instead of the square ones. It's cheaper than a raise, and it has just the same effect as a carpet on the floor.'

'Don't give up hope, Norman,' said O'Toole. 'We'll make the big time ourselves, one day.'

In the train, O'Toole read the letter Barr had given him. It was written in purple ink on mauve paper, and said that the writer had recently changed sex, and thought there might be many people in Britain who had been told they were men, but felt themselves to be women. The writer said that an account of his/her experiences might give such unfortunate people the courage to proclaim openly that a mistake had been made, and live happier lives in consequence. It was signed, 'Henrietta Marsh (formerly Henry Marsh).'

O'Toole had a lot of trouble finding the address: it would probably mean something to a postman, but there were none about, and the writer had evidently intended to conduct negotiations by mail. O'Toole's feet hurt after a mile walk down lanes flanked by bare trees, when he was driven to conclude that the address could only apply to a ploughed field, half-hidden by hedge. Doubtfully he pushed open the gate and walked a few yards into the field, wetting his shoes in pools lying in the furrows, already edged in the bleak late autumn dusk by rims of ice. Then he saw a caravan, half concealed behind a hedge, with a dim light burning inside. He knocked.

The door of the caravan was opened by what seemed to be a woman, thirty or so, with long bleached hair.

'O'Toole of the *Sunday Sun*,' O'Toole said up to the personage. 'You Marsh?'

'Miss Marsh, yes,' said the personage in a deep contralto.

'I'm here to discuss your story,' said O'Toole.

'Come in, please,' said Marsh.

The personage backed into the caravan and O'Toole followed. He/she was holding the collar of a huge Alsatian dog which studied O'Toole with angry yellow eyes.

'Down, Bruce,' said Marsh. The dog obediently crouched in a corner, a yard or so from O'Toole's foot, which it measured hungrily.

'Do sit down, Mr O'Toole, and let me make you a cup of tea,' said Marsh, not so alarming when O'Toole saw her in a better light and heard the familiar invitation. Half-consciously, he judged that, although her hands were on the square side and her face was rather wrinkled for her apparent age, if he'd met her by accident he would have taken her for a woman, and so he decided to treat her as one, conversationally if in no other way.

'I'm rather hard to find here, aren't I?' she said. 'I didn't really expect you to call in person.'

'Oh, we're used to difficult addresses,' said O'Toole. As his hostess made tea, he looked round the caravan. Bruce certainly hadn't changed his sex, and O'Toole saw that he was a normal enough dog when you got over the surprise of meeting him. He risked a pat on the head, and Bruce made no objection.

The decor of the caravan was desperately arty. A guitar hung on one wall, with a Spanish comb and lace underneath it: nearby was a hand, hanging from a nail, made of black-painted plaster with the finger-nails blood-red, the sort of thing which would have been considered pretty daring by Aleister Crowley's set forty or fifty years ago. On the opposite wall was a drawing involving tigers, women and curved shapes tinted in dim rainbow colours which might have come from an *avant-garde* cafe in Wagga Wagga. O'Toole was speculating on what sort of painful or poverty-stricken life, how many shop-assistant's jobs, provincial coffee-houses, public libraries and last buses had driven Miss Marsh to these frantic straits, and the ultimate castration, to be different, when his hostess put a cup of tea in his hand and sat down opposite him.

'It's very good of you to come so far to see me, Mr O'Toole,' she said, and even in the bizarre surroundings there was Elizabeth's kind and business-like manner. 'I hope I will be able to repay you by giving you something interesting to publish. You understand, I don't ask any payment, but I do ask for your assurance that you will treat my problem seriously, and not as a joke.'

O'Toole stirred his tea.

'Cub's honour,' he said reflectively.

'You were a Scout?' asked Miss Marsh.

'No,' O'Toole lied, irritating himself. 'Tell me, Miss Marsh, why did you write to the *Sun?* Why us,?'

'Your paper is sort of human, interested in people and their problems, if you know what I mean,' said Miss Marsh. 'I never miss it.'

'I see,' said O'Toole.

'Now let me tell you something of my story,' said Miss Marsh. 'Of course, people in my position come in for a lot of ignorant abuse, you understand, but I can see that you are an intelligent person, and you must be tolerant or you wouldn't have come all this way to see me. Briefly, I first began to have the feeling that a terrible mistake had been made about me when I was at school in Ilkley...'

O'Toole wasn't listening. The details of Miss Marsh's pilgrimage, school, Air Force, break with family, clergymen, psychiatrists, finally surgeons, were irrelevant to the story he had been sent to get: when you got down to it, all Miss Marsh could tell him was what it was like to be a human being in a tight corner and fight it out alone, and he couldn't take that angle back to the office.

If only, he thought, Barr had given him a routine story, something funny about dogs or comical foreigners or a man who loved his mother-in-law, something he could like himself for as he wrote it. But on the end of the wish, without a paragraph break, came the recognition that this *was* a routine story, vastly entertaining to the nasty readers of his nasty paper, O'Toole making his mark as the hammer of homosexuals and champion of sound, clean British sex, practised by numbers wherever the Union Jack waved and the sun never set.

'Is something amusing you?' Miss Marsh interpolated into her story, a trifle aggrieved. O'Toole discovered he was wearing what must have looked like a dirty smirk.

'Nothing you said, just a passing thought,' he explained lamely. 'Please go on.'

'I suppose it has its funny side,' said Miss Marsh. 'Well, as I was saying, this Harley Street doctor told me...'

But something had to be done, thought O'Toole. Miss Marsh was obviously a pushover: trusting him, not at all afraid of him or the paper, he/she could no doubt be induced to say anything at all, and if he/she wouldn't come at the proposition that she had had her cock cut off for a new thrill, words to that effect could be invented and put into her mouth without the slightest risk at all. No doubt she would visit the office and complain, but very likely she would accept the explanation that O'Toole hadn't written the story which was published: O'Toole could see himself in the waiting-room telling her about the mysterious higher-ups who are always responsible for the villainies of the popular Press. And if she didn't like it, she could sue: O'Toole saw the jury which had put Eileen down listening to him, clean-cut, truthful, colonial, generated the British way, and Miss Marsh, the living representative of the sordidness and horror of life which the jurors themselves were anxious to forget. She didn't stand a chance. It was easy.

But, O'Toole decided, he wasn't going to do it. Barr had been right in selecting this as a test case. This sort of operation was the heart of his business, and no one could get far in it who didn't whole-heartedly disapprove of Miss Marsh, even having met her and seen she was a human being. Miss Marsh hadn't asked for money, hadn't been sly, hadn't been frightened: she actually believed the paper was what it purported to be, and so, presumably, did thirteen million readers.

But confidence trickery on this scale, thought O'Toole, was worth more than a pony a week. It was worth more than Barr's salary, even, whatever that was. Anyone who could lie, and play-act, and angle and slant and rearrange week after week and never be caught, and who was prepared to do it for a bank manager's wages was himself the victim of a confidence trick. A rogue who is another rogue's fool is a pitiable object.

'...and that brings you more or less up to date,' said Miss Marsh. 'I live in this caravan because no one bothers me here, but it's a lonely life, and I thought that someone should make a start toward breaking down the terrible barriers between people over things like this. Don't you agree?'

'I'll see what I can do,' said O'Toole. 'I'll have to be getting back now, but I'll discuss your problem with my editor.'

'Are you sure you have the details? I didn't see you making any notes.'

'Don't have to,' said O'Toole. 'Fantastic memory.'

'Oh!' said Miss Marsh doubtfully.

'You'll be hearing from us,' said O'Toole, rising to go. 'I've been most interested in your story. I'd like to talk to you about it sometime.' He was outside, on the snowy ground, and Miss Marsh was standing puzzled in the lit doorway of the caravan with her hand on the dog's collar.

'Thanks,' said O'Toole, and turned and walked rapidly over the field. Final service to the industry, he thought, I left her sweet for someone else to have a go.

He almost ran to the station and was alone in the carriage up to London. From Blackfriars he again half-ran up Fleet Street to the office, coming close to bowling over three or four homing typists, but

203

he never saw them. The newsroom, as he crossed, was deserted, but the light was on in Barr's office and the editor was bowed over a proof. He looked up with a start as O'Toole, breathless, came in.

'What is it, laddie?' asked Barr. 'I was just on the point of leaving.'

'I won't keep you,' said O'Toole. 'I just want to tell you that I made a mess of that job, but it doesn't matter to me. I resign. I quit. I'm through.'

'Now there's no need to be hasty,' said Barr. 'I may have sounded a trifle harsh this morning, perhaps...'

'No, it's not that, Mr Barr,' said O'Toole. 'This has been growing on me. I'm just not cut out for this business. I don't know what I am cut out for, but it's not this.'

'You don't want time to think this over?' Barr asked.

'No,' said O'Toole. 'I just want my cards.'

'I see,' said Barr. He rose from his desk. 'Well, I don't say I disagree with you, O'Toole. If you'll pardon my saying so, you seem to be somewhat unstable for our kind of organisation. There's a touch of the prima donna about you which doesn't go well in a team. I'll have your cards sent to you, but don't hesitate to drop into the office if there's anything you want to talk over... Take a few weeks off, eh, and get things sorted out? You've got ability, O'Toole, and when you settle down in the Old Country you'll find your niche, all right. I'd be glad to give you an introduction to the *Pic,* or the *Graphic,* or indeed any paper which you fancy might suit you.'

'Thank you, Mr Barr,' said O'Toole.

'Well, laddie, perhaps you're doing the right thing,' said Barr, holding out his hand. 'No hard feelings, eh?'

'None at all, Mr Barr,' said O'Toole, shaking. 'Thanks for the chance, anyway.'

'I'm not sorry,' said Barr. 'Good luck, laddie.'

It seemed superfluous to wish Barr good luck, so O'Toole said 'Thanks' and left his office. There was no sign of Starsh or Knight, Jacobs or Sprogg or any of the staff in the newsroom, and O'Toole wasn't sorry: he didn't want to see any of them for the time being, perhaps forever.

Passing the waiting-room for the last time on his way out, O'Toole thought of all the people he had seen there, and for some reason the pale, collarless, crucified face of Father Sweeney lingered longest in his mind.

On his way home, he thought that Barr was the man he had met in

Fleet Street whom he least understood: he had been unexpectedly decent about O'Toole's leaving, and his last offer of introductions was probably quite genuine: yet he must have met people other than sycophants and shareholders some time in his life, he must have some idea, however dim, that the world was not as the *Sunday Sun* presented it.

Probably not, O'Toole concluded. Very likely, the only mystery about Barr was that he had long since become a machine: there was nothing to understand.

There was no one at home when O'Toole arrived at the flat, but there was a telegram, sent from Dunkirk that day:

ARRIVING VICTORIA 2030 MEET ME JOWLS

O'Toole ate alone in the coffee-shop in South Kensington where he had kept his first appointment with Elizabeth, and then walked to Victoria to meet his friend. Outside the station, he studied the scene. Marshal Foch, the disposals stores and the rubber goods shops: Jowls was going to ask him what he thought of London, and he hadn't the faintest idea. He knew of nothing in Jowls' experience with which he could compare it.

The Dover train was punctual, and one of the first off was his friend, loping eagerly over the platform to meet him, big, burly, loose-jointed, with the hooked nose and hooded, deep-set eyes he remembered, now mere points in the crinkles of a joyous smile of greeting. The newcomer wore the wide baggy trousers and broad lapels of too thin material for the English winter, which mark the Australian visitor.

'Hello, Jowls,' said O'Toole.

'Shoulders, me old cobber, it's good to see you,' said Jowls, wringing his hand.

O'Toole was startled. It was many months since he had heard an Australian voice: it was true, it sounded like lock-jawed Cockney.

'You look fit, Jowls,' said O'Toole.

'I'm ready for anything,' said Jowls. 'The night-clubs, Buck Palace, the Cliveden Set, lead me to 'em.'

'I've got a few things to discuss with you,' said O'Toole. 'Let's get your bags home, shall we?'

'Okay, the penthouse,' said Jowls. 'I hope this clobber is good enough for your friends. This suit set me back sixty rugs just before I left.'

'It's adequate,' said O'Toole. 'Let's get a cab.'

Jowls was bubbling with excitement as the cab took them to South Kensington. 'I see you're splashed all over the papers, Shoulders,' he said. 'I picked up the London papers in Dunkirk this morning. The big vice exposer, eh? I'm really looking forward to meeting Norman Knight and all the Fleet Street big-shots, I can tell you.'

'Don't get too eager,' said O'Toole.

'What's the trouble, cobber?' said Jowls, turning to look at him. 'You look pale, come to think of it. Climate getting you down, eh? I'm all fixed for that. I've got a couple of sets of long woollen underwear and some tinned butter and a load of vitamin tablets, just in case.'

'The war's been over for fifteen years, you know,' said O'Toole. 'Still, you'll learn.'

They had arrived at the flat, and the two friends carried Jowls' luggage upstairs. There was still no one at home as O'Toole led the way to his room, opened the door and said, 'This is it.'

'Good God,' said Jowls. 'This joint's unfurnished!'

'It is a bit bleak,' said O'Toole. 'You can sleep there for the night.'

'But it's a bus seat!' said Jowls. 'This is staggering.'

'It's a tough country, you know,' said O'Toole.

'I never expected anything like this,' said his friend.

'You might as well know the worst,' said O'Toole. 'I'm out of work.'

'But you had a job yesterday,' said Jowls.

'I know. I quit today.'

'You quit?'

'That's it. I walked out.'

'In trouble?'

'Not particularly. Let's say, it was a matter of values.'

'Values? You mean you don't know what things cost?'

'I'm beginning to find out.'

'I don't know what to say,' said Jowls. 'What's happened to Jenny?'

'I haven't seen her,' said O'Toole. 'Painful subject.'

'Didn't you find another girl?'

'She's gone, too.'

'This is crazy,' said Jowls. 'The country's lousy with good sorts. I knocked back three or four offers on the boat coming over because I thought you'd have something special lined up.'

'You find your own, and good luck to you,' said O'Toole.

'What on earth's happened to you, Shoulders?' asked Jowls. 'If I had a job paying a pony a week I'd have my own place and you wouldn't see my dust. Where's your get up and go? It sounds like it got up and

206

went. This Jenny bitch has leucotomised you, by the look of it. You've got to snap out of it, sport, and get on with your life.'

'It's more complicated than you think, Jowls,' said O'Toole.

'This job you left, is it still going?' asked Jowls.

'I suppose so. My seat's hardly cold.'

'Expenses reasonable?'

'Not too bad, by London standards.'

'Your own by-line?'

'That's easy here,' said O'Toole. 'Even on things you don't write.'

'Could they use a good man?'

'There are never enough.'

'Well, that will do me, for a start... You've let the Poms get you down, mate. How did you get the job?'

'I just wrote a bright, snappy letter to all the papers, and they were the first one to reply.'

'There's not a second to lose,' said Jowls. 'We'll starve to death if one of us doesn't get off his arse straight away. I'll get my typewriter and you can dictate me a letter.'

Jowls unpacked his portable and found a sheet of paper. 'Okay, let's have it,' he said.

'I would suggest something like this,' said O'Toole. 'Dear Sir: I wonder if there is an opening on your staff for a young Australian journalist looking for a break in Fleet Street after a few hours in the Old Country. Then say you know he's a busy man, and give a list of your details and qualifications with sideheads like age, experience, ambition and so on. I'd stress that you are a sincere specialist in human interest.'

'You think it will work?'

'I wouldn't be surprised,' said O'Toole. 'In fact, nothing would surprise me any more.'

'I can see I'm going to have to have a serious talk with you, Shoulders,' said Jowls. 'You can't just spend the rest of your life mooning on a bus seat in this crummy little room waiting for something to surprise you when the biggest city in the world is out there waiting for you to take over. What are you going to do?'

'I don't know,' said O'Toole. 'I don't know at all.'

...ends...

Lightning Source UK Ltd.
Milton Keynes UK
23 September 2010

160269UK00009B/221/P